GOOD DAYS, BAD DAYS

GOOD DAYS, BAD DAYS

Selected Stories

Stew Mosberg

Full Court Press
Englewood Cliffs, New Jersey

First Edition

Copyright © 2017 by Stew Mosberg

Published in the United States of America
by Full Court Press, 601 Palisade Avenue,
Englewood Cliffs, NJ 07632
fullcourtpressnj.com

ISBN 978-1-938812-94-1
Library of Congress Catalog No. 2017941270

"White Ghost" first appeared in *Arts Perspective,*
Winter 2011

*Editing and book design by Barry Sheinkopf
for Bookshapers (bookshapers.com)*

ACKNOWLEDGMENTS

The process of writing a book does not happen without the support and advice of many people and resources. I am forever grateful to Barry Sheinkopf, my writing mentor, editor, book designer, and publishing guru. Thank you to McCarson Leigh Tafoya and Jennaye Derge for their work on the cover photo, Sherry King for her early read and positive feedback, to Bill Grimes for his creativity on the book jacket, and to the Durango Arts Center Micro Grants program for their support. To my beautiful Sharon Krinsky, thank you for being my muse and "cover girl," and for your always honest criticism and encouragement.

—*Stew Mosberg*
Bayfield, Colorado
June 2017

TABLE OF CONTENTS

A Bad Idea, *1*

A Cannon's Roar, *17*

A Good Birthday, *21*

Bench Buddies, *27*

Betwixt, *32*

Carmine's Fight, *39*

Copies, *51*

Cracker Box, *57*

Douglas And Louise, *65*

Fire Fight, *74*

Fraterna Caritas, *79*

Hidden, *88*

Ingénue, *118*

The Carousel, *125*

Life Forms, *132*

Mateo, Enrique, And Carlos, *138*

Memories, *149*

Mr. Abaddon, *156*

Restitution, *163*

Resurrection, *171*

Siblings, *184*

Subversive, *194*

The Organist, *202*

The Plan, *208*

Together Again, *224*

Torment, *229*

Tough Times, *239*

Transparent, *244*

Traveling Companion, *253*

White Ghost, *266*

Forever, *275*

A BAD IDEA

DAVID STARED ABSENTMINDEDLY at the cars cruising passed their Park Slope apartment. "I've decided to write a story about child prostitutes of Thailand." He said it quietly, without looking in her direction.

Caught by surprise, not sure if she'd heard him correctly, she blurted, "You're what?"

"I decided," he said more authoritatively, "to write a story about child prostitutes in Malaysia."

"Where the hell did that come from?" she asked, more amused than angry.

"I don't know." He shrugged. "I heard about these kids, some only eleven years old, girls *and* boys, orphans or run-aways, who are sold into slavery." He paused, turned away from the window, and finally looked into her eyes.

"Listen—"

She cut him off with a wave of her free hand, the other tightly gripping the back of the dining room chair, her knuckles bloodless white.

"David, what the hell are you talking about? You know nothing about Thailand—you've never even been there."

"What difference does that make? I write a lot of things I

don't know anything about——at least until I research it."

"David," she started, but this time he was the one to cut in.

"It sounds interesting and the kind of story that should find plenty of readers and more than a few magazines who'll print it."

"That's just it. . . ." She was beginning to get angry and took a breath before continuing. "You don't know that. You're telling me you're going half way around the world to write a story about something you know nothing about and have no assignment from a magazine to cover expenses or know if anyone will even print it?"

"Bridget, I already queried a few editors. Just haven't heard back yet."

She pulled at the chair and sat down. Lowering her head, she began nervously twisting her long, henna-tinted hair, still wet from the shower.

"David, it's a bad idea." She shook her head. "I assume you were planning on going alone, right?"

"Well, yeah. Can't see any point in you straggling after me through the back alleys of—"

She waved him off again. "When, may I ask, were you planning to go? And for how long? And when were you going to tell *me*?"

The questions shot out of her, staccato-like, harshly, not waiting for a response. Then she abruptly stood up and headed toward the bedroom. He waited a few minutes, took a deep breath, and exhaled slowly, then repeated the process, before following her.

She was sitting on the edge of the bed, hugging a pillow, her knees pulled up against her. She didn't look up.

He started to explain, "Honey, I'm sorry—"

"No, you're not!" she shot back. "You *want* to go. You *want* to go by yourself. I know what's going on."

He reached for her, but she pulled away. He placed a hand on her shoulder. She stiffened.

"David, you're the most self-centered, inconsiderate. . .I gave up on the idea of us getting married. I let go of the idea of having a child with you. Everything's your way, everything." She stopped, exasperated, hurt, tearful.

"Honey," he began. "I. . .I. . . . Look, you knew what I was like when we moved in together. Didn't I ask you to come with me to—"

She raised her hand again. "David, that was then. I *work* now. You know I can't go with you. Even if you asked me to—which you didn't."

They both fell silent, contemplating what to do or say next.

She looked fleetingly at the clock on the night stand. "I have to get ready."

He reached for her. "Please don't leave like this. We have to finish this—"

She rose from the bed, smoothed the duvet, and turned to the dresser. Suddenly there was a pleading urgency in his voice: "It *can't* wait."

That stopped her cold.

"Why the hell not?"

"Because I already booked the flight."

Her demeanor instantly shifted. Shoulders drooping, arms dangling heavily at her sides, lips quivering, she screamed, "David! How *could* you?"

In the awkward silence that followed he heard the refrigerator humming, the click of the hot water heater, the wind rustling the leaves outside; he could smell the breakfast coffee wafting in from the kitchen.

Tears began to pool in her eyes. After a full minute she straightened her tall, slender body, pulled her hair back, entered the bathroom, and gently closed the door. He heard the squeak of the spigot and a stream of water surge into the sink.

Not knowing what else to do, feeling like a dismissed child, he poured the last bit of coffee into his mug, the one that had the words *Author! Author!* written on it, and heaved an enormous sigh. He sat down and put his elbows on the chrome and Formica retro-kitchen table, and considered Bridget's state of mind.

SHE TOOK ALMOST TWENTY MINUTES to emerge from the bedroom. Dressed for her job at a downtown art gallery, her hair slicked back with gel, the obligatory black ensemble hugging her torso, she squinted at him, trying to comprehend his motives—this man whom she fell so hard for the moment their eyes met at the museum three years before. "David, I have no idea what makes you the way you are, but I know that we are worlds apart in this relationship. We do need to talk." For emphasis, she added, "And soon."

He nodded, said, "You're right," and looked away, adding a sarcastic, "When would you like to do that?"

Reaching for the door and not looking back, she said, "I can't tonight. We have the Cuercia opening."

"Oh, right, you wanted me to come to that."

As she opened the door, she turned to face him. "Under the circumstances, it's—-don't you think it would be a bit awkward now?"

"Yes, I suppose so."

"Perhaps," she said as she headed out, "we can talk about this in the morning?"

He didn't respond, but watched her march down the corridor out of sight. He stood there for a few seconds and then closed the door.

David spent the morning thinking about their relationship, where it had faltered, when it had changed from fun, laughter, and hot sex to a few mumbles, cursory conversation, and compulsory lovemaking. Hard as it was for him to concede, he knew she was not at fault. He spent most of the day and early evening rehashing his choice to go to Thailand, his role in the discord with Bridget.

When she got home that evening, he tried to smooth things over, but she wouldn't have any of it.

"So how was the opening?" he asked.

"Fine."

She was tight-lipped, unsmiling, still pissed from the morning.

"Um, big turn-out?"

She sighed and slowly shook her head from side to side. "David, I'm tired. I just want to go to sleep. We can talk in the morning."

HE STAYED UP LATE, sitting on the sofa, the TV on without sound, considering his life, his career, what she had said about him. He knew Thailand was an ill-conceived attempt to escape, not so much from Bridget, but from himself.

In time he crept into the bedroom, undressed in the dark, and slid under the blanket. He was reluctant to move, afraid of waking her, but the urge to nestle closer overtook him, and he pressed gently against her back. She stiffened but made no attempt to pull away. Satisfied by the proximity and warmth of her body, he closed his eyes and was asleep within minutes.

HE WOKE SEVERAL HOURS LATER after realizing she had gotten out of bed. The sun was up and the coffee made; Bridget was sitting at the kitchen table, scratching her head, working a crossword puzzle. She was still in her sleep pants and a T-shirt. Their eyes met, and she muttered, "G' morning."

Well, that's promising, he thought. He mumbled a rather sheepish "Hi" and sat down opposite her, watching, waiting for a sign it was safe to speak, to offer some words of reconciliation.

She wrote down a few letters, erased them, shook her head, and put the pencil on the table. "You have something you want to say to me?" she asked.

"You mean about the trip?"

"Yes, about the trip. About why you didn't say anything sooner. Why you think it's okay to do that to me."

He was silent, framing his response, not sure exactly what it was he wanted, or was about, to say. They stared at one other, she somewhat incredulously, he with mind racing, trying to read her expression until he blurted out an answer that surprised even him. "I won't go."

"*What?*"

"I'm not going. It's a dumb idea, and. . . and I don't want to lose you. I want to get back to where we used to be, and I'm sorry I was so insensitive."

Bridget's lips parted, but no words came out. She had been caught completely off guard. "Where is this coming from?" she finally asked.

He pressed his lips together, smirked, shrugged, but offered no reply.

"You sure?" she asked. "You were pretty adamant yesterday. What about the ticket? I thought you said you already booked the flight."

"I can cancel up to a week before."

"Uh-huh. So when were you supposed to go?"

"A week from tomorrow."

"That only gives you one day. You sure, David? You sure you want to cancel?"

He nodded. "Yeah. It's the right thing to do."

"I've never known you to let that get in your way."

He took a deep breath, said, "Well," and then stopped.

"How long were you planning on going for, anyway?" she asked.

"I didn't have a plan."

"Really?" she asked skeptically. "You have no return ticket?"

"Yeah, no. I didn't get one."

She cleared her throat, peered out the window, and considered the exchange—a more civil conversation than she anticipated. She sat upright and brushed her hair away from her face. "Maybe. . . maybe you *should* go. I mean, would you be able to get it done in a few weeks?"

". . .You mean that?"

"Well, could you?"

"I don't know," he said, warming to the idea, grateful for her turnaround.

"What would it take?"

"Well, I need to make a few contacts in Bangkok before I go, and I'm not sure what I could accomplish or how long it would take once I got there."

She hesitated, peering into her coffee cup, hoping she wouldn't be sorry for what she was about to say. "David, go. It would be good for you. . .and for us. Just go, but please, please be careful, and I mean it. . . . Don't stay more than a couple of weeks, or I might not be here when you get back."

She knew it was harsh, but a day earlier she had been ready anyway. Now they might just have a chance. Give him some space. Give the two of them room, and maybe they could work it out, and maybe he'd settle down and make the commitment.

"Wow! You are *somethin'*," he declared. "I don't know what to say."

He reached across the table, stood up, and walked around to hug her, kiss her, and then hug her again.

ENERGIZED AND FOCUSED, David secured an editor's approval to write a four-thousand word exposé on "The State of the Thai Sex Trade." He spent hours at the computer downloading data, maps, and a "sex guide" to the Soi Cowboy district in Bangkok, notorious for the sex clubs and the child hookers roaming the crowded streets. He was disgusted by what he read, horrified by the statistics.

Disturbed but not dismayed, he plodded along gathering information, sharing with Bridget from time to time what he had learned.

"It's inconceivable," he told her one night. "There are hundreds of thousands of kids under eighteen forced into prostitution. Boys too, only ten years old, are forced to engage in sex acts with men."

Repulsed by what he was telling her, Bridget finally raised her hand in protest. "Why in god's name are you doing this,

David?"

He was beginning to question it himself, but he had the assignment from the magazine and was already too far into it. He convinced himself that it could publicize the practice and perhaps even help the agencies trying to end sex trafficking.

THE EMIRATES FLIGHT FROM JFK to Bangkok took twenty hours, and he arrived exhausted. Sex tourism, as it was known locally, was a thriving business and his taxi ride to the hotel included procurement pitches by the driver.

And so it begins, he thought.

Relieved to be in his hotel room, he fell onto the bed and slept in his clothes for the next five hours, woke at 6:00 PM Malaysia time, and started his voyeuristic journey into the underbelly of hedonism.

It wasn't hard to find a taxi; they were bright, almost fluorescent colored. He climbed into a magenta pink one just outside the hotel and asked to be taken to the *Soi Cowboy* district; the streets were choked with traffic, making the trip twice as long, for which his cab fare was increased thirty-five *baht*, as allowed by local authority.

Within seconds of being dropped off among the vendors, the tourists, the seedy-looking bars and tiny shops, he spotted several street children selling flowers and gum. The purple, red, and green neon lights cast an eerie glow on everything and everyone along the street.

One boy, who looked to be no more than ten, grabbed his sleeve and pleaded for him to buy a flower.

"You buy! You buy!" he squawked.

Then he offered something else. He rolled his tongue around and made sucking sounds. "Blow job, twenty *baht*.

You like good." He said the words as if in a trance, his pupils dilated, a few bruises visible on his arms.

David, stunned and frozen in place for a moment, finally put up his hands, shook his head, and walked away. The reality of what he had chosen to write about suddenly sickened him, and he felt as though he would puke. He took several deep breaths to clear his head, but the comingled odors of strange food, garbage, petrol, and throngs of people plugged his nostrils. The flashing signs and blaring music added to his nausea, and he looked for a place to sit, if only for a few minutes. What have I done? he wondered.

He found an empty stool at a food shop, was immediately approached by the counter man, and pointed at the first thing he saw with absolutely no intention of eating it. He turned to face the street. Directly across from where he was sitting stood a bar named Club Insanity. Next door to it, a flashing sign read *Ap Ob Nuat* and, in English, *Steamy Hot Shower Massage.*

There must have been two dozen young girls standing outside, all in very, very short skirts, halter tops, and heavy eye make-up; some had tattoos; none looked more than fourteen. Some made gestures to lure passers-by, gyrated, or assumed suggestive poses; others appeared vapid and disconnected. Looking both ways, David saw the scene being repeated all along the street.

He studied the girls across from where he sat, trying not to be conspicuous or look like a potential customer. It took awhile for him to realize they were being carefully watched by two heavily tattooed men near the doorway. One stood with his arms folded, and the other smoked a cigarette, neither taking his eyes off the girls.

David regained his composure, paid for the uneaten bowl

of food, and headed down the street. The scene he'd witnessed was repeated along the entire strip; he was propositioned a few times and wondered how he could get interviews with some of them, or *if* he could. He decided to return to the hotel, get a good night's sleep, and engage the services of an English-speaking guide.

THE GUIDE TURNED OUT to be a goldmine. He spoke fluent English, Malay, and Japanese, and was a law student familiar with the government's arcane rules on prostitution and sex trafficking. They met in the hotel lobby.

"My name is Thuanthong Aromdee, kind sir. You may call me Thong."

"I am pleased to meet you, Thong."

David explained his mission and what he needed, not the least of which was to keep safe and avoid actual sex with a minor, or anyone else for that matter. The plan was to identify a few subjects, pay them their normal fees, and engage them in conversation.

Thong's knowledge of the "industry" was encyclopedic and David learned more than he expected. "There was big studies by United Nation," Thong explained. "They say maybe two million sex workers in Thailand. Most prostitutes come from far away, sold by parents for promise of job in big city. Others are taken by *Yakuza* from Japan, maybe Philippines, other place."

"*Yakuza*? You mean Japanese Mafia?" David asked him.

"Not mafia. They very old Japanese group. Work for owner. Make sure girls okay, get paid, not get hurt. Pay police to keep business working."

David smiled and nodded that he understood.

Thong assessed his client's cultural ignorance and added, "*Yakuza* work together with other gangs and government officials."

They decided to start interviewing "bar girls," and to gain their confidence that it was okay to talk.

After repeated attempts and buying them a lot of watered-down drinks at exorbitant prices, David's naiveté became apparent. None of the girls would share information; most didn't understand what he wanted, and he was attracting the attention of the Yakuza protectors.

He and Thong tried again in different bars, but without success. David considered hiring the girls for private sessions, but he needed Thong to be there to translate, and none of the girls would allow two at a time.

Standing outside Happy Place Hotel, they were approached by "freelance" prostitutes, but Thong had a hard time convincing them that David was legitimate and would pay them just to talk. Some laughed and walked away; others refused, afraid to go with two men.

DAVID GREW MORE FRUSTRATED as the days went by, and he was beginning to think he might have to give up. He called Bridget to let her know he was alright. "Hey, it's me."

"David! I'm so glad to hear from you. Are you okay? How's it going?"

"Heya, Bridge. Yeah, I'm okay, but it's not going anywhere. I can't get what I need. I'm beginning to think you were right. It was a crazy idea."

"What's the problem?"

"I'm having trouble getting interviews."

"Well, just stick with it. I know you'll succeed. How long

do you think you'll need?"

He was ready to go home right then, but wouldn't say so, not after what had happened before he left. "I don't know, Bridge. I'm not sure. Look, I'll call you in a couple days. I should know more by then. Okay?"

"Sure, of course." Wanting to talk more but not knowing what to say, he was about to hang up when she said, "David, I *do* miss you."

He instantly felt better. "I miss you, too. If nothing else, being away from each other was probably a good thing, right?"

"Yes, I suppose so. We'll talk in a few days then?"

"Yes. Bye for now." He was about to hang up, thought better of it, and said, "I love you," but she had already disconnected.

Afraid he would come up empty-handed, have nothing to show for his effort, and lose out on the assignment fee, he released Thong, who was genuinely sad and thus offered his services at no charge.

David, in good conscience, apologized but didn't accept the offer and for the next two days went it alone, with no results—until he was approached by a girl who looked older than the others, maybe sixteen, and spoke some English. When he explained what he wanted, she seemed to understand most of it.

"We no fuck? Just talk? You no like me?"

"No, no, you're very. . .pretty. I just want to ask some questions."

"Maybe you want boy."

"No, no. I want *you*," he said it with as much conviction as he could muster.

She looked at him askance, cautious, unsure, and then

agreed to be interviewed as long as he paid full price for her and the room for one hour.

He showed her the money, assured her that he would pay in advance, and she asked him to wait while she talked to her "boyfriend" and then disappeared into the Hotel Jasmine.

He could see her in the lobby, pointing over her shoulder, talking to someone just out of sight. She came back, took hold of his arm, and led him into the hotel and down a dimly lit corridor into a tiny room.

David sat on the one chair and took out his tape recorder.

"You pay now," she demanded.

"Oh, sure. Hold on."

He reached for his wallet, counted out one thousand *baht*, twenty-eight dollars American, and handed them to her, stuffing the remaining 53,000 *baht* back into the billfold.

She sat on the bed and began to undress.

He held up his hand. "No! Just talk."

"Just talk," she giggled, and then stood up. "I use bathroom."

She closed and locked the door behind her, which seemed odd to him, but the whole scenario was strange, so he let it go.

A minute passed, but before he could ask her what was going on, there was very loud, agitated knocking on the door and a foreign voice shouting, "You finish now. Time over!"

"I just got in here," he shot back. "Go away!"

The knocking continued, but louder this time, and then two men burst in. One of them slammed into David, knocking him to the floor. The other kicked him in the head. Dazed and frightened, he tried to get up but was kicked again, this time cracking a rib. Before he could regroup, the other assailant pulled him to his feet, punched him in the face, and threw him onto the bed.

"You pay now!" he screamed.

"I p-p-*paid* her already," he stammered, wiping the blood streaming from his nose.

"More! You pay more. Everything, now!"

The girl shouted something in Thai from behind the bathroom door, and the guy grabbed him by the hair. David tried to cover his head with his arms, but the attacker pummeled him, yanked him to his feet, and started pulling at his pockets. He located the wallet and tore it open, and took all the bills before he smacked David hard across the face.

As suddenly as they had entered, they left, the girl with them.

It took him ten minutes to stand up, the pain in his side awful, his head throbbing, blood continuing to drip.

At the front desk, he tried to explain to the clerk what had happened and asked him to call the police, but the man seemed, or pretended, not to understand. David became belligerent and started shouting at him, which ironically brought a policeman. He told David they could do nothing, and that he was wrong trying to buy sex and better off forgetting about it.

With no money to get back to his hotel and unable to speak Thai, he was in a panic. Out on the street, he frantically searched for someone who looked American or British and was fortunate to find an Australian couple who took pity on him and helped him get back to his hotel.

Shaken, bruised, and broke, he crashed onto the bed and cried himself to sleep. In the morning he was able to get through to the American Consulate and walked the eight blocks to the office, where he told them about his experience.

They allowed him to call Bridget to wire money and arrange for his return to the States. To his great relief, while she was horrified by what had happened, she was sympathetic. Her last words before they hung up were, "It was a bad idea."

A CANNON'S ROAR

A FLURRY OF ACTIVITY occurred after the stage manager called, "Places, everyone!" followed by, "Places! Thank you," from several of the actors as they located their marks and held them until the audience settled down.

It was June and quite warm, and Thomas Havershire felt the familiar tug of stage fright in the pit of his stomach. But he was only a bit player and would likely go unnoticed by critics and audience alike, so his jitters were for naught. At that moment, lines from a previous Shakespeare play ran through his mind: "a *poor player who struts and frets his hour upon the stage, and then is heard no more.*"

Upset by the thought of his own anonymity, he murmured under his breath, "Damn you, Will."

The spectators hushed as one of the players took a small step forward. Surveying the people pressed against the stage and leaning over the tiers above, he launched into his opening lines: "*I come no more to make you laugh: things now, that bear a weighty and a serious brow, sad, high, and working, full of state and woe. . . .*"

The play, *Henry VIII*, went well that evening, yet the company's founding members called a cast meeting afterward and made an announcement.

"You are to be commended on a fine performance," Burbage began. "Alas, the audience was restless. And you may have noted that attendance has dwindled since our last production, perchance because some of our competitors have added more gimmickry to their performances, and with great success. And so. . ." he paused to glance at the assembly, cleared his throat, and turned to give a signal, at which point two attendants rolled a cannon onto the stage. They ceremoniously loaded it with gunpowder and wadding and fired off a loud and piercing volley that reverberated off the rafters. There were startled gasps from some of the actors, followed by applause and cheers.

Burbage continued, "And so, you see, we now have our very own contrivance with which to entertain our audience."

More applause followed before young Havershire asked, "And, good sir, just how and when will this. . . this contrivance, as you call it, be used in the play?"

"A fair query, my good fellow," replied Burbage. "We are to use it at the very opening, so as to seize the complete attention of our audience."

Nods of approval followed the proclamation, including Havershire's, who understood that to protest would lead to cries of insurrection.

The next performance was scheduled for a few days hence, and as word spread that something new was planned, it generated a full house of almost fifteen hundred vociferous souls.

Audience anticipation that night was palpable, and the crowd in the upper section began to stomp its feet and clap hands rhythmically before the performers took to the stage.

Vendors circulated through the theater, selling meat pies and sweets. A number of attendees stacked rotten vegetables, which would be used to pelt actors who forgot their lines. The gang of theatergoers was in a raucous mood, which added an element of impending doom.

The cannon had been rolled onto the stage before the public arrived and was draped in brocade to keep it hidden. Cast and crew were convinced the gimmick would be a resounding success.

At the appointed moment, just as the performance was to begin, two attendees, the same two who had fired the device at the cast meeting, quickly exposed the already primed cannon, lit the fuse, and stood back. The entire maneuver took less than five seconds, catching most of the audience off guard. While the explosion was great enough to elicit screams as well as howls of laughter, no one had anticipated the trajectory of the ball, which shot to the top tier and immediately set fire to the thatched roof, spreading rapidly to the wooden frame.

Panic ensued, and everyone scrambled to get out, but there was no planned evacuation route, no fire extinguishers or fire brigades. Spectators leapt from the highest seats, others were trampled underfoot, and acrid smoke filled the air and blinded those trying to leave; pandemonium broke out. Within twenty minutes the Globe Theater had burned to the ground.

The very next day, Thomas Havershire walked among the ashes, reflecting on the irony of the previous night's performance and the play's opening lines: "*I come no more to make you laugh: things now, that bear a weighty and a serious brow, sad, high, and working, full of state and woe . . .*"

It was June 30, 1613, and the Globe, utterly destroyed, was

rebuilt within a year, this time with a tiled roof, and remained open for the next twenty-nine years.

AUTHOR'S NOTE: The original Globe Theatre, built in 1599 by the playing company The Lord Chamberlain's Men, to which Shakespeare belonged, was destroyed by fire on June 29, 1613. The fire was caused by an accident with a cannon during a production of *Henry VIII*. Richard Burbage was a principal player and shareholder in the company. To the best of my knowledge, no one named Thomas Havershire was ever associated with the Globe.

A GOOD BIRTHDAY

YOSHI MATSUKI RAISED the tiny cup of sake and tipped it toward his father. "*Kanpai, chichioya. Otanjo-bi omedetou.*" He said it with a slight bow of his head.

The older man responded quietly, with the serenity Yoshi had come to revere, "*Arigato. Kanpai!*"

They sat with legs crossed on a mat in a local restaurant, celebrating the elder Matsuki's seventieth birthday.

Shegesi, Yoshi's father, had come to Oregon from Hawaii in 1908 to work and, he hoped, send for his wife Asako and their four-year-old son.

Industrious and with a strong back, Shegesi soon found employment, but he had an arduous journey to get to it. Following throngs of his countrymen east, away from the Pacific Coast, he took work on sugar beet farms in the Snake River Valley of Idaho, then joined a railroad crew laying track near the town of Nampa. Living quarters at the work camp were dismal and crowded, wages were low, and hours long, but Shegesi still managed to save his money and planned to buy a piece of land to farm and send for his family.

It didn't work out that way.

As hordes of foreigners came to the West and took jobs for lower pay, attitudes toward them changed, and with them Shegesi's dream. It wasn't long before new laws and regulations were created by the United States government to curtail the influx of Asian immigrants and, most disheartening for Shegesi, making it illegal for the Japanese to own land.

He wrote letters to Asako every week, but they took months to arrive, and the two became more estranged as his time away turned into years. Asako and her mother, along with Yoshi and an uncle, lived together in a rented house near Oahu. As the years slipped by, she became less willing to leave the island, but Yoshi was becoming a man and the family agreed that he should join his father in America.

Raised in a traditional Buddhist and Shinto home, the young Matsuki dutifully accepted his fate and arrived in America by steamer in the late summer of 1920; he was sixteen.

As his father had done, Yoshi signed on with a work crew and gradually headed east to reunite with him. It took sixty-eight days to get to Nampa, where the winter introduced itself with a vengeance to the Hawaiian-born Yoshi—conditions he had never experienced and was ill-equipped to deal with.

Chilled to the core, on the verge of exhaustion, and emaciated, he barely made it into the work camp where his father lived.

The camp's small barrack buildings were on one level and housed a dozen men each, with a small stove for cooking, one sink, and a shower and toilet facility outside. Each man had a cot, a shelf for his belongings, and a rod to hang clothing. The camp had a large separate dining hall that doubled as a communal meeting space.

The night he arrived, as crews shuffled back into camp, Yoshi stumbled from one barrack to the next, calling out his father's name.

At first he shouted in Japanese, then in broken English, then in Japanese again, "Matsuki Shegesi, are you here?"

Yoshi had only seen a photo of his father from ten years before but had no memories of the man. By the time the young Matsuki arrived, Shegesi was almost sixty, gray- haired, and considerably weathered from being outdoors every day for years. His furrowed brow and crestfallen frown disguised him even further.

Hearing his name being called out in Japanese, Shegesi was confused at first; then, as he realized it must be Yoshi, his heart beat faster. Leaping off his cot he shouted, "*Hai! Sumimasen desu Matsuki!*"

Overcome with joy, relieved to finally have been reconnected, the two men shed all customary Asian formality and uncharacteristically embraced. Allowing their tears to flow, the years of separation to dissolve, father and son stepped back to look at one another, then embraced again and started to laugh.

Embarrassed by his display of emotion, Shegesi suggested they go to the meeting hall to be away from prying eyes and ears. They sat for hours, close to one another, knees almost touching, quietly telling about their lives apart from each other.

"Your mother Asako, is she still so beautiful? Does she speak of me? Is she happy?"

The questions came slowly, the answers more so.

The Japanese do not share feelings easily, and Yoshi had little idea of how his mother felt, but he did say to his father, "*Hai, chichioya-san,* she is still beautiful, but I am afraid when

I left she was not well. Her mother, my *Sobo,* died, and it was hard for her because *Oji-san,* my uncle Hanshiro, was no help to her. He was—" he hesitated, searching for the English word, then in Japanese offered, "*Chinsui!*" and lowered his gaze. "I am sorry I do not know how to say he drink too much sake."

His father chuckled, then nodded slowly and became serious. "Drunk. That is a dishonor to the family," he grumbled. "I am ashamed."

They didn't discuss it further.

Yoshi, already hired to work on the railway, was given a bunk next to his father, and the two were put in the same crew, which included Chinese and Japanese, as well as an Irishman, and a Canadian. It was the warmth and love they developed for each other that helped Yoshi endure his first harsh winter.

The following year, he received a letter from his uncle Hanshiro that Asako had died of influenza. On hearing the news, Shegesi quietly cried while Yoshi, who missed her greatly, let loose a torrent of bitter tears.

Bonding more like siblings than father and son, the two men shared everything; money, food, and clothing. When the railroad was completed, they migrated to California and worked on the farms until it became too much for the aging Shegesi.

Yoshi then found work in the vineyards of Napa Valley and worked his way up to foreman, allowing him to rent a house where Shegesi and he could live. When the Depression came to the Valley, his position as foreman was eliminated; some time later, the vineyard failed, and he lost his job.

Ironically, a few months before joining the growing ranks of the unemployed, Yoshi had met a *Nisei,* a second-generation Japanese girl named Miyuki, eleven years younger than he and born an American citizen. Afraid that his father might not approve, or that he might think Yoshi would soon leave, he waited before introducing her to him.

Miyuki worked as a bookkeeper in her father's grocery store, which weathered the financial collapse by extending credit and allowing customers to pay as little as fifty cents a week.

When Yoshi knew he wanted to marry her, he couldn't hide it any longer and introduced her to his father. Miyuki was a combination of old-world Japan and new-world America. Like a school girl, she often giggled behind a cupped hand, yet she possessed a natural grace and beauty. Not surprisingly, Shegesi was captivated by her and elated for Yoshi.

"Miyuki is like a pearl," he told him. "You *must* marry her. She is right for you."

As the Depression eased, Yoshi found menial jobs and eventually asked Miyuki's father if he could marry her. Yoshi was thirty-one, she just twenty. As a wedding present, her father bought them a house, and, as tradition called for, they insisted Shegesi move in with them; it was 1935, and Shegesi celebrated his sixty-fourth birthday.

They lived quietly, Yoshi working whenever he could, Miyuki helping at the grocery, Shegesi tending a vegetable garden in back of the house. It was a peaceful life, and the years passed quietly; the three of them were oblivious to the outside world.

"I AM OLD," SHEGESI TOLD THEM one night. "I would like grandchildren before I die."

Miyuki giggled but remained quiet.

"*Otou-sama!*" exclaimed Shegesi. Then, ashamed for raising his voice, he softened and bowed his head a little. "If I may speak, please?"

"Hai, Yoshi," said his father.

"*Chichioya*, forgive me, but we cannot afford children. You. . .you were already an older man when I was born, and then you came to America. Time is not right for us."

Shegesi looked sad but understood. After a few moments of contemplation, he responded, "It would be honor to name child after me when it comes."

On hearing him, Miyuki turned toward her husband. "May I speak, Yoshi-san?"

"Always, Miyuki."

She turned her delicate face toward her father-in-law. "*Gifu*," she said softly, "if we have a child I would be *honored* to give it your name."

Shegesi made a grumbling sound and nodded once in appreciation, but offered no words. For him, the matter would not be brought up again.

The following week the three of them went out for Shegesi's eightieth birthday. As the sake flowed, he became particularly jovial, talking about growing up in Nagasaki, where much of his family still lived, how he had met Asako and of their time together in Hawaii, and of what he remembered about Yoshi as a little boy.

Miyuki was delighted and giggled much. Her husband sat with a faint smile on his face, happy that his father was so fond of Miyuki and how much he seemed to be enjoying himself.

It was a good birthday—December 6, 1941.

BENCH BUDDIES

WEATHER PERMITTING, Charlie Grossman and Em- mett Pitt met on a bench facing the Seventy-second Street subway entrance every morning at ten o'- clock, just a few blocks from where Amsterdam and Broadway split off from Columbus Avenue.

They used to sit further down, near Sherman Square, but it got too noisy to hear each other. Since Morris died (they called him the third musketeer), the fun had gone out of their conversations.

Morris had been their comic relief; the old vaudevillian lived to be eighty-nine and for thirty years made a living work- ing the Borscht Belt. Without his youthful exuberance and good-natured chiding to keep them in check, Charlie and Em- mett often bickered and one time even stopped talking for a whole week. They'd just sit there pretending they didn't know each other, until one morning a young man sat between them and opened a container of coffee and a newspaper. Charlie glanced sideways at Emmett, cleared his throat, and growled at the interloper, "Hey, we're saving this seat for Morris!"

The fellow stifled a laugh, put the lid back on the cup,

stood up, and smiled. "Have a nice day, gents," he said, and walked away. Emmett nodded in Charlie's direction, and the two began talking to each other again as if they had been interrupted only a minute before.

Charlie looked across the street, in the direction of Zabar's delicatessen, and said aloud, "Susan Hayward, now she was a dish!"

"Whatta ya talkin'?" responded Emmett. "You mean Rita Hayworth."

Charlie sighed exasperatedly. "Hayward, Hayworth, what's the difference? They're both gone anyway. Besides. . . it was Ava Gardner who got me all hot and bothered."

"She was a tramp," grumbled Emmett. "She married 'em all. That skinny guy, what's his . . .oh, yeah, Sinatra. And the little guy? Uh—"

"The Andy Hardy guy. . . Rooney," answered Charlie. "Yeah, yeah, Mickey Rooney. I could never understand that. Shrimpy little guys, both of 'em."

"Yeah," said Emmett. "But Artie Shaw I could get. Handsome like Errol Flynn, bandleader, could play a mean trumpet."

"Clarinet," said Charlie.

Emmett pondered which instrument and floated off into his own reverie. Several minutes passed and neither spoke, but Charlie watched him, wondering where his memory had taken him. He knew the feeling all too well.

Often sitting in front of the television in his rent-controlled apartment above Fairway Market, Grossman would drift for long spells; no thoughts, just emptiness, and then back again. It happened more frequently of late, but he didn't tell anyone, not even Sarah, who lived out on the island in Syosset. "Come live with us, Pop," she implored. "We have room. You'll get to see the kids more. You know we love you, Pop. Please?"

But the idea made him uncomfortable. Yes, he missed them, but he would lose his independence. She'd hover and baby him, and lonely as he was, at least he was his own man.

Emmett came back as suddenly as he had left and spoke mid-sentence like he'd been talking the whole time. "Margaret and you, married fifty-six years?"

Charlie sighed, a deep, guttural sound, as if exasperated by the remark. "Yes, fifty-six years. Can't believe it. The same woman. Watched her get old in front of my eyes, that dainty little thing, a wisp of a girl. Oy!" His thoughts trailed off, and a moment later he turned toward Emmett. "How come you never got married?" he asked for what must have been the umpteenth time.

"How many times you ask me that, Charlie? What'd ya, forget?"

"So remind me."

Emmett sighed. "It's not like I didn't have anyone in my life, y'know? There were women, lots of 'em, in fact."

"Yeah, but I mean how come none of them stuck around?"

Emmett scratched at his full head of white hair, contemplating the question as if it had never been asked before. "They didn't all leave me. Some I gave up." He paused a moment before shaking his head from side to side in despair. "There was one. Del. Delores Finkelstein. Jewish. A real beauty, but when her mother heard about me, oh, boy. 'Emmett? Pitt?'" she asked. "'That's a Jewish name?' It got so bad," he continued, "we had to meet in the park by the boat house after school, or at the Thalia movie theater on Saturdays, just so we could spend time together without her parents knowing."

"Hypocrites!" Charlie protested. "Jews of all people should know what bigotry and prejudice is."

Emmett exhaled loudly and absently brushed at his coat with one hand, as if wiping the memory away. Grossman waited and watched for the appropriate moment to ask his next question. "So? What happened? How come you just didn't elope?"

"I got drafted. Went to war. Came back four years later, and she was married. She died in child birth, y'know."

"Ach, I'm sorry, Emmett. I didn't mean to stir it up again. I forgot."

"So that's what happened. Never married 'cause I was still in love with her. Still am, I guess."

Changing the subject, Charlie turned to face him. "You still play pinochle? I mean, since Morris passed away?"

Emmett was clearly perturbed by the inquiry. "Who would I play with? You don't play."

"Just asking," Charlie replied. "Don't get so testy." After a minute of silence he added, "So what *do* you play?"

"Gin rummy. Now that's a game. Simple. Too many rules in Pinochle."

"Gin rummy, huh?" Charlie considered the idea. "Okay, we should play sometime."

Surprised, Emmett looked Charlie squarely in the eye. "You mean it?"

"Sure, why not? Come to my apartment on Thursday, I'll set up the card table. We'll play awhile. You like sturgeon?"

"Too expensive," replied Emmett. "You see the price at Barney Greengrass? A sturgeon appetizer and a bialy with a schmeer, twenty dollars! No, thanks. A nice turkey sandwich and a glass of tea. I'm good."

Charlie rose from the bench. "Okay. Thursday. We'll play. We'll eat. We'll enjoy."

Emmett nodded. "So I'll see you tomorrow?"

"Why not? I'll see you tomorrow. Same time."

BETWIXT

URING THE LUNCH HOUR and again during his coffee break, Henry perused his messages on the dating site. There were three—one from a woman in Daytona who was eleven years older than he was, one from a woman in Sanford whom he didn't find very attractive, and the other, a very good-looking brunette from Casselberry, a little north of where he lived. He "favored" her, but waited until he was home before sending her a response.

Hi, he wrote, *I read your message on Datesight.com and love your picture and your profile. I think we have lots in common and a similar outlook on life. Please write back if you agree, H2.0.*

The signature was his screen name, *H* for Henry, *2.0* for "to Orlando," which is where he had lived since moving from Minnesota.

She replied almost immediately, and they started a string of emails over the next few weeks that eventually led to a phone call, and then another and another, until they finally agreed to meet in Winter Park, mid-way between their houses. She suggested the café inside the Cornell Museum on the campus of Rollins College, as mutual ground.

AFTER THEIR SECOND CUP OF CHAI TEA, they walked through the galleries and discovered that they both loved Impressionism and the work of Frederick Childe Hassam. They lingered in front of his "The French Tea Garden" and soon discovered they shared more than just the same taste in art. They ambled through the rest of the afternoon holding hands.

It wasn't long after that first date, which lasted well into the evening, that they started seeing each other regularly.

Alexis was vivacious, attractive, and she had a slender figure, an engaging smile, and a hearty laugh. She possessed large hands and feet for a woman, but they somehow fit her. Her choice in clothing and accessories were understated yet very feminine. Henry fell hard. Also tall and thin, he had the same color hair and hazel eyes as she did.

A month into their courtship, while strolling around Lake Kathryn near her condo in Casselberry, he remarked that, if they ever had children, everyone would look alike. She sighed, took his hand, and pulled him to a park bench and sat down.

"Henry, honey," she said almost in tears, "I love children, but I can't have them."

He listened attentively, waiting for a more comprehensive explanation, but she stopped short of sharing the details.

"Why not?" he finally asked.

"It's. . .a medical condition, that's all."

He took hold of her hand and brought it to his lips, held it there for a moment, and then quietly, almost conspiratorially said, "It's okay. Besides, I'm not sure I want to share you with anyone else, anyway. You know, I—I don't even know . . . Alex, were you ever married?"

"Yes, I was. To a lovely, gentle person. Jamie had a sweet disposition and was very understanding."

"So what happened?" he asked.

She seemed to be measuring her words, her eyes downcast. "I wanted. . .something different for my life. I-I wasn't comfortable in who I was."

". . .How long were you together?"

"Six years."

"When?"

"Five years ago."

She turned to face him. "And you?" she asked. "Were you ever married?"

He frowned at the question. "No, no, never married," he said, and added almost inaudibly, "Just couldn't find the right one, I guess."

Alexis nodded but said nothing more, and they dropped the subject.

Over the next few months their relationship progressed to stronger feelings and eventually to sexual intimacy, and soon afterward they began to spend weekends together and then a vacation on St. Croix, where Henry asked her to marry him.

At the time, he was cradling her in his arms while she floated languidly in the tepid, turquoise water; the setting sun casting an orange-pink aura on the sails of a schooner in the distance. The scene was sublimely idyllic for a proposal.

She didn't answer right away, and he wondered whether she'd heard him or was stalling, or perhaps considering how to say no.

About to ask her again, he noticed she was crying. "Is that a yes or. . . ?"

She remained silent, her eyes closed, tears mixing with the sea water. Henry didn't know what to do, so he turned around slowly toward shore and let go of her.

She stood up and took his hand. "Let's go back to the room, okay?"

"Sure. Are you feeling alright?"

She nodded and half-smiled. "I want to talk to you about what you just asked. But in the privacy of our room."

Not sure what to expect, Henry resigned himself to bad news. Nothing could have prepared him for what was to come.

ALTHOUGH THEY HAD A LOVELY BALCONY overlooking the beach, she sat inside on the tiny sofa and beckoned him next to her. He stood for a few moments, then took a chair a few feet away.

"What happened?" he pleaded. "Did I ask too soon?"

She shook her head and took a very deep breath.

He gave a little chuckle, "Y'know, this isn't exactly the response I was hoping for."

"Henry, I love you. I do—more than anyone I have ever known, but. . . ."

"But what?"

"Henry, darling I—I-"

"Alex, out with it! I can take it. What are you trying to say?"

She reached for his hand, but he remained motionless.

"Okay. . .this isn't easy for me, and I know it isn't going to be for you." She inhaled deeply again and then looked directly into his eyes. "Remember when I told you I was married to Jamie?"

"Yes. Wait—oh God, you're not still *married* are you?"

"No. No I'm not. Henry, Jamie is a woman."

He stared at her, trying to comprehend what she had said.

"What are you. . .what do you mean, he's a *woman?*"

"Henry, listen to me. Jamie is and always was a woman."

"Are you telling me you're a lesbian?"

No. . .well, not exactly—Henry, my real. . .my birth name was Alexander!"

"What? What are you saying?"

"Henry, I'm. . .I used to be a man."

He sat there incredulous. His mind was reeling, and he felt sick to his stomach. "Alexis, I don't understand. Why are you saying this? If you don't want to get married, just say so. I mean—"

"Look, I know this is a blow—"

"A *blow!*" His face flushed as he squeezed the arms of the chair. "What are you *talking* about?"

Tears began to run down her cheeks, and her lower lip trembled.

"This is ridiculous, Alex. I mean, we had *sex*. You have a *vagina,* for Chrissake. You have *boobs.* How could you be a man?"

"Henry, Henry my darling, Henry. I am so, so sorry. I should have told you sooner, but—"

"No! *No!*" He was growing angry. "It can't be. How? How is it possible? Are you telling me you're. . .you're *transgender?*"

"It's called a sex reassignment."

". . .When did you do it?"

"It took three years, and many operations, and a lot of money."

He sat with his mouth agape.

Unsure if he was going to cry or lash out at her, she quietly asked, "Henry, do you want me to leave?"

It took him some time to collect his thoughts before he rose from the chair. She leaned back against the sofa, afraid he was going to hit her, but instead he walked toward the door and turned, tears in his eyes.

"I need to think about this. I'm going for a walk."

He left before she could respond.

DARKNESS HAD OVERTAKEN THE ISLAND. Palm fronds rustled in the evening breeze, the moon shone off the placid sea, and Henry had been walking down the beach for a long while before he finally tired, sank onto the sand, and wept. He pondered what he found so incredible, so shocking, not knowing how he truly felt about her. . .him, whatever, whoever, and most of all, who Alexis was supposed to be to *him*.

He eventually found his way to a hammock, and, staring at the stars, making bargains, he pleaded with the heavens to show him, what to do. He dozed on and off until nearly morning and, when he felt he knew the answer, hoisted himself up and went back to the room.

Alexis was asleep on the sofa and woke with a start when he entered the room, thinking he was still angry, expecting to be told to get out. She pulled a cushion against her chest.

He slumped onto the sofa and heaved a sigh, then reached for her hand, which she cautiously slid into his.

He swallowed hard, looked into her eyes, and in a tremulous voice, uttered something he would never have believed could come from his mouth.

"Alexis, this is crazy to me. It is so surreal that I cannot fathom what lies ahead. All I know is I fell in love with *you*— not who or what you once were, but *you*. And I *still* love you. I can only imagine what your life was like as a m-man, and what you went through to be true to yourself. . .and now I love you even more for your courage."

She started to sob, shaking with emotion, threw her arms around his neck, and pressed her face against him, speechless.

He whispered into her ear, to be sure she heard him, "I don't know what happens from here on, but I know I can't give you up, and if you will have me. . .I still want to be your husband."

It was difficult to hear between her sobs, but he was absolutely certain she replied, "Yes! Yes! *Yes!*"

CARMINE'S FIGHT

D RESSED IN A PINSTRIPE SUIT and alligator shoes outside Vito's Restaurant, an irritated customer yelled to the parking attendant, "Hey, Punchy, move your dumb ass and get me my freakin' car?"

The valet was wandering among the vehicles, searching for it. He kept looking at the ticket in his hand and then at the row of cars, not knowing which belonged to the irate patron.

"Jesus!" the man barked. "It's the blue Coupe De Ville, you moron"

A tall, peroxide-tinted blond standing next to him, snapping her gum to some hidden rhythm, griped, "Augie, why doncha just go get it yourself?"

"Hey," he shot back, "why doncha just shut your face."

The valet finally figured out which car it was, drove it the few yards to the canopy, got out, and held the door open. "Sorry, Mister Dominick, I-I couldn't re-remember."

Dominick shook his head and slipped a five into the guy's hand. "Here, this is for ya *troubles!*"

Before he slid onto the seat he looked up at the hulking figure and smiled. "I remember when you was at the Garden.

Knocked that colored guy right outta the ring. You was *good*. What happened to you, anyway? Too many head shots, huh? Bees in ya bonnet?"

CARMINE BEVILACQUA WAS TOO BIG for a middleweight, at least now, years after he'd lost the title to Jorge "The Puma" Mendoza. But at 160 pounds, Carmine was a trim, quick-on-his-feet, hard-punching knock-out artist with adoring fans and a sure bet for the Boxing Hall of Fame in Canostota, New York.

Growing up in the Bronx, not far from Yankee Stadium, he had a broken nose and two knife wounds by the time he was fourteen.

One blistering hot summer day an Italian police sergeant arrested him for stealing a car out of the parking lot during a double header between the Yankees and the Red Sox. The cop, Angelo Pileggi, was on a crusade to save kids from a life of crime or early death at the hands of a rival gang. And if the kid was Italian, he ramped up his efforts.

Seizing Carmine by the shirt collar with one hand, his other wrapped tightly around the kid's wrist, Pileggi muttered, "Listen, kid," in a harsh whisper but with a touch of compassion. "You got a choice. I take you to lock up, and you're looking at hard time in Dannemora for grand theft." He breathed in through his nose. "Or you can come to the PAL, Tuesday night at the precinct."

Carmine squirmed, trying to get loose, but the cop was stronger than he looked.

"Listen to me," Pileggi went on. "I know your mother and I know Father Ruggio, so don't think you're gonna get away and I don't know who you are. . . . You think you're tough?"

He let go of the collar but held onto the wrist tight enough to let Carmine know he was serious. "I'm gonna give you a chance to prove it. We'll put you in the ring and see what you're made of."

Carmine had been a good child growing up, but he'd gone astray not long after his dockworker father was crushed to death by a falling shipping container, leaving his mother a heartbroken mess unable to take care of her young son because she had to work to support him and herself.

The boy was left in the care of an aged, widowed grandmother who didn't speak much English and spent most of her time in bed or at Saint Teresa of Avila Holy Catholic Church. He grew up largely by his wits and a winning smile, fighting when he had to and running when he needed to get away from a gang or the cops.

His first time in the ring at the Police Athletic League gym, Carmine was knocked flat by one punch delivered with lightning speed by a Puerto Rican kid five inches shorter than he was. It was just one of many to come over the next eleven years, but he always got up and always stayed in the fight, until one day he couldn't.

PILEGGI WAS ALSO THE BOXING COACH at the local PAL, which met in the basement of St. Theresa. He'd solicited funds and equipment from local merchants and the church youth club to set up the gym and boxing ring, and he brought youngsters into the program with considerable care and sensitivity. He gave encouragement and basic defensive skills to those who lacked real talent, so they wouldn't be bullied in the school yard. He spent time with the kids who showed aptitude and gave them every opportunity to excel at something they could use to build confidence and maybe a way out of a dismal future.

As the program progressed, Pileggi entered a team of young boxers into amateur fights with other clubs and brought the gifted kids, Carmine among them, into the PAL championship bouts. The first was in the Bronx, then the other boroughs; eventually, they made it to the state championships.

Carmine had twenty-three amateur bouts the first year, winning nineteen, plus one draw; the three losses were close decisions. Knockouts were all but impossible in those three-round events, because the fighters wore protective headgear, and the referees stopped the fight if blood began to trickle.

By the time Carmine turned sixteen, Angelo Pileggi had been promoted to Detective Grade but insisted on staying with the boxing program. By then his star pupil, Carmine Bevilacqua had grown into a solid welterweight with skill beyond his years. He was also old enough to enter the Golden Gloves, a time-honored stepping stone to the professional ranks.

Angelo knew it was time to get Carmine a better, more experienced trainer. The kid had tears in his eyes when he told him. "But, Angie, you're my mentor. You been like a father ta me. I can't do this without you."

Pileggi teared up as well and reassured the youngster that he would be at all his fights, telling him, "No matter what, I promise you, kid. I'll always be in your corner."

He was true to his word for the next six years. Carmine won the welterweight division golden gloves in his second-year attempt, and two years later, at nineteen, turned pro.

Angelo begged a trainer from upstate New York, who had a stable of contenders and two world champions, to take Carmine into his fold. If Angelo Peleggi was the boy's mentor and father figure, then Christopher Harlow became a surrogate role model and took him under his wing. He carefully, thoughtfully brought him along, revealed the nuances and science of boxing to him, building his strength, speed, and accuracy, and even taught him a few dirty tricks, mostly so he could avoid them when his opponents got frustrated.

Chris, after some coaxing from Carmine, agreed to let Detective Peleggi manage the kid's career. It turned out to be a wise decision. As a cop, Angelo could always smell a raw deal or phony offer; he was also someone both trainer and boxer trusted without question.

In that environment, and with his deep-seated desire to become a world champion, Carmine flourished, listened to advice, worked out religiously, stayed clean, and focused on his goal.

His professional career started with four-round matchups and moved on to six-and eventually eight-round fights. By the time he was twenty-one, he had the physique of a middleweight and travelled from state to state, winning one battle after another until his *Ring Magazine* ranking reached number two and brought him the offer of a title shot.

Entering the ring as the eight-to-one underdog, he electrified the fans with a fourth-round knockout and became the Middleweight Champion of the World.

His mom was at ringside that night, and Carmine stepped through the ropes and went to her seat to kiss her and raise her hand in triumph. The crowd went nuts, and his fan base exploded.

CARMINE WAS A GOOD CHAMPION, taking on all comers, never ducked a fight or complained to the ref if hit below the belt or behind the head. He defended his title often, sometimes three times in a year, and invariably came away victorious, though not without close calls.

He made enough money to buy a house in Yonkers and gave it to his mother as a birthday present. When her health began to fail, he hired a live-in caregiver. When he wasn't training for a bout, he lived in the house, too. He kept a small house for himself too in upstate New York, near Chris, and occasionally took the trainer's niece out for dinner or to a movie, but his focus was always on boxing, and he told Chris, "Don't worry, I ain't gonna be trouble for her. I like her, but I know she's too classy for me."

CARMINE'S NINTH TITLE DEFENSE, against an Argentinean boxer, changed him forever. Little known in the United States, southpaw Carlos Galíndez was a problem from the opening bell. He grabbed, punched to the body with ferocity, and took an early lead by outpunching Carmine two to one.

In the corner after the fourth round, Chris looked into his fighter's eyes and saw Carmine was not focusing. "What's wrong kid?"

The champ didn't immediately respond but stared into Chris's chest while the cut man worked a gash under the fighter's right eye. When he pressed the hard, ice-cold, metallic anti-swell to his cheek bone, Carmine winced.

"Carmine, listen to me," Chris barked, "stay away from this guy. Don't let him get inside. Keep your jab in his face. You're takin' too much punishment. And keep your *hands* up, goddamit!"

The trainer leaned in to whisper, "What'sa matter with you?"

Carmine shook his head very slowly from side to side, "Nuthin'. I'm okay."

He managed to stay away in the fifth and landed a few hard rights of his own in the sixth. At the close of round seven, he sent a crushing blow to Galíndez's temple that rocked the South American back on his feet, and the man would have gone down if the ropes hadn't held him up. Carmine was about to go in for the kill when the bell rang.

The Argentinean came out swinging in the next round, and the two fighters went toe-to-toe in the center of the ring, bringing the crowd to its feet. Two minutes into the round, Carmine got tangled up in the corner while Galíndez pummeled away at his mid-section, landing punishing blows to Carmine's liver while holding the champion's arm on the side opposite the referee.

Carmine tried slipping the punches and heard Chris screaming from across the ring, "Get outta there! Get off the ropes!"

Thirty seconds before the bell, Galíndez stepped back and landed an enormous left hook that sent Carmine's sweat flying into the third row. It looked as if Carmine was going down, but he shook it off and swung back, missing the target by a foot only to get hit with a counter punch that landed on his jaw with a cracking sound just as the bell rang.

In the corner, Chris got a close look at his fighter. Carmine's right eye was almost shut; the anti-swell was not working. Worse than that, he realized Carmine's jaw was fractured. "Kid, it ain't your night. I'm gonna call it quits. You can't take no more of this."

Angelo worked his way to the ring apron from three rows back, leaned in through the ropes, and said to Carmine,

"Maybe it's time, son. Don't take any more of this than you have to."

Carmine sat on the stool, taking deep breaths, looked up at his trainer, and shook his head. "No, you're not stoppin' it. I'm okay. I got this guy."

The ring doctor came over as well.

"One round," pronounced the physician. "One more round. If he keeps getting hit, I'm stopping it."

"I'm good," said Carmine, lifted himself off the stool, and faced his adversary across the ring.

Galíndez stood up, smiled, and winked at him. The bell sounded, and the two men met center ring. The South American threw a sweeping left at Carmine's head, but the champion stepped away and answered with a powerful uppercut that sent Galíndez teetering backward, and then Carmine was all over him and began hammering away with both hands to the body and then to the face. The Argentinean was overwhelmed by the viciousness of the onslaught and tried to get away, then tried to tie up Carmine in a clinch but was pushed off and hit with a barrage of lefts and rights that slammed him into the ropes.

Carmine didn't pursue his prey, but waited for the man to come to him. As Galíndez moved in, Carmine stepped to the side, rammed a brutal left hook into the man's solar plexus that doubled him over, and hit him with an explosive right that sent him to the canvas, out cold.

It was a tough win for Carmine. More significant was the damage he had sustained—a torn retina, a ruptured spleen, two broken ribs, a fractured jaw, and fluid on the brain. Both Angelo and Chris told him it was time to quit while he was still undefeated and able to "walk and talk," as Chris put it.

CARMINE'S MOTHER DIED of renal failure a few months after the Galíndez fight, sending Carmine into a depression that took months to shake. By the time the boxing commission pronounced him fit to fight again, Chris could tell that his fighter was a step behind, his reflexes slowed—and, most important, his enthusiasm for training had dulled. Chris began scrutinizing his fighter's every move in the training ring, during workouts, and socially when given the opportunity. He asked his niece if she noticed anything unusual in his behavior. "He drifts off sometimes," she told him. "Once in a while he forgets and gropes for a word when we're talking. Otherwise he's the same loveable guy as always." She smiled meekly and then added , "Maybe he moves slower than he used to, and. . . well, he doesn't seem to be there all the time. You know what I mean?"

Chris knew exactly what she meant but didn't want to alarm her. They were telltale signs, and he again considered asking Carmine to vacate the title, but the public was clamoring for a rematch with Galíndez, and the boxing bigwigs had other plans. It was important for Carmine to give a title shot to the next guy in line, and so he did, winning by a narrow margin. Then another fight eight months later with a British fighter he stopped in the sixth by TKO.

Each time he stepped into the ring Chris feared for him, but he didn't let on, just watched more intently from the corner, ever vigilant.

CARMINE DEFENDED THE TITLE twice more after the battle against the British boxer, once in Chicago when he exhibited some of his former skills and banished the challenger in the fifth round with a one-two combination that laid the guy out face-down on the canvas.

Then came the heavily promoted combat between Carmine Bevalaqua, the "undefeated, undisputed Middleweight Champion of the World," against a young, fast-rising star and Olympic gold-medal slugger from the Dominican Republic, Jorge Mendoza, nicknamed "The Puma." The odds makers had it at five-to-one for Carmine by a knockout in the sixth. It didn't quite turn out that way.

By the end of the third round Mendoza had to be helped onto the stool, and it looked like Carmine would beat the betting line by two rounds.

Having told Angelo privately that he would retire after this one, he was primed for an easy victory and all but jumped out of his seat when the bell rang for round four.

Whatever his trainer said to the Dominican must've invigorated him, because he practically ran across the ring and met Carmine only a few steps from the corner.

Starting with a right cross, the young fighter spun the champion around with a follow up left that almost decked him. Knees buckling from the force of the punch, Carmine grabbed his opponent and locked his arms around him for a few seconds of relief in order to collect himself.

The ref separated them and had the two step back for a split second before they clashed again. This time Mendoza unleashed a savage flurry to Carmine's stomach and then pushed him back before charging in again, not giving Carmine time to recover and hitting him in the head with a left-and-right combination before swinging from his shoe tops with an uppercut that lifted the champion off the floor.

Carmine fell like a tree, flat out, arms spread wide, his head banging onto the canvas with such force it bounced twice. The crowd gasped in horror at the power and at their hero sprawled on the floor, his eyes unfocused, blood leaking from his mouth and ears. The ref waived off the fight, pulled out Carmine's mouthpiece, and yelled for the doctor.

Chris was hovering over his fallen fighter before the doctor got to him; Angelo jumped into the ring immediately thereafter. It took two agonizing minutes to get Carmine into a sitting position before calling for a stretcher.

He was on the way to the hospital before the announcer declared, "Winner by knockout, and the New Middleweight Champion of The World, Jorge 'The Puma' Mendoza!"

CARMINE WAS IN THE HOSPITAL for four weeks, the first ten days in an induced coma to help the brain swelling subside, a hole drilled into his temple to reduce the pressure. He also suffered sclerotic-coating eye damage and a busted cheek bone.

Neurosurgeons stated the obvious, that Carmine would never fight again, but they were most concerned with how much brain damage there was and whether he would be able to function anywhere close to normal.

On release from the hospital he was placed in Chris's charge and began extensive rehabilitation and occupational therapy. After eight months he was able to care for himself and moved back into his house. He never fully recovered and suffered periodically from excruciating migraines. He had virtually no recollection of his last fight and at times had no idea that he had been a world-champion boxer. Eventually he understood his condition and only by sheer force of his fighting spirit was he able to function enough to work somewhere.

Pillegi got him the job as a parking attendant at *Vito's Italian Cuisine,* which was owned by former boxer Vito Carlucci, another of Angelo's early pupils.

True to his word, Angelo stayed in Carmine's corner and helped out when he could, but he could never bring himself to step foot inside the PAL gym again.

COPIES

AFTER SEVERAL AGONIZING MONTHS of thinking it through, Carl Hagen finally felt certain about his decision and made the call. The voice was not unpleasant, just a bit detached. "CloneX Corporation. How may I direct your call?"

"I'd like to speak with a sales representative."

"Sorry, was that salary reputation?"

"No! Sales. . .rep-re-sent-a-tive."

"Sales representative?"

"Yes."

"One moment, please. I will connect you to the salary department."

"No!" Carl screeched.

"Good afternoon, Salary Department."

Carl sighed deeply, exasperated. "Can you connect me with a sales rep-re-sent-ative, please?"

". . .Please hold."

Dreadful Fifties music was piped into his ear while he waited. I hate that crap, he thought.

After several minutes on hold a voice interrupted the cacophony. "Sales Department, good afternoon."

Carl sighed. "Are you human?"

"As close as it gets," was the reply. The female voice was carefully cadenced, devoid of emotion, perfunctory.

He shook his head and then launched into his inquiry. "I'm interested in purchasing, uhhh. . .model number 840."

"Do you have clearance, sir?"

"Yes. YK7."

"Thank you, sir. One moment."

"Please don't—"

The awful music started again, but thankfully lasted only thirty seconds before the voice returned. "Is this Carl Hagen?"

"Yes."

"Thank you for holding, Mr. Hagen. We need you to answer a few questions for verification purposes before we can proceed, and you do understand that this call is being monitored by NWSA. Is that okay?"

"Do I have a choice?"

As soon as it came out of his mouth he regretted saying it. "Never mind, just let's get on with it. . . please."

"Is your present address Region 521 Strata Plateau, Tundra-Meadow?"

"Yes."

"How may I help you, Carl?"

"I'm interested in acquiring an A-840F, and I want to know what's involved, how much it will cost, and how long it will take to get an accelerated version."

"Well, sir, the model you are requesting is in great demand since it was introduced back in 2163. The waiting time is approximately seven months before procedure initiation. An accelerated model—" she paused and then asked, "What age are you requesting?"

"Eighteen, I should think, maybe twenty."

He could hear her breathing while she searched for additional information.

"Ah, here it is. An A Model 840F—uh. . .our accelerated maturation process for eighteen to twenty-four is approximately three months."

"Okay," he said, "can you tell me what the known side effects are for an A.M.?"

"Limited, sir. We've had very few complaints and only two returns of the two hundred produced."

"What were the complaints?"

"Um. . .both were contaminated and exhibited second-generation trait discordance."

"Do you offer a guarantee?"

"Yes, sir, we offer a ninety-day return policy on proof of process negligence."

"What do you do with the returns?"

"I'm sorry, sir, I'm not authorized to give out such information. Would you like to be connected to our service policy representative?"

"No, not now. What's the cost?"

"Model 840F Accelerated is currently listed at sixty-two thousand, plus delivery."

"How is it shipped?"

"By drone pod, sir. Unless the client requests P.E.T.—a Personal Escort Transport."

Carl pressed the transcribe button on his communication tablet to download the call to a snag file.

"This all sounds good to me," he said, "How do we proceed?"

"You can select attributes and details from the replication link on Network CapConnect. You can order from it as well. However, unless you take personal possession of your model at our facility in Primordia, sign the release forms, and verify satisfaction, the guarantee is nullified."

"How much notice do you give for direct personal possession delivery?"

"Up to two weeks in advance, sir."

"Okay, thank you. You've been very helpful."

"Will there be anything else?"

"No, thanks, I'll access through CapConnect. Good day."

"Good day, sir, and thank—"

Carl hit *Cyber Clear*, tapped off, and sat back. He considered the options, the amount of GovScrip he had squirreled away, and smiled at the prospect of soon having the GC of his dreams.

Having researched a number of Copy Processors, Carl had learned that CloneX was the very best in the business. In 2050 they had been sanctioned for "progenization" by the Global Genetic Federation and subsequently produced the entire copy population for the Mars program—sixty each of model number R-11, male and female. Since then, the variations in DNA manipulation techniques had allowed CloneX to produce copies that retained the required critical aspects yet provided each with enough visual differences to be considered unique: hair and eye color, breast and penis size, height and appendage variance, and so forth.

By the time the world got wind of the human cloning experiments, it had been too far gone to stop. Processing facilities had been set up to salvage, harvest, and catalog DNA samples, cerebral fluids, and stem cell tissue.

The Genetic Federation had been forced to convene and ultimately approve the procedure of nucleic transfer, basing it on the fact that the genetic copies were not the robots envisioned in the late twenty-first century but were instead more like Dolly, the sheep, cloned in 1996 from an adult somatic cell. Dolly had been deemed a bona fide member of genus *ovis* and an exact "copy" of her parent. By 2115, the company had been able to eliminate host wombs entirely and produce genetic copies outside the body.

This historic information was relayed to Carl via the CloneX site, and he verified it on four secure Bibliolopedia net sites.

Following his call, Carl spent the next three days selecting and deselecting attributes, appearance characteristics, activity traits, and a gamut of behavior functions he had been conjuring for the past two years. Finally satisfied with what he believed would be his life companion, he placed the order, routed prepayment, and then fretted for the next twelve weeks until finally being contacted by CloneX's GCE division. A representative from the Genetic Copy Emancipation Department told him his order was in final gestation and would be ready for possession in nine days.

He had decided to have "Chandra" delivered to him rather than make the journey to Primordia to pick her up. The added expense and time involved was too great, even though, in having her delivered, he had to waive the guarantee. Carl could barely contain his excitement.

Like all private clone transactions, the genetic copy would have been programmed with a chip implant to help get her to Carl's location, after which the memory insert would be automatically erased.

ONE EARLY AFTERNOON, WITH THE TWO SUNS shining brightly, a lovely Model A-840 appeared at the doorway of the Tundra-Meadow dwelling belonging to model number 432M, otherwise known as Carl Hagen, a lonely inhabitant of the planet Cepheus in the Andromeda galaxy, 2.5 million light-years away from what is still known as Earth.

CRACKER BOX

D ONCHOO BE TAKIN' NUTHIN from nobody, boy! You hear?" Lil' Boll Weevil—that's what everyone called him—sat smirking on the cabin's dirt floor, afraid to look up at his father.

The verbal assault continued. "You jus' a sharecropper boy, you got nuthin', ain't nevuh gonna have nuthin', and better not be takin' nuthin'! Understan'?"

Boll nodded a few times, pushed the dirt around with his hand, and glanced at his father. "Why don't we got nuthin', Daddy?"

"'Cause we po', stupid."

His tiny face looked confused, "Why is we po'?"

"Cause we niggas, boy. Thas away it is. Now get up and go fetch some watuh."

Boll scrambled to his feet, hitched up his ragged, hand-me-down trousers, and headed outside to the rain barrel.

His father, Juba, watched him for a moment, swatted at the flies buzzing around his head, and mumbled to the spot where his son had been sitting, "Damn, Boll, why you gots to be so much trouble?"

Boll came back with the leaking pail, water sloshing over the top and dripping out of the bottom. He trudged to the metal basin, emptied the container into it, and wiped his hands on his pants. Juba seized the boy's thin shoulders and slowly turned him to look into his brown, cow-like eyes. Saddened to find tears staining the youngster's cheeks, his demeanor softened. "Listin', I don't mean to be hollerin' all the time," he said, and noticing the child's runny nose, added, "'N wipe yoself."

Boll drew a sleeve across his face and sniffed.

Containing his anger, worried what might happen if the boy had been caught stealing the bailing wire from the big house barn, Juba asked, "How much wire you take?"

"Six."

"Six what, boy?"

"Six pieces."

"'N whachoo gonna do wit dem?"

Boll shrugged and looked at his feet.

"You be knowin'," grumbled his father. "I 'spect you tellin' me by suppa time. Or you ain't gettin' none."

He peered down at him, dismayed, and left to sit on the rickety steps outside.

Boll, seriously conflicted about what to tell his father, sat on the chair under a calendar by the open shelf where the few food items were kept in tin cans and cotton sacks. The 1922 calendar had only the month of December left and was three years old. It was the month and year his mother's body had been found burned and hanging from a tree a mile from the still. No one had ever been charged.

Juba's people whispered about hooded men dressed in white who ravaged the farms and churches at night, burning and beating people, "Jus' cause we darkies," they said.

Juba had seen them on horseback late at night up on the ridge past the Civil War cemetery. They had been carrying torches, and it'd scared him enough that he had taken Boll and hidden in the swamp until dawn.

By suppertime, the only real meal of the day for the two of them, he eased up on Boll and asked him to come to the table and eat. The boy sat quietly, hungrily spooning possum stew into his mouth until the plate was clean. Juba watched him the whole time, a tiny smile in the corner of his mouth.

"You got somethin' you wanna tell me, Bo?"

The boy licked at the plate and then wiped a hand across his mouth. "'Bout the wire?"

"Yes."

Boll fidgeted in his chair, not wanting to anger his father yet somehow still hold on to his secret. "I wants to tell you, but I scared."

"Why you scared?" The boy didn't answer, and Juba could see he was worried. "Maybe you tell me t'morrow."

Boll slowly moved his head up and down and shrugged.

"Go n' wash y'self and go t'bed. We goin' to de sto in de mornin'."

Once a week Mr. Nathan, the farmer he sharecropped for, lent him a mule and cart to travel the three miles outside Milltail Creek to buy supplies and get mail and a newspaper. He'd stare at the Buffalo City Gazette for a long time, trying to understand what it said, but he had never been taught to read.

If there were other sharecrop kids in the Colored part of town, he would let Boll play with them as long as they promised not to stray too far.

When Juba was able to stretch the time in town, he would

sit inside Moses's Tonsiltorium, the Colored Only barbershop, and listen to what others had to say. It was there that he first heard about migratin'.

"Juba, why you still here?" one of them asked. "You got dat boy, he need to be up in Dee-troit."

"Dat right, Issiah? How we gonna get dere?"

"Lotsa people goin'. They goes by train. Some o dem walkin' all de way. Don't mattuh none how you get dere. Long as you get dere."

The others laughed and then suddenly fell silent.

Moses, the ironically bald-headed proprietor, had stopped snipping at the man's head who was sitting in the chair. No one spoke, knowing Moses was a man of few words who, rather than participate, preferred to listen to the rabble, the chiding, the idle gossip of the patrons and loiterers.

When he did offer a comment, it was generally accepted as gospel, and the five customers waited for whatever was about to be said. "I knows," he started, "that some make it, others don't. I hear dat them Klanspeople finds 'em and strings 'em up or puts tar all over dem and stick feathers on dem. Some even get set afire."

He drifted off and then solemnly raised the scissors and returned to his trade, the very thing that separated him from the menial life of his customers.

He paused for a moment and wiped tears from his eyes, peered out the window, and sighed despairingly. "Juba, I thinks they right. You got Boll, and he need to have mo' den dis. His momma woulda done it."

Juba scratched his chin but didn't respond. He slowly stood up. "I gots t' be gettin' back to Missah Nathan. He be waitin' on me."

He went to get Boll, but the boy wasn't where he left him. "Hey, boy," he called to one of the kids chasing a chicken. "Where be Boll?"

The boy stopped running, stared at him as if he didn't understand the question, then pointed to the alley behind the barber shop. Juba knew what went on down that alley, and it was not a good place for a boy of eight.

He found the child peering through cracks in a wooden door of a ramshackle building. There was music coming from inside. Juba moved quickly to pull him away. Boll was so engrossed he hadn't heard his father approach. Juba was about to yank him back but stopped short when he heard the child tapping out a rhythm, trying to imitate the sound from within. He waited until the music stopped and then snapped, "Boll!"

The startled child reared up and whirled around to face his father, a look of terror in his eyes.

"Whatchoo doin'?" demanded Juba.

"Um, um—" he stammered. "I be—"

Juba took hold of his arm and, lifting him off the ground, pulled him away from the door. He didn't say another word until they were a mile out of town on the way to the farm. "You be doin' dat all de time when we in town?"

Boll nodded.

Juba was unsure what to say or if he should be angry, so he said nothing.

The next time they went to town, Juba kept Boll with him. At the feed store, he saw the boy eyeing an empty wooden cracker box. When he had finished getting the supplies, he asked Boll, "Whatchoo want wit dat box?"

"I likes it."

"Fo' what?"

Boll looked away.

Juba turned to the store owner, a decent man, slow of step, almost toothless, born into slavery and emancipated when he was five.

"'Zekiel, how much dat box?" he asked, pointing to the object of Boll's attention.

Ezekiel turned as if moving were a chore, looked where Juba was pointing, and saw Bo transfixed.

"Hm, dat? Dat dere box is uh, uh. . .relic."

Juba didn't know what that meant but figured a relic must be expensive, so he motioned to Boll. "Put dat down, Bo. We ain't got no money for dat."

"No," chuckled Ezekial, "I jus' jivin' ya. You can take it."

Bo bent down, scooped up the box, and ran out of the store, shouting over his shoulder, "*Thank* ya, Mr. Zekial!"

Juba smiled at the old man, nodded gratefully, and left.

On the journey home, Boll sat with the box on his lap, stroking it as if it were a cat, never looking up. By the time the farm came into view and Boll still hadn't said anything, Juba finally asked, "Whatchoo gonna do wit dat?"

"Gonna do music."

". . .Music?"

Before Juba had a chance to ask him more, the mule came to an abrupt stop, brayed, and refused to take another step. Juba shouted at the animal, handed the reins to Bo, and jumped down from the wagon. "Hoold tight, Bo. Donchoo let go."

"Dere it is, I sees it!" cried the boy, pointing to a crook between two branches of a gumbo limbo tree. Juba's eyes followed the length of the trunk up its waxy, red bark until he spotted the cougar. It was fifteen feet up and poised to spring.

Had the mule not stopped, the big cat would have pounced right on top of them. Juba grabbed the cloth covering the groceries in the wagon and began to swirl it over his head, shouting, "Yah! Yah!" over and over while the frightened mule brayed louder and louder. Bo, afraid the mule would bolt, began yelling at it. The commotion brought Mr. Nathan running, brandishing a shotgun.

Spotting the creature, he didn't speak a word, just raised the gun, took aim, and blasted the cougar out of the tree.

"That's the sumbitch been stealin' my hogs!" He turned to leave, then stopped to face Juba. "Git it out the road," was all he said before heading back to the farmhouse.

Juba took Nathan's demand to mean he could get rid of it anyway he wanted to, and he couldn't have been happier; for the next six days, he and Boll feasted on the big cat.

LIGHT BEGAN TO FADE EARLIER and with it the work day. Juba set to plugging holes in the walls of the house while Boll gathered and stacked wood for winter heat. A couple weeks after the cougar incident, Juba noticed that the cracker box Boll so coveted was nowhere to be found. That night he asked him. "Bo, whatchoo do wit dat box?"

"I show you tomorrow," he said with a mysterious grin.

The next morning Juba was awakened by a strange plinking sound. Fearful it was the jangle of Klansmen on horses, he instinctively turned to the corner of the room for Bo and saw the straw mat was empty. The sound continued, alternating between loud and low. Reaching for the ax handle he kept under the bed, Juba warily got up and crept silently to the doorway.

There, sitting on the steps, was Boll. In his hands was the

cracker box to which he had added an extension, fastened four pieces of the stolen wire, and stretched them across an opening he'd somehow cut into the top of the box. Holding it on his knee the way he had seen the music makers in town doing it, Bo pulled at the metal strings and improvised a crude melody. He looked up at his daddy, brimming with pride. Juba nodded in awe and said one word, "Music!"

IN TIME, "BO' WEEVIL" JACKSON left Juba and the farm and brought his music to the juke joints and jazz clubs of Detroit, Chicago, and New Orleans. His recordings delighted legions of devoted fans and drew admiring audiences wherever he performed.

DOUGLAS AND LOUISE

THEY WERE IN THEIR SEVENTIES, married fifty-two years, with children and grandchildren, assorted illnesses and recoveries, and tragic losses of siblings, other relatives, and friends. Like most marriages of that duration, they'd had their share of fallings-out, but when people asked how they lasted so long, Louise would reply, "My sense of humor."

Now, however, try as she might, it became more difficult to laugh. First it was finding out that she had multiple sclerosis. "We can slow it down," they said, "But we can't stop it."

In the years following that verdict, her movements became tedious, her steps tiny and cautious, yet she muddled through, dealing with it: no complaints from a woman who had been crowned *Best All-Around Athlete, Camp Gold Crest, 1948.*

Douglas, her husband, had also been an athlete, a high school swimming champion and later, at college, a boxing star. Over the years, alcohol consumption had wreaked havoc on his flyweight physique, and he'd gradually added fifty pounds and lost interest in working out, preferring instead to "socialize," as he called it.

Conversely, Louise had stayed much the same; her tiny,

well-proportioned body remained thin, largely because she smoked. "It curbs my appetite," she said, which was not something she'd ever had much of anyway.

In time, it wasn't the MS that took her, but the lung cancer. Her mother had succumbed to the disease, although no one had ever seen *her* with a cigarette in her mouth. It was probably a foregone conclusion that Louise too would develop it, and the cigarettes didn't help.

Eventually, the scourge metastasized, and chemotherapy was prescribed, but having witnessed a much-loved nephew suffer through the debilitating side-effects, Louise refused the treatment. She didn't want to endure the pain and hair loss, or the weakened body and nausea.

Doug knew she could not be dissuaded from her "action by inaction," as he put it. They discussed it, but her decision to let the chips fall where they might was heeded. Douglas wasn't happy, but he knew after more than half a century with her that she had the resolve and strength of her convictions and was not to be trifled with once her mind was made up.

As the seasons changed and she became weaker, Doug's anxiety was harder to suppress; he drank even more than before, at lunch, after work, at dinner. Once at home, after she went to sleep, he would have another drink and often pass out on the sofa with the TV on mute, the sound of his own snoring waking him just long enough to crawl into bed beside her.

One Saturday morning she sipped a cup of coffee and nibbled on a bagel without the cream cheese or nova he'd picked up at the deli.

"I think I want to have my hair done," she said.

He glanced at her gray roots, nodded, and smiled. "Sure, why not? It'll make you feel better."

"I'll call the salon and see if they can take me."

"They'll fit you in," he reassured her. "I'm sure they will. Do you want me to call Selena?"

She nodded almost imperceptibly, and he went to the phone on the kitchen counter but reached for the coffee pot instead and poured some for her while she gazed wistfully out the window, unaware he had filled her cup.

He succeeded in getting her a two o'clock appointment, which allowed her time to get ready and have him drive her there. He promised to return by three-thirty, and headed back home. Parking on the street rather than in their garage spot, he climbed the stairs to the boardwalk and sat on a bench, listening to the surf and the cawing gulls circling the trash bins. The sun warmed his balding head, and he turned his face upward to catch a few rays of April sunshine, but not before brushing a tear from his ruddy cheek.

Prompt as always, he picked her up at precisely three-thirty. She was sitting in a chair near the appointment desk, her roots colored, hair washed, cut, and dried into a chin-length bob, a small self-satisfied smile on her creased face.

Douglas crooked his arm and leaned in to help her rise. She seemed reenergized by the afternoon's pampering and stood up without his support.

"I'll bring the car around," he offered.

"No, that's okay," she said, "I'll walk with you." And she did. The parking space was only a block away, so it wasn't a chore for her, and in those few minutes, a stranger seeing them would have thought they were a couple of spry seniors out for a stroll.

Returning to the house, she told him she was going to lie down for a bit. Douglas pulled the cover back, helped her onto the bed and kissed her forehead, then took a seat on their small balcony overlooking the beach. A minute later, he went back to the kitchen and poured himself a pre-mixed martini, tossed one pimento-stuffed olive into the glass, and plopped an ice cube in for good measure. He swished it around with one finger, brought it to his lips, and licked it.

Back on the balcony, he eased onto the plastic chair, took a deep breath, and felt the sea-scented air fill his nostrils. He closed his eyes and drifted off.

When he opened them again he was unsure how much time had passed. His drink, ice cube long since melted, remained at his feet, untouched.

Peering at his watch through half-closed eyes, he saw that half an hour had ticked by. He shuffled to the bedroom and stood in the doorway, careful not to wake her.

She was lying on her back with her mouth slightly open, as if she had just exhaled; her eyes were closed.

He watched quietly from a few feet away before taking a step closer—and then another. He couldn't hear her breathing, and he looked at her chest to see if it was moving. "Lulu. . .you awake?" He sat on the edge of the bed, placed his fingers an inch from her lips, and feeling no air escaping, gently touched her arm, and then pushed it a few times.

He stared blankly for a minute before leaning over and kissing her softly. He examined her slender, freckled fingers and placed them at her sides, rose to his feet and left the room.

A full minute went by before he slumped onto the sofa and wept. Panic never took hold of him; he knew instinctively that she was gone, and wanting more time alone with her, he waited before making the calls. The first was to 911, the second to his middle son Geoff, who lived in the city an hour away.

ATTENDANCE AT THE FUNERAL was standing room only, with people from around the country arriving to pay tribute and to express their love for Louise, for Douglas, and for the family.

The first two weeks after the burial were a blur to him. He spent much of that time despondent and feeling drained, empty of emotion or the ability to focus.

He continued to drink during the early days of the *shiva* period, so it wasn't long before he was back to his two-martini lunches and the after-work cocktails, and then again at dinner whether out or at home alone.

He took to sleeping on her side of the bed and frequently called her name as if she were in the next room. At work he found he could function well enough and, from time to time, even experienced moments of great clarity. More often, however, he succumbed to bouts of depression, made worse by gin and vermouth.

Always an early riser, Douglas was typically dressed for work, impeccably turned out, and onto his second cup of coffee by seven in the morning.

ON A SUNNY MORNING SIX MONTHS AFTER Louise took her last breath, Douglas got out of the shower, toweled himself off, and headed back to the bedroom to get dressed.

In an instant, his entire right side went numb, and he crashed to the floor. He lay crumpled in the narrow hallway, unable to move, the telephone visible but impossible to reach. It was six-thirty. Incapacitated, imprisoned in his mind, unable to make a sound, Douglas remained naked on the floor, wedged against the wall, for an hour, trying to drag his body across the carpeted floor, but with no success.

Geoff made it a ritual to call his Dad at the office a few minutes before the market opened to check-in and see how he was getting along.

The day Douglas had the stroke, Geoff made the call but was told, "Your dad hasn't come in yet." Not wanting to appear alarmed, he said he would call back, and he did. When he heard that Douglas still hadn't arrived, he searched his memory for some appointment his father might have mentioned, and when nothing came to mind he hit the speed dial number for his parents' home. It rang four times before the answer machine kicked in. Geoff hung up and immediately called his father's neighbor.

She breathlessly picked up the phone on the third ring, her newborn wailing in the background. "Oh, hi, Geoff, what's up? Sorry 'bout the baby—she's cranky today."

"Marlene," he began, "Can you do me a favor and ring my dad's doorbell?"

"Sure. What's the matter?"

Containing his emotions, he explained his father's absence from work. Marlene held the baby in the crook of her arm and cradled the remote against her ear, took the two steps to the doorway across the hall, and rang the door chime. No answer. She tried the door and finally called out, "Doug, it's Marlene!" and then into the receiver, "There's no answer, Geoff."

"Do you still have a key to his apartment?" he asked with the first sign of real apprehension.

"Yes. Do you want me to go in?"

About to agree, he had the presence of mind to hesitate and consider the probabilities of Douglas being inside, and if he was, what she would find if she entered.

"Marlene," he suggested, "Maybe you'd better have the

super go in with you."

She quickly agreed. "Okay, I'll go find him and call you back."

Hugging her infant to her chest, she didn't wait for the elevator and walked down the flight of stairs to the lobby. Spotting Alvin, the security guard–doorman, she asked him to follow her back to Doug's apartment. He entered first, and, two steps into the foyer, he discovered Douglas lying on the floor where he'd been for almost three hours.

Alvin quickly determined that Douglas was alive but couldn't move anything. Fortunately, he was able to talk, more like grunts, and Alvin knew professional assistance was needed before trying to do anything further. He called 911 while Marlene called Geoff and explained the situation. She promised to let Geoff know what hospital they would be going to.

"A STROKE, HE'S HAD A STROKE!" Geoff sobbed into the phone, and then, "Shoreham," in response to his brother's question about what hospital their father had been taken to.

"Bernie, call Jake and let him know. I'll get back to you soon as I have more information." Bernie lived upstate, four hours away, Jake, the youngest son, on the other side of the continent.

Geoff's wife Fran was a doctor at a large hospital complex in the city, and she began the process to have her father-in-law transferred there as soon as it was practical and safe.

A few days into his hospitalization, Douglas became belligerent, bellicose, and agitated, pulling at IV tubes and yanking the oxygen tubes from his nostrils. Apparently delirious, he experienced a bout of dementia and began tossing his excrement from the bed pan.

It wasn't long before doctors recognized that Douglas was undergoing symptoms of alcohol withdrawal and detoxification.

A week later, he suffered a heart attack that required insertion of a stent. Following that, Doug's youngest brother Stan arrived and spent a few days at the bedside while Doug incoherently ranted and had to be sedated to the point he didn't recognize him. Stan left to go back home to Montana, promising his nephews that he'd return to take care of Douglas for the first week whenever he was released.

The most significant visitors had yet to arrive: Jake and Doug's two grandsons, ages six and nine. Significant because, as Stan would much later learn, it was the seminal moment in Doug's recovery.

"When Jake and the boys came to the hospital," Doug later said, "the two little ones climbed onto the bed and hugged me. One on each side, they told me they loved me and wanted me to stay their Pop-Pop."

When he finished acknowledging his epiphany he looked Stan squarely in the eye and said, more clear-eyed than he'd been in years, "It was right then and there I stopped drinking forever and vowed to stick around as long as I could."

It took months of physical therapy and training for Douglas to learn to use his left hand instead of his right, and to maneuver a cane so he could walk with limited use of his paralyzed right leg. He would never regain the use of either of his right-side limbs, but through strength of will and defiance he adjusted enough to be self-sufficient.   He would never drive a car again or ride a bicycle on the boardwalk. But he found his enthusiasm for work was as dead as his arm and leg.

A year later he moved to the opposite coast to live in a "facility" a mile from Jake and his young family. He welcomed, relished in fact, the chance to sit in the sun, as he did for a few more years.

FIRE FIGHT

SERGEANT PARKER HEFLIN looked at his watch and decided it was best to leave right then. "Okay, listen up. We're goin' out the same way we came in. Lopez, you're on point. Washington and Cartwright, you bring up the rear. Monahan, Weiss, and Martin, fall in behind me."

When Lopez didn't move, the Sergeant hissed at him, "What's your problem?"

"Cuñio, man! Why do I gotta be on point?"

Parker became enraged. "Do it . . . *now*!"

The recruit shook his head, shuffled to the front of the column, hitched up his webbing, and headed into the jungle. As they continued to slog their way forward, they stopped every so often to listen for signs of the enemy. The late afternoon heat was roasting, their clothes soggy with sweat. A few small birds flitted from tree to tree, and insects made their presence known by chirps and bites.

Parker slapped at his neck, fanned the air around his face, and moved to the head of the column, going faster as the brush began mercifully to open up. When the lighting changed, he knew the river was up ahead, and he stopped until the others caught up.

"We're gonna follow the river to our rendezvous point. You guys okay?"

A few of them nodded. "Cuñio, man," Lopez complained. "I need a smoke." He reached up to remove the pack of cigarettes from the band around his helmet. As soon as he had taken it off, a shot rang out. He stood frozen in space for a moment then crashed to the ground. The bullet had entered the front of his skull and come out the side of his temple just above his ear.

Parker shouted, "Everyone *down!*" He threw himself to the ground and crawled to the edge of the tree line.

"Anybody see where that came from?" several of them shouted at the same time.

"Behind us!"

"Over to the left."

"Across the river!"

Lopez's body was lying flat on the ground; face up, his eyes and mouth wide open. Liquid had begun to flow from the wound in his forehead. There was a gaping hole above his ear where the bullet had exited, and the blood was beginning to sink into the soft soil, staining it dark brown. Anxious minutes passed in which nobody moved or made a sound. Parker looked at his watch and realized that the chopper would soon be flying directly overhead on the way up river to the prescribed rendezvous.

"Weiss, give me the radio!"

Private Weiss pushed the field phone toward Parker but couldn't reach far enough, so he got up on one knee to stretch closer. Another shot shattered the air. Birds shrieked and flew out of the trees.

Weiss fell backward and, still holding the radio, tumbled over twice and came to a stop. His arms were spread wide. Blood squirted from his neck. His legs shook violently. His mouth was moving, but no sound came out. Parker swung around, looking for a sign that would reveal the shooter.

One of the men shouted, "Oh, fuck! We gotta get *outta* here, Sarge."

Parker's mind was racing, his stomach tight, and he had started to feel sick. "Everyone back into the bush!"

They scrambled on their hands and knees and took cover out of the line of sight. Specialist 4th Class George Cartwright came up alongside Parker and, looking back at the two bodies said, "Weiss is still moving. We can't leave him there."

Parker squinted. "Hold off! Not yet. You wanna' get—"

Cartwright turned toward the river and motioned with his chin. "I see somethin'. Eleven o'clock."

Parker peered across the water, searched the shoreline, and scanned the trees looking for movement. He saw nothing. Cartwright looked back at Weiss's body. The soldier's mouth had stopped moving, but his legs were still twitching. "We need the radio," he whispered.

Parker motioned for him to keep quiet. After a few more seconds he said, "We have to find the shooter," hoping that there was only one.

"When I say go, we'll all move down to the water. Washington, you get Lopez. Basso, you get Weiss and the radio. The rest of you lay down heavy fire. Go! Go! Go!"

As they came out into the open they all dropped to their knees and raised their weapons toward the opposite side of the river. Each peered across the water, scanning the banks and treetops. Basso tugged on his helmet to pull it lower on his

GOOD DAYS, BAD DAYS

head. Washington shifted his utility belt and then smacked the bottom of the M-16 cartridge magazine to make sure it was seated. Hoping the sniper might give his location away, Parker held up his hand to keep Basso and Washington from moving forward. All of them were breathing heavily, sweat pooling in their clothes.

Parker lowered his hand.

Washington, staying in a crouch, moved as fast as he could; Basso quickly followed. Like cockroaches scurrying in the light, trying to avoid getting squashed, each moved erratically toward his destination.

Basso reached Weiss within seconds and, yanking at the pack strapped to his back, struggled to get to the tree line while dragging his fallen comrade. Washington got to Lopez a few seconds later. He was pulling him by the shirt, scrambling back toward the squad, when another shot rang out. It sliced into the ground and kicked up soil, missing him by inches. The entire squad began to fire their weapons; the noise was deafening.

Parker yelled, "Cease-fire! Stop firing!" For an agonizing few moments it was deathly silent. Then the jungle erupted into an unbelievable explosion of sound. Automatic weapons, machine-gun fire, single rifle shots all responded to the squad's volley. On all sides of them, the ground was kicked up by the impact of bullets. Leaves and branches flew in every conceivable direction. The barrage continued to rain down on them, keeping them pressed against the ground. Bullets flashed over their heads and ricocheted off the trees and burrowed into the jungle floor.

"Carter's hit!" shouted Basso.

"Me, too!" shouted another.

Parker moved further into the bush and closer to the squad. "Anyone else?"

"Carter and Martin," answered Cartwright.

Parker looked around. "Any more?"

"Monahan!" came a voice. "Monahan's hurt bad."

The shots began to slow down to sporadic pops from an AK-47. Taking the momentary silence as a sign the enemy couldn't see them, Parker looked at his watch. It was almost sixteen-hundred. Time to rendezvous with the helicopter, which would pass overhead any minute on its way up river. They had to send it a signal somehow. He called out to the squad, "Smoke grenades?"

At first there was no response; then just as the sound of whirring rotor blades became audible, someone cried, "Lopez had 'em!"

Parker jumped up, raced toward Lopez's dead body, and tore at a canister clipped to the kid's webbing. Pulling the pin, he threw it toward the sound of the Huey. Just as the grenade burst into the air, he spotted the 'copter.

At the same moment a mortar shell exploded a few yards away, sending shrapnel and debris in every direction, followed by a torrent of bullets, engulfing them in a firefight from hell.

Sergeant Heflin and his men would not live to tell about it.

FRATERNA CARITAS

M ARCELLUS AND FLAVIUS, young sons of a legendary Samnite warrior, grew up in a household filled with love, nurtured by their mother Calpurnia. Living in the remote Umbrian hills, far from other children, the two relied on each other as friends and confidantes. Just two years apart, they looked like twins, with dark curly hair and penetrating, alert eyes. They played and laughed, chased through the villa, engaged in athletic competition, and mastered the use of weapons taught to them by their father Titus.

By 84 BC, the close-knit pair had embraced the family business and grown into young men ready to burnish their father's legacy. As they prepared to take the helm, war broke out against the Romans. Better equipped, with superior weaponry and more experienced officers and soldiers, the Romans were the most powerful military force in the world, and the Samnites were defeated. The boys' father was killed defending his home, and as the Romans descended upon the villa, his Calpurnia was raped and murdered in front of the brothers' eyes. The two were loaded into separate ox carts and hauled off to be sold as slaves on the road back to Rome.

With tears in their eyes, they waved goodbye. Flavius, the eldest, cried out, "Farewell, Marcellus, my brother, we will be together again!"

Marcellus had no idea where his brother had been taken, only that their parents were dead, that he was separated from him, and that, for the first time in his life, he was alone.

After several days' travel, he and a few other Samnites appeared at a stone building in the dark of night. Shackled to one another, they were led down a long hallway and thrown into separate, windowless cells. For the next few days Marcellus was treated harshly and fed only thin gruel and rancid wine once a day.

Unsure of where he had been taken, he listened to the sounds from beyond the wall. During the day he heard the clash of metal against metal, the muffled strike of wood on wood, the grunts and howls of male voices, the barking of commands— sounds familiar from his early days learning combat from his father.

Several days later, he was visited by a stocky, muscular man with a long scar across his face and several broken teeth, whose hair was a tangled mat of accumulated grime held back by a sweat-stained leather band.

"I am Thraex," he said gruffly. "You have no name. You are here to die." He shrugged powerful shoulders indifferently and added, "Or perhaps not. My job is to keep you alive, to fight another day for the glory of Rome and the entertainment of the populace."

In that instant Marcellus understood he was to be a gladiator, and that Thraex was the *lanista,* the owner and probably chief trainer, of the *ludus,* the school.

"Today," said Thraex, "you will be allowed to bathe and

eat a full meal. Tomorrow we will see what you are made of."

Marcellus clenched his jaw, knowing very well what he was "made of" and angry that he had allowed himself and Flavius to be captured. We should have battled to the death, he told himself.

Thraex leaned against the wall and stroked his chin, studying the man before him. "Have you ever seen gladiatorial combat?"

Marcellus shook his head.

"Listen to me, Samnite!" the other said angrily. "Your entire culture has been destroyed. You are now my property. In the arena your role is as the enemy of Rome. You will be taught much here, and we will train you well. If you learn and survive for three, for five, years, you might be freed and even become a Roman citizen."

Marcellus was not comforted by the assertion. What good would freedom be, if it was granted? He had no family; he had nothing left.

"Sleep, Samnite," Thraex suggested as he turned to leave. "Tomorrow you begin to die."

Marcellus spent the night mourning his murdered parents and wondering where Flavius was, or whether he was still alive. By daybreak he vowed to himself that he would learn everything he could to remain alive and be freed. He would find his brother no matter what it took.

In the beginning, Marcellus and four other captives were given a meal of stale bread softened in wine, some dates, honey, and hard cheese. Brought into a small practice arena they went through a series of exercises and paired off to wrestle. After this they sat along the edge of the ring to observe practicing gladiators awaiting their call to mortal combat. The *lanista* was paid well for the competitors sent off to large arenas. Thraex had been very successful since earning his own liberty in the arena, and his gladiators often went on to be famous; a few had also won their freedom.

The weeks that passed were agonizingly slow for Marcellus, but he practiced with a vengeance and became highly skilled as a retiarius. With only an arm and shoulder guard to protect himself, he learned to wield the weighted fisherman's net, a trident, and a dagger.

"You are skilled," Thraex told him one afternoon. "Neptune himself would be pleased." Marcellus gave no reply, offering only a wry smile.

"Tomorrow," continued the *lanista*, "you will face one as equally skilled as you, but a *secutor*. If you win, you will be moved into a larger room and eat in the dining hall."

In the late afternoon of the next day, with shadows bisecting the sand, a few dozen spectators observed the student combatants from wooden stands encircling the ring. Thraex would point to two trainees, already dressed for their respective roles, and summon them forward. He gave a signal, and the clash of metal and grunting began. These were not fights to the death; it was too expensive to train and lose a man before he could be sold.

To prevent a trident from being thrust through his face, a *secutor's* helmet had only two small eye-holes. It also had a rounded top, so as not to get caught in the net.

Thraex carefully matched opponents so they would learn as well as provide good entertainment for the spectators who paid a *denarius* to watch. Boisterous and out for a good time, they would taunt, laugh, and offer advice on who should live or die, though lives were always spared at the school. Only one combatant was encumbered by heavy armor, the other lightly armed, which gave one more freedom of movement but limited protection.

The *secutor*, brandishing a short sword and curved shield, rushed at Marcellus. He dodged the sword swipe and cast his net at the feet of the charging, masked figure. It caught on the warrior's foot, but he was able to disengage and pushed hard against Marcellus with his shield.

Marcellus stumbled backward with the force of the blow, lost his footing, and crashed to the ground. The *secutor* lunged at him with his sword. Marcellus twisted sideways, raised the padded practice trident, and jammed it into his rival's chest.

The crowd howled and a chorus of pleased voices shouted, "*Mortem! Lugula!*"

Thraex waved off the contest and dismissed both men. Marcellus reached down to help the fallen foe, but Thraex pushed him aside: Acts of kindness were a sign of weakness, a fatal flaw in combat.

Marcellus continued to hone his skills with the net and was able to throw it with great accuracy, often rendering an opponent immobile within the first minute of battle. He achieved victories against *secutors* but lost to *murmillos*, who carried a long shield and a sword, the *gladius*, which gave gladiators their name.

Marcellus was visibly proud after winning his twelfth fight, but an irate Thraex said to him, "Do not think you are ready for the *femminile*. In the sport arena, a fallen gladiator is a dead gladiator. You fight a *murmillo*, and you are meat for the pigs."

Marcellus soon noticed that trainees would often disappear without a trace, and rumors spread about what arena they might have been sent to; the empire was so vast it could be anywhere, hundreds, even thousands, of miles away.

Thraex was harsh and unrelenting with Marcellus, working on his weaknesses so that he would be a formidable gladiator and, in time, bring a higher price.

One night, roused from a deep sleep, Marcellus was chained together with two others, put into an enclosed cart, and driven away. There was a tiny window at the back through which they could see the countryside as they jostled along the rutted road.

After three days they caught sight of the sea, which most had never seen before, and then a single mountain with a plume of smoke rising to the sky. *"Vesuvio!"* one of them cried out.

Marcellus remembered his father speaking of the wondrous place where the ground sometimes shook and hills rumbled high above a fabulous city filled with people and marvels befitting the gods—Pompeii. But Titus had barely mentioned the awful place in the city where slaves were mauled and devoured by wild beasts, where men, and sometimes women, were forced to fight to the death. Marcellus sensed that was where they were going. Oh, dear brother, he thought, what has happened to us? Do the gods approve? How could this be? I miss you so very much, Flavius.

THE CART AND ITS CARGO pitched and rattled forward through a gateway. Marcellus and the others became alarmed by the cacophonous clatter of hooves and voices shouting in dialects he had not heard before. As they inched along through the throngs, people would peer inside, taunt them, and throw rotten fruit through the window.

The wagon shuddered to a halt, and the driver greeted someone and laughed, and then climbed down from his seat; a few minutes later, the door swung open. Blinding sunlight fell into the tiny space, forcing the chained prisoners to shield their eyes. Prodded to get out, they crouched one by one through the opening and jumped down. With their legs weakened from the journey, all fell onto the dusty ground.

Standing before them was the tallest man Marcellus had ever seen, a Nubian as dark-skinned as a raven and muscled from neck to sandaled feet. He poked at them with a spear and motioned toward an alley, which they passed through into a long tunnel lit by torches.

Marcellus counted seventy strides before the men stopped at another doorway and were brought into a large hall, where their chains were removed. The Nubian motioned for them to sit, to be quiet, and to wait. In time, three slave girls entered with bowls of hot water and an amphora of oil. They stripped the men of their loincloths, bathed them, anointed each with the oil, and left as quietly as they entered. Within minutes, they returned with platters of fruit and meat, and poured chalices of wine. Glancing furtively at one another the men devoured the offerings.

Following this welcome, their stomachs full for the first time in months and lightheaded from drink, each dozed off like sated lions after a kill.

DUSK DESCENDED ON POMPEII, painting it with an orange and pink glow, the clamor dissipating as people cleared the marketplace. Still unsure of exactly where they were, and hoping Marcellus was wrong about it being the belly of the gladiatorial arena, the three men were finally visited by the *lanista*

Attilio Cassianus.

"Salute, Gladiators! You are in Pompeii, the most beautiful city in all the empire. The only way you will see beyond these walls will be to earn your freedom. Otherwise you will die and never know its marvels. So fight well, battle to win, kill to live, and you will be treated generously, as you have just seen. The best of you will be praised by all of Rome, by the populace, by women, by children, maybe even by Caesar Augustus! Each of you is here because you are a trained fighter with your weapons. There are others in this place you do not know who are better than you and have already survived in combat."

He pointed to one of them. "You! You will be a *secutor* known as Vicinius." He motioned to Marcellus. "You will be called Antonius, a *retiarii*. And you," he said to the third, "You are now Cato, a *murmillo*. I have paid many *denarii* for each of you and expect to be repaid. You may each meet in the arena and kill the other, or you may fight one of those unknown to you. Either way, you will die a gladiator. . .or maybe not." He gave them time to absorb the words, and then sardonically added, "Or perhaps you will live to see our great city. But if you refuse to fight, you will be killed on the spot by Maxima—" he gestured toward the Nubian— "and fed to the lions."

WHILE MARCELLUS, NOW CALLED ANTONIUS, waited to do battle he was allowed to practice in a large, high-walled courtyard adjacent to the main arena. As many as twenty gladiators trained at the same time, some in pairs, others alone.

He was called to enter the arena in early summer, during the festival of *Fortuna*. Perspiring from fear as much as the heat, he gathered his net and trident, adjusted his arm and shoulder guards, and tightened a wide leather belt around his mid-section. He was led through a tunnel to a doorway that opened into the arena.

The boisterous crowd of already wine-soaked holiday revelers and blood-thirsty spectators shook the alleyway walls and was like nothing he had ever heard. His heart raced; his legs felt weak and he could barely hold the trident. Staring straight ahead, he suddenly felt the presence of another gladiator and stole a glance sideways to see who it was. The man wore a *secutor's* helmet with a rounded top and fin-shaped flanges to avoid getting caught in the net and to protect his neck. The figure, unnerving in appearance, hidden behind the face cover, froze in place when he saw Marcellus and began to pull frantically at the helmet, shouting incoherently. Suddenly the doorway swung open and the two men were pushed into the arena by the Nubian. The crowd roared as the two lurched forward.

Marcellus raised his trident to give the traditional salute, then stepped away from his opponent and began to circle him, his net set to ensnare.

Rather than lunge toward him or take a fighting stance, the *secutor* remained in place, continuing to shout unintelligibly from inside the helmet.

Confused by the display, uncertain how to proceed, Marcellus stood at the ready, thinking it might be a tactical ploy to catch him off guard. Angry shouts of "*Mortem! Vigliacco!*" rose from the audience, followed by a barrage of eggs and vegetables.

Suddenly the *secutor* threw down his sword and shield, yanked at his head gear, and at last threw it to the ground. "Marcellus!" he cried out. "It's me, Flavius!"

HIDDEN

F RANK WELLS ROSE STEADFASTLY through the ranks of law enforcement; he walked a beat, went to night school at John Jay College of Criminal Justice in New York, made friends in the department and, once he reach Detective Grade, was given the plum assignments.

By the time he was thirty-six, he was in the U.S. Marshals Service, working in the Witness Security Program more commonly known as Witness Protection.

In time he was promoted to assistant director of Witness Security and, aware of the inherent danger in his line of work, never got married.

His reliability and devotion to duty, along with an unblemished record, made Frank the ideal candidate for a highly classified assignment. After being summoned to the office of Crossfield "Cross" Eagen, III, the director of the Service, Frank was asked to close the door and sit down.

A Yale graduate and from old money, Crossfield had only recently been appointed. He wasn't much older than Frank, had impeccable credentials, and had worked his way up the ranks of the Justice Department in a number of highly regarded positions. He could be gruff when situations irked him but also engaging, charming, and very persuasive when he wanted to be.

Behind his desk, on a long credenza, sat citations and photos of Cross with the current President and attorney general. On the wall were a few pictures and newspaper clippings of him leading perps away in handcuffs or shielding jurors and witnesses from harm.

"Frank, what I'm about to tell you," he began, "is confidential and just between us. Do you understand?"

"Absolutely, Cross, whatever you need."

"Good. Here's the situation. . . . You know that protecting the lives of the people placed in our program is the single most important objective of our work."

"Of course. I've devoted the past ten years of my life to that premise."

"I know that, and that's one reason why I am entrusting you with this information."

Frank nodded and leaned in.

Eagen sucked on a tooth, then looked directly into Frank's eyes. "In our entire history, not one witness security program participant has been killed. At least not while following program guidelines under active protection of the Service."

Frank shifted in his seat. He knew all this and wondered why the director was delivering the sermon. Then it came.

"Frank—" Eagen seemed to pause for dramatic effect or perhaps just to find the most appropriate words— "Frank, in the past four months nine program participants have turned up dead."

Wells, stunned by the revelation, remained silent.

"Yes," offered his boss, "I felt the same way. No words.

Just shock and. . . ."

"Uh, *how? When?*"

"The first deaths occurred two days apart and both were in California."

Frank was on the edge of his seat. "And the others?"

"A couple more were taken down the following week. One in New Hampshire, another in Minnesota."

"Do you think they're mob hits?"

"Could be. The most disturbing part is that they were located and identified at all—I mean, these people'd been squirreled away from everything and anyone they ever knew—family, friends, associates. Been given new names, new ID's. Even cosmetic changes."

". . .It *is* pretty odd and very, very disturbing. And the rest?" asked Frank.

"Spread out over a few weeks, some a couple days apart, others a week or so."

"What were the circumstances?"

"All shot in the back of the head. . .and all over the country, all over. California, New Hampshire, North Dakota, two in Iowa. . . ."

Frank scratched his chin. "Cross, why are you. . .I mean, I appreciate this, but why me? What do you want me to—"

"I want you in charge of the investigation, but you'll have to go it alone. No one else can be privy to it. Word gets out, and the department is screwed. No one. You understand?"

Wells nodded. "Yes."

Eagen reached down, opened a drawer, and removed a stack of files, all marked *Classified—Eyes Only.* "Take these. Keep them under lock and key, and make no copies. We'll only correspond verbally, understand?"

"Yes, sir."

"Good. As of now, you're off any other case. You report to no one but me. We'll meet in this office at 3 o'clock every Thursday for updates. Expenses go directly to me. You do what you need, get what you have to, and travel when you must."

Frank stood up, gathered the files, and held them tightly under his arm. "I'm on it, sir. Thank you for your confidence."

"There's nobody else I want for this, Frank. Don't let me down. I want these killings to stop, and I want the killer."

Frank was about to leave but stopped at the door and asked, "How do you know it's one?"

". . .One what, Frank?"

"You said 'killer,' not 'killers.' How do you know it's only one?"

"Uhh, figure of speech. Sure, sure, it could be more than one. Always the details, Frank. That's what makes you right for this job."

Frank smiled and turned down the hall to his office, closed the door, and dropped the files on his desk. Sitting down, he exhaled loudly. *"Whoa!"*

Perusing the folders, it was abundantly clear that the information they contained was of a highly sensitive nature and demanded total secrecy. Better to do this somewhere else, he thought. He pushed back from the desk and returned to the Director's office. Eagen's door was open, so Frank signaled that he wanted to talk privately.

"Come in. Close the door."

"Cross," he began, "given the sensitivity of this assignment, I think it would be wise to move it off premises—I know, I know it's risky letting it out, but I need to keep all this material visible, set up image boards, spreadsheets, you know the routine. I have to find a link, similarities, possible motives, the works."

"Where're you thinking?"

"My apartment."

"How will you explain your absence?"

"Just say I'm on authorized department business. Nobody will suspect."

Cross considered it for a moment and nodded. "Okay, do it. Make arrangements with Melanie, so she doesn't ask a lot of questions or know where you are or why. Say you'll check in with her for mail and messages. How much time you thinking?"

"I have no idea. You know how these things go. And it's complicated because I'll be on my own. I'll have to do everything—interviews, travel, research, coordinate with local law enforcement, the AG's office. He's gonna need to know."

Cross glared at him. "No! Hold off on him."

"But—"

"Frank, I'll take care of him. You just dig into the case."

Frank hesitated, but Crossfield Eagen was his superior, and you didn't question the chain of command. He nodded. "Okay, Chief, I'm on it. I'll see you next week."

Eagen, who was watching him from across the room, looked away, offering a perfunctory, "Good luck."

FRANK SPOKE TO MELANIE about his pending absence, and that he would check in with her every day or two but was on a classified assignment and couldn't say anything further. She was a study in restraint, not prone to probing or poking her noise where it didn't belong. She and Frank had been working well as a team for four years. Both had felt the physical attraction but kept it completely professional, difficult as it was.

He set himself up at home—put a large bulletin board on the living room wall, added leaves to the dining room table and spread everything out. He read through all the folders twice and made notes as he went along, then took each separately and began pinning photos and pertinent information to the board. He went about his work methodically in the old-fashioned way.

It was early into the third day when connections and similarities began to emerge. All nine victims were male, all had joined the protection program within the past ten years, and none lived with families. Four were former mob members, three drug traffickers, and two terrorists. The last two didn't make sense to him until he discovered they had also worked for the Iranian and Syrian governments before being caught by CIA Operatives. After enhanced interrogation, they both turned and were promised immunity and new identities. They became high-value clients in divulging terrorist cells in the U.S. As a result, Middle Eastern factions had put a $10 million price tag on their heads.

Frank couldn't figure out whether all nine victims were somehow related, and whether the killer, or killers, were hired assassins. And if so, hired by whom? It wasn't much of a stretch to link the wise guys and the drug dealers, but the two foreign operatives? He pondered that for a long time before finally making the connection—at least in theory.

FRANK REPORTED HIS PROGRESS TO CROSS during their first Thursday meeting. When he got to the part about the operatives, he paused, took a deep breath, and said, "This is purely spec at this point, but I think it's plausible and I intend to verify it."

"Go on, let me hear," Eagen said.

"I'm not sure where it will lead, but our two foreign clients were caught in Afghanistan. They had large amounts of U.S. currency on them at the time."

The director nodded. "And?"

"The poppy trade is a mainstay of the Afghan economy. The four dead syndicate guys were prominent in the East Coast drug business. The traffickers were procuring the stuff for them, who in turn paid with laundered money and weapons, which then found their way back to the two terrorists who were getting the drugs from their Afghani resources."

Eagen listened attentively but said little and didn't ask any questions. Frank waited. The silence began to unnerve him. After a full minute he asked, "Well? What do you think, Cross? Does it sound right?"

Eagen was tight-lipped, scratched at his cheek, and slowly moved his head up and down. "Yes, Frank. You're doing a fine job. . .as usual. Stay with it." As an afterthought, he added, "Anything you need?"

Frank opened his note pad and went down a list of things. "I want to look at the homicide files at the local police departments where the murders occurred."

Cross nodded.

"I want to visit CIA in Langley—" he looked up from the pad and haltingly went on— "and I still think we need to bring the AG into the mix."

Cross was steely-eyed and grim; he studied Frank's face, fingers drumming on the desk. "No no, not yet."

Confused by the absence of protocol and uncertain of

Cross's motive, Frank rapidly considered what reasons his superior might have for keeping the Attorney General of the United States in the dark.

Eagen made a move to stand up and Frank, afraid he was going to lose the chance to ask, just blurted it out. "Sir, what, if I may ask, is the reason for keeping the AG out of this?"

"No, Frank, you may not ask." On seeing his assistant director register shock, Cross added, "I have my reasons, Frank."

"Sir, I don't mean to be insubordinate, but—"

"But you *are* being insubordinate. So let's just leave it off the table for now. Okay?"

Dismayed but undaunted, Frank rose from the chair and gathered his paperwork. "Okay, I'll see you next week. I'm off to Salinas and Fresno to check out the files on the first two—" he made little quote marks with his fingers— "accidents."

ALL THE HOMICIDES FEATURED a single bullet to the head. The victims were found in their cars or on a deserted road, and most executions had occurred in the late evening or early morning. That was interesting but led him nowhere. Frank dug in, starting with the first two of the nine victims. He learned that the cases the two were involved in had been tried in New York, but three years apart and seemingly unrelated, other than they were both linked to organized crime. Both had been made men.

He moved on to the next, and then the next, turning up nothing useful. By the time he had explored six of the nine murders, he was frustrated by the lack of any links and said so to Eagen. "I have nothing useful. This is coming up short at every turn, and I think I need some help."

"What kind of help, Frank? You're better than any help you'd get elsewhere."

"I appreciate the compliment, Chief, but I could use a few sets of eyes—and brains—here."

The director cleared his throat. "I don't care how much time it takes, you work this one by yourself."

Frank considered resigning. The investigation was getting him nowhere and left him feeling inadequate, an attribute he didn't welcome.

"I'm sorry to bring it up again, Sir, but the support of the AG, and all the assistance he could muster could clear this up—"

"*Frank*! Goddamn it, I said no!"

Wells' jaw tightened at Eagen's outburst, but he somehow managed to stare at his superior without uttering a word. Eagen glared back at him. A deathly silence pervaded the room as seconds ticked away. Finally, Wells began to feel as if his skin was tightening around him, and he stood up. "Sir, it is unrealistic to think I can do this by myself, and I'd like to put a time frame on the assignment."

"You stay with this, Frank. You don't quit until I say so. Is that understood?"

Frank rose, shook his head, and quietly said, "Next week then."

He left the room without looking back.

THE FOLLOWING DAY, circumventing the chain of command, he called in a lot of favors and was able to get an unprecedented appointment with the Attorney General of the United States.

Given only fifteen minutes to brief the AG, he cut quickly

to the chase. Aghast at the news, the AG held all his calls and delayed his other meetings. "I understand the implications of this on all levels," he told Frank.

"Thank you, sir. I am fully aware that what I have done is a breach of protocol. I am willing to jeopardize my career because I recognize the potential consequences for the Marshal's Service, for WIDSEC, and for its credibility. I believe the very existence of the program is at stake."

"Marshal Wells, you are a brave man, and the country is in your debt."

Frank scanned the pictures behind the Attorney General's desk; Supreme Court Justices, President of The United States, and one he knew well, John Jay, the nation's first Chief Justice.

The AG came around his desk to sit next to Wells. "Marshal," he said in a lowered voice, "I am of the opinion that coming to me is out of line, since you didn't have approval, but I also understand your predicament. For now, at least, tell me what it is you need to get to the bottom of these, uh, incidents, and I will do what I can to maintain confidentiality while you conduct further investigation." He placed a hand on Frank's shoulder. "I will choose a trusted member of my staff as your contact, so I stay at arm's length. Is that agreeable?

"Yes, sir."

"Good. Do you have a secure contact number that we can use?"

"I do, sir."

Frank placed a card on the desk—no name, no address, just a phone number. The AG glanced at it and dropped it in a desk drawer. "Prepare a list of what you need—the minimum number of agents you absolutely must have, and a timeline. When my agent makes contact, you can convey that information."

"Thank you, sir. I am grateful for your assistance more than I can say."

They shook hands, and Frank left.

HE FELT A MIX OF RELIEF AND ANXIETY when he got home but wasted no time preparing his list. He knew the agents he was given to work with would have to be unimpeachable, and discreet beyond a high security clearance.

The most disquieting aspect was that he couldn't say a word to Cross about what he had done and would be doing. It made him terribly uneasy and would take all his resolve to maintain the secret when discussing his progress with him.

When the phone rang, Frank was so deep in thought he almost jumped out of his chair. It was a female voice, and at first he thought it was a wrong number.

"I'm calling for Marshal Wells."

"Who is this?" he asked.

"Special Agent Larkin," she replied. ""I'm calling on behalf of the attorney general."

". . .What is this in reference to?"

"Your meeting concerning WIDSEC."

Frank exhaled. "I wasn't expecting, uh—"

"A woman? I know, I get that a lot. Where and when do you want to meet?"

Frank liked that. "Tomorrow, ten A.M.," he said. "Meet me in Union Station across from the Center Café, the West Hall entrance."

"I have red hair," she offered. "I'll be wearing a green hat and scarf."

"Works for me. See you tomorrow." He hung up, tried to

visualize the caller, and smiled about her being a woman.

WHEN HE GOT TO THE WEST HALL, she was already there, red hair and green accessories eminently visible—but she had neglected to mention that she was almost six feet tall without heels. They exchanged a knowing glance.

On seeing how attractive she was and wanting to keep everything above board, Frank realized that working so closely together would require a place other than his apartment.

He motioned her toward the Café, found a corner table, sat down, ordered coffee, and they spent the next half hour getting to know each other before turning to the case.

Her first name was Helen, she was married, had no children and had been with the Justice Department for nine years, the last three directly with the AG. Wells asked her to find a workplace that would accommodate several people and provide enough space to spread out.

OVER THE NEXT FEW WEEKS they put together a team of three others, all with top clearance, fully vetted, sworn to secrecy, and sensitive to the mission.

Clarence Switt was an NSA computer whiz who immediately went about setting up a firewall, wrote code, and developed a secure site. Justin McAvoy was a seasoned FBI crime investigator with previous experience collaborating on witness security. The third, Marvin Burke, was a former CIA operative who had a record of hunting down terrorists and bringing them in alive. Helen was a superb researcher, a gifted CI, and was also tirelessly upbeat—a major asset for the team.

Eventually they came to believe that only one killer was involved, and that whoever it was had to have inside information about the mechanics of WIDSEC and the individuals who were killed. That narrowed down the options.

Their photo file grew from the original few to dozens of images gleaned from local and state police files, as well as from Justice Department archives. They combed through each, seeking connections and links, trying to find suspects. They were looking for a serial killer who might have known the victims, was aware they had been government informants, that they had been placed in the witness program, and, most important, knew how to find them.

They became obsessed with the case, none more than Frank, who frequently spent nights in the "office" combing through files, trying to connect the dots.

At home one night, after eighteen hours of staring at photos, he woke abruptly with the image of one in his mind, a picture he remembered seeing somewhere other than in his office. He sifted through his memory, trying to recall where he'd seen it, and finally got dressed and drove to the covert workplace.

Arriving before sunrise, he discovered the office door ajar. Expecting to find one of his team at work inside, he was shocked to see the office had been broken into.

There was no sign of forced entry, no overturned furniture or damage, but things had definitely been rummaged through.

He was careful not to move or touch anything and waited an hour before calling Helen. She showed up within forty minutes, and they discussed the possibility of a random break-in versus someone knowing what was going on in the room.

"From the looks of this, Frank," she suggested after examining the lock and the condition of the office, "whoever it was knew *exactly* what they were looking for. They were methodical and cautious and either had a key or were awfully good at picking a lock."

They put up coffee and waited for the others. First thing Frank asked them when they arrived was, "Were any of you here last night?"

Marvin and Justin shook their heads. Clarence was the first to speak. "What? No, hi or good morning?"

Frank turned his attention to Switt, "So *were* you here?"

"No. Why, what's up?"

"We had a visitor last night."

The three of them looked at each other, than at Helen.

"Who locked up?" asked Justin.

"I was the last one out," announced Frank. "I left around eleven."

He looked each of them individually and then took a deep breath. "Alright, let's look around and see what, if anything, is missing. Helen, check the bulletin board. Justin and Clarence, split up the files and look through them. Marv, you and I take care of the rest. Let's get to work."

"Wait a second," cried Helen. "If this wasn't random, then someone knows we're here and why. . .and came looking for something in particular."

"Who the hell knows we're here?" questioned Switt,

and answered the question himself. "The killer. Or someone working for him?—or her."

They turned to Frank, but he wasn't looking in their direction; his eyes were fixed on the bulletin board. Suddenly he squeezed his eyes shut, held up a hand for silence, and remained perfectly still. He opened his eyes and walked to the wall, both hands up, index fingers moving up and down, left and right.

"They're missing!" he exclaimed.

"What's missing?" asked Helen.

"The *pictures!* There are three photos missing."

They crowded around the board.

"Which ones?" asked Justin.

Frank scratched his chin, trying to remember the exact subject matter, who or what was in the photos. He closed his eyes and, almost as quickly, opened them.

"Damn! I woke up thinking about one. I knew I'd seen it somewhere, but couldn't figure out where."

Their eyes were on him now, expectant. "Eagen!"

Heads turned to each other, than back to Wells. "Eagen?" repeated Helen.

"Director Eagen," Frank said flatly. "The department head. My boss."

"What about him?" asked Justin.

Frank sat down on the edge of the folding table they used for conferences. "The photo. I saw the same photo on the wall behind his desk."

They instinctively looked at the board where the photos would have been, trying to conjure the one he was talking about.

Frank continued, "Remember? The picture of the perp walk? Eagen leading 'Peppers' Pastelli out of the courthouse following testimony against the Carlucci family? That was nine, maybe ten years ago."

"Yeah, so Pastelli's one of our dead guys. We know that." said McAvoy.

"That's right," agreed Frank, "and if I remember correctly, Crossfield Eagen appears in the other missing photos, too."

"Right," said Larkin, "I remember. One was with Benny Scalia, Benny Bananas, and the other was Paul Segretto."

"Uh, yeah," confirmed Wells. "All three of those guys were in the program and sent to. . .where were they sent?"

Helen went to retrieve the witness files.

Shuffling through the folders she turned to the group and stammered, "They're—they're gone."

"What the fuck!" barked Switt.

Helen was watching Frank, waiting for him to comment. Seconds ticked by. Everyone held their breath.

"Where were Scalia and Segretto living?" Frank finally asked.

A hush fell over the group, the computer drive hummed in the corner of Marvin's desk, a car alarm wailed in the distance, a cat screeched in the alleyway. Helen pulled a chair away from the desk and sat down. She ran her fingers through her cinnamon-colored hair.

"North Dakota," she offered, almost inaudibly.

"What?" asked Frank. "North Dakota. Scalia was killed in North Dakota. . .and Segretto was found in New Hampshire. Pistelli was shot in. . . um, Fresno."

"Okay. All of you, let's reconstruct what we know. Reconfirm the dates of their deaths and the nearest airports to where their bodies were found. And I want to know the caliber weapon used in the shootings. Let's go. I want this *yesterday!*"

The activity took on a dizzying pace, the chatter and the clacking of their keyboards caroming off the walls. Frank busied himself studying the remaining photos with a magnifying glass, searching for things he might have overlooked, maybe some other recognizable people.

In less than fifteen minutes, heads popped up, and the chairs rolled back.

"Okay, let's have it," commanded Frank.

Justin glanced at a printout in his hand. "Nearest airport to Concord, New Hampshire, would be Portsmouth, but an alternate access would be through Logan—it has more options, and it's an easy drive to the crime scene. Location number two . . .Grand Forks, North Dakota. There's an airport right there. Fresno also has one."

"That's good," said Frank. "Marv, what've you got?"

"Delta is the only airline into Grand Forks. American flies into Portsmouth. A dozen others fly out of Boston. Six service Fresno."

Frank tugged at his ear, an old working habit. "Clarence, I want to see the ballistic reports. What was the—"

"The first two were .40-cal. The others were .357s, maybe a SIG Sauer P229."

Frank turned to Helen and motioned to the door. "Take a walk with me."

She got up without a word and put on her coat.

At the door, Frank turned toward the others. "We'll be back in a few minutes."

On the street, he stood very close to her and said, in a voice just above a whisper, "I need to see the AG as soon as possible."

"What are you—"

"I have a gut feeling, and I hope to God I'm wrong."

"I think I know where you're going with this," she said, "I'll set it up soon as possible.

HELEN IMPARTED THE GREAT SENSE of urgency to the AG and he agreed to a clandestine early-morning meeting the following day.   He and Frank met across from the Justice Department, near the steps of the Smithsonian, shook hands, and started walking.

"Sir," Frank began, "I have a disturbing. . .call it an edu-cated guess. . .that might be too bizarre—"

"What do you have?"

"There are some odd coincidences. Someone broke into our office yesterday."

The AG stopped walking and stared at him. "What was taken?"

"Three files and some photos."

"What significance do they have?"

"Photos of the murdered witnesses."

"Details?"

"Benny Scalia, Jimmy Pastelli, Paul Segretto. Scalia was facing life plus one hundred twenty-five for eleven mob hits, racketeering, loan sharking, the works. He served two and then turned informant, entered the program, new identity, all the trimmings."

The AG nodded.

Frank continued, "Segretto was a capo in the Stefano crime family. He had a rap sheet as long as Pennsylvania Avenue. He was looking at life without parole and opened up about the family's entire operation. Two years after his relocation, with a new ID, he was arrested on a rape charge, which was dismissed, and was picked up again the following year for drug trafficking and assault and battery."

"Nice people. And Pistelli?"

"An enforcer. Admitted to six hits, probably involved in four others. Mandatory life sentence.

". . .Well, what's your theory, Marshal?"

Frank stopped in his tracks. "Can we sit down? This is difficult for me."

They found a bench. "Sir, there are very few people who could've known the witnesses' new identities and where they were living. Whoever wanted them dead was probably out for more than vengeance. Whoever broke into our office knew what was in there. It wasn't random. One of our team was probably followed, and I think it was me. No one but you and my crew know about this investigation—" he paused, cleared his throat, and looked directly at the AG— "except for Cross Eagen."

The AG remained calm and expressionless. "That is a very dangerous accusation, Marshal Wells. Are you sure you want to go down that road?"

"Sir, the pieces fit. I know it sounds crazy, but we have to pursue it. Eagen assigned the investigation to me and only me. He must've followed me after one of our Thursday meetings, discovered our HQ, and then come back when no one was there so he could snoop around and confirm his suspicions. He removed whatever might implicate him personally."

The AG was silent for a long while. "Have you voiced this idea with the others?"

"Just Helen. As you said, it's a dangerous road to travel down, and I wanted to talk to you first."

"Let me ask you this. If the director is guilty, which I cannot fathom, why would he assign you to investigate? He had to believe you'd eventually uncover it."

Frank's eyes met his. "I have been wrestling with that, and I think he insisted I be the only one to work on the case so it would be prolonged. He was hoping he'd covered himself, that nothing could be traced back to him."

The AG nodded. "What do you need from me?"

"Approval to access Eagen's expense records, travel log,

days out of the office, anything that might place him in the crime scene arena."

"Frank, do you think you could get in without JD support?"

"You mean do we have the ability to hack in?"

"Yes, because I can't give you official approval. You need to have more than reasonable suspicion. If Director Eagen is innocent, and this was to get out, well—you'd need a court order, and that would open this up to even more people. At any rate, whatever you find will be considered illegal evidence if you do this on your own, and I'm afraid I can't condone it." He hesitated. "All right—do what you need to do, but you didn't hear it from me. Is that understood?"

Frank sighed, nodded, and shook the AG's hand. "Thank you for your time, sir. I'll get back to you when I have more."

They walked off in opposite directions.

WHEN HE REACHED THE OFFICE, Frank found everyone already engrossed in work, though it was only eight A.M.

"Okay," he said, "everybody, heads-up." He sat at the big table, a pained expression on his face. "I believe we are at a point in this investigation where we have to step over the line. I am about to say some things that may not sit well with you. It will put you at risk legally and possibly jeopardize your careers. I admire your integrity and will understand if you want to be released from further involvement. But once I share this with you, there's no turning back." He stopped and looked at each of them to see their reactions.

Clarence cleared his throat. "I think I speak for all of us, Frank, when I say we signed on knowing there might be risks, and that it was a clandestine mission from the beginning." He turned to look at the others. "Everyone?"

"I'm in," announced Helen.

Justin and Marvin simultaneously declared, "Me, too."

"Okay, then," Frank began, "here's my hypothesis. For whatever reason, Director Eagen wanted those witnesses gone. Maybe they had something on him, maybe he had a vendetta, maybe he had them killed—or maybe he's the killer."

Justin barked, "That's *preposterous*, Frank. I mean, come on—"

"Hear me out. Who else but us and the AG know about the investigation, or the murders for that matter? Who had access to the IDs and backgrounds of all the victims?"

"It's a crazy idea, Frank," Marvin replied.

"I know what it *sounds* like, but I want to explore it. We have nothing else. . .and the office break-in, and the missing photos with Cross Eagen in them, are just too coincidental."

"So what next?" asked Helen.

"Clarence, do you think you can get into the admin files of the Marshal Service?"

"Uh, yeah, but—"

"It will be critical to verifying my theory, and yes, it falls into murky legal waters. Look, if we determine Eagen is innocent, than no one has to know about this. And—and if it's the other way around, well. . . ."

"What do you want to access?" asked Clarence.

"I want his expense and travel records and his day-to-day activity log for the past four months. I want to know when he was out of the office, and for how long."

"It'll take me time to get in. I'll have to create an algorithm and let it run."

"How long?" asked Frank.

"I have no idea. . .could be a couple days, maybe longer, maybe not."

"Whatever it takes. Go for it."

He turned toward McAvoy. "Justin, I want you to access airline schedules for all flights to and from the places we talked about. All that originated out of Dulles or Reagan on those dates. Marv and Helen, when Justin has the list, I want you to check the manifests for Eagen's name. Remember, he's brilliant, so stay alert to any discrepancies or even remotely coincidental pieces of information."

They went to work.

Frank was apprehensive about his upcoming Thursday meeting with Eagen, knowing he had to give the impression that nothing had changed. Cross would have to think he wasn't a suspect, though he knew Frank had disobeyed him and gone rogue. It was a dicey situation.

ENTERING THE OFFICE OF THE DIRECTOR, Frank offered his customary innocuous greeting. "Good morning, Cross!" He assumed Eagen would listen to everything he said and wouldn't believe any of it.

"So, how're things going, Frank? Any news, breakthroughs, what do you have?"

"Well, I have a few leads—nothing concrete, just hunches, really."

The director was probably enjoying the pretense. "So what can you shed light on? What're you thinking?"

Frank glanced behind the desk at the wall and the credenza; the photos of Eagen were gone. "Sir, I've been struggling with motive, but now believe the killer, or killers, were out for retribution, for disrespecting *omertá*—at least as far as the mob hits. For the others, I'm still baffled. I believe there is a link between all of the victims. The manner in which they were killed are similar. . . . It's more than likely a couple of hit men. Perhaps hired by one guy—a mob boss, maybe."

Eagen didn't take his eyes off Frank. It was a dance of deception, and for the moment Crossfield Eagen seemed to be doing the leading. "So," he asked, "you still feel you need to get the AG involved?"

"I still think it could expedite the investigation, yes, but—" he hesitated before adding, "no, I guess not."

"That's good, Frank. I agree. I think you're doing just fine by yourself."

Frank wasn't sure how long he could keep the progress reports going—and then a disturbing thought occurred to him: Perhaps Eagen wasn't involved at all.

CLARENCE HAD THE ALGORITHM RUNNING day and night, and it took eighteen hours to unlock the code and the passwords. After that, it was just a matter of collecting data, which they did.

Before too long it became apparent that Eagen had either covered his tracks supremely well or just wasn't their guy. Department expense records revealed no charges or other relevant information on or around the dates of the crimes. Eagen's daily appointment log had no entries on those days.

A conflicted Frank Wells sat deep in thought, doggedly sifting through the collected information while the others conversed quietly in a corner of the room; the investigation had stalled. He suddenly shoved back, almost knocking over the chair. "Wait a minute! Clarence, let me see Eagen's day planner for the week prior to, and just after, the murder dates."

The log showed Eagen had a very full schedule leading up to and immediately following the key days, but no appointments on the exact dates.

"The *only* way he could be out and back in that short a time would be to fly," said Helen.

"Recheck the flight manifests," Frank ordered. But before she could run down the lists, he abruptly shouted, "I got it!"

All heads turned to him.

"Air marshal! He boarded as an air marshal. It would allow him to carry his weapon—a SIG Sauer P229, the air marshal weapon of choice."

"And the slugs used on Scalia and Segretto," shouted McAvoy, "are SIG loads. Boom!"

"Helen," Frank called out, "air marshals board incognito, but the crew knows who they are and where they're seated; typically first-class, aisle seat. That will narrow your search."

Helen rifled through pages of flight manifests while muttering, "No. No, no. . . wait! Here he is. . .Dulles to Logan. September 12, the six P.M. shuttle."

"Keep going. I want more," Frank demanded.

She rummaged through the pile, scouring the lists until she found another, and then another, each going in and out of the crime scene locations around the time of the murders. A lengthy search of the car rental companies turned up rentals by Eagen at the airports on the same days.

"We have him!" Frank shouted, and then he slumped into a chair. "Jesus! I can't believe it. Why? What in God's name . . . ."

The others said nothing and glanced at each other before

sitting down at the table, waiting for instructions. "We have to question his secretary, Paula," he suggested. "She can verify whether he was out for any period of time on those days. We need to build a case."

"How we gonna get her to do that without him knowing?" asked Burke.

"Look," Frank offered, "she and Melanie have a good relationship. They often work together. I'll have Melanie ask her if I had a meeting with him on one of those dates."

"Why would Melanie be asking Paula about something that took place months ago?" Clarence wanted to know. "What possible—"

"I'll tell her my cell crashed and I can't recall."

"Why wouldn't you just ask him yourself?" asked Helen.

"I wouldn't bother him with that. Besides, he'd only tell me to talk to Paula."

"Might work," she said, "but if it doesn't and word gets back to Eagen—"

"Helen, he already knows I'm working around him. . . . Look, people, we have to move on this—fast! Right now there's no other way to confirm his absence, and all we need is to tie one of the murders to him. We have him listed on the flights as an air marshal. How can he explain that?"

Knowing they only had the one lead, he waited for an answer to the obvious. None came.

"We need to corroborate that he was out on those days," he continued. "Circumstantial evidence it's not. He'll never have to know how we accessed the information, and the manifests and appointment books are not classified information."

He called Melanie and told her what he needed. She didn't question him other than to ask how soon he wanted it. He had to smile at her loyalty. "Thanks, Mel. I'll call you tomorrow, but you can reach me on my cell if you have something sooner."

Melanie called back in twenty minutes. "Hi. Paula was very accommodating. I thumbed through the date book and scrolled through the director's calendar. There were no appointments with you; in fact, he had a totally clear calendar on the dates you gave me. Does that help?"

"Mel, I owe you dinner! No, *two* dinners!"

"I'll take you up on that. You need anything else?"

"No, that's it for now."

"By the way," she asked, "when're you coming back to the office?"

"I can't say for sure. Soon, I hope."

"Been pretty quiet around here without you," she remarked.

"Yeah, well, it won't be for too much longer."

As soon as he said it, he wished he hadn't, but she didn't comment other than to say good-bye.

Frank turned to face the others. "I think we have probable cause." He turned to Helen. "The AG will have to decide how and when he wants to proceed with an arrest. This is a very delicate situation, and it's going to be explosive!"

"I'll set up a meeting with him, but he may want to get others involved, and it will probably be in his office, not in the park this time."

Frank was looking off into the distance, and although he heard her, he was thousands of miles away—North Dakota, California, Iowa, and New Hampshire.

Helen interrupted his reverie. "Frank? Are you listening?"

He refocused. "I'm still having trouble understanding his

motive."

McAvoy hesitantly raised a hand. "I, uh—I have a theory."

"Let's hear it," ordered Frank.

"Somebody got to him. They threatened him and his family. Whoever it was needed to know where the victims were hidden and brought Eagen along for insurance."

Burke shook his head, "No. Threats wouldn't scare him, and he'd have brought the full force of the Marshal Service down on whoever it was before becoming an accessory to murder."

"Listen," Frank said, "anything we come up with at this point is pure conjecture. If an arrest is made, there'll be an interrogation and disclosure of evidence. Proving that he's the murderer, no matter what the motive, will be the toughest part. There were no witnesses to any of the crimes. All we can do is match ballistics to his service weapon, place him in the location at the time of the murders, and pray to God we're right about this, or a lot of heads will roll, mine first."

The mood in the room was somber. Helen finally broke the silence. "What's next?"

Frank heaved a sigh. "We have to meet with the AG and present our case against Crossfield Eagen as convincingly as possible."

They called it a day and decided to regroup at ten in the morning to prepare the presentation.

"Get some sleep," said Frank. "You have all done a masterful job. There is no way I could have done this alone, and I will never apologize for going to the attorney general for support. Thank you."

He shook hands with everyone and said good night.

FRANK SLEPT FITFULLY THAT EVENING and woke with a

start, his T-shirt clammy, his shoulder muscles tight. Glancing at the clock while gulping a second cup of coffee, he felt terribly uneasy and unsure of what he was embarking upon; the 'what ifs' filled his head. Self-doubt was not a trait Frank Wells was comfortable with. It wasn't doing him any good to be sitting at home, so he got dressed and went to the office, well ahead of the others.

He busied himself making a pot of coffee, perusing the wall images, and revisiting the hacked information. He was still unsettled over the direction things had taken, secretly hoping he was completely wrong about Crossfield Eagen, that the man was somehow innocent of any wrongdoing.

His cell phone vibrated, and a terse text message glared back at him: *Urgent! Call Office Now. Melanie.*

He looked at his watch, it was 9:20. There wasn't enough time to head over there before his team assembled. What, he wondered, could it be?

He keyed in the speed dial, and Melanie picked up on the first ring.

She all but cried, "Frank! You gotta get in here."

"What's the matter?" he shot back. Her reply was much worse than he could have imagined.

"Director Eagen is dead!"

"...What? When? What the—"

She was sobbing so much he couldn't understand her.

"I'll be right there."

"Frank," she managed to blurt out, "he shot himself in the head. Last night. Please, hurry."

"I'm on my way!"

He propped a flashing red dome light on the roof of the car and flew up Constitution Avenue to Tenth Street, zipped into the garage, and rushed through security. The scene in the office was organized chaos, swarming with marshals, JD personnel, and DC police.

Quickly cleared to enter, he sought out Melanie. She fell into his arms, visibly shaken and distraught.

"Okay, okay, calm down. What can you tell me?" he asked her as consolingly as he could.

EAGEN HAD COMMITTED SUICIDE the previous evening when no one else was in the office. He was found in his chair, his head, what was left of it, thrown back by the force of the .357 cartridge and had broken his neck. Pieces of his skull and brain had all but obliterated the photo of him and the President. There was a suicide note on the desk:

> *I ask only one thing, forgiveness from my family. I know how this will affect them, but I cannot put them through the endless spotlight of the media, the lengthy trials and appeals, and my heinous and shameful acts.*
>
> *To my colleagues, I believe, given the chance, many of you would have done the same thing. Of the thousands of witnesses we have been charged with protecting over the years, the nine informants I assassinated were all those I had first-hand knowledge of and safeguarded during their trials, confessions, and entry into the WIDSEC program.*
>
> *These were the lowest of the low, scum who did not deserve the treatment we gave them or the new lives they got to live when so many others died as a result of their monstrous behavior, their psychopathic lifestyles, and their chosen path to hell. I only did what should*

have been done in the first place.

Crossfield Eagen, III

SIX WEEKS LATER, Frank wells was appointed director of the WIDSEC program. As promised, he took Melanie to dinner—and does so pretty regularly.

INGÉNUE

THIRTY-TWO-YEAR-OLD LYLE PADAMORE felt weak in the knees the moment he saw her lounging on the big sofa chair at the Rivington Street Bean 'n' Brew. He couldn't take his eyes off of her, even when she caught him staring. Her demeanor was serene, not aloof; not remotely off-putting, she simply appeared comfortable in her space, in the moment; all of which made her that much more alluring.

Her hair caught his attention first—thick, raven-colored tresses resting on her shoulders. And then her complexion, honey-colored, smooth, and radiant, catching the shaft of light streaming through the window behind her, adding luster to her tawny skin.

Peering up from his laptop he spied her blowing softly, with sensuous lips, into a steaming mug. He was captivated, and not only with lust, although that too was quite evident when their eyes met.

The coffee house was generally quiet on Monday mornings; most of the patrons placed orders to go and hastily retreated to catch the subway uptown to their jobs. Only a few regulars, the would-be novelists, the unemployed musicians and poets, the night-job people, sat at tables murmuring to their neighbor or tablemate, some perusing the *Village Voice* or *New York Times*, while others sat transfixed by their Macs and iPads.

Wait, was that a smile? Did she smile? Lyle was sure he had seen her smile. He glanced backward on the chance she was looking at someone else, the smile meant for another. But there was no one behind him. Could it be a subtle invitation, a flirtatious moment, or a mere pleasantry shared with a fellow caffeine addict?

Lyle felt his heart pumping faster, adrenalin coursing though his veins; he swallowed hard, digging deep to find the courage to approach her. He wasn't bad looking, and according to some women, even considered handsome. He certainly didn't lack confidence, but for some reason, the vision of loveliness before him made him feel like a school boy, sweaty palms and all. And he hadn't spoken a word to her or even knew her name.

What the hell is wrong with me? he wondered. He took a very deep breath and tried to calm his nerves—or find them.

Trying to be the picture of self-assurance, not too suave, not ultra-cool, he sought just the right touch of confidence without arrogance or swagger.

Sincere, witty, with a hint of sexiness, that's what was called for. Could he muster it in the five steps it would take to walk to her table?

"Hi," she said.

Dear God, he thought, a voice to match the rest of her, a little throaty but soft, girlish, but not silly, a young woman with warmth and a touch of worldliness. . .wait, all that in just "hi"?

His desire was getting the best of him. He tried to settle

down. Better cool it, dude, he said to himself, and wondered if he had spoken the words aloud, because he was certain she laughed.

"Hi," she repeated and then put out her hand.

He took it gently, shook it twice, and cautiously asked, "Mind if I sit down?"

"That's the idea, isn't it?" She smiled. Oh, man, dimples too? Okay, stay calm. Think of something funny. No, clever. "Uh, hi," he barely managed to stammer.

"I'm Andrea," she added. "Who are you?"

"Um, hi, Andrea, I'm Lyle. . .Lyle Padamore. You new here? I mean, I haven't seen you before."

She nodded slowly. "Yes, very new. My first time. I mean here, at this coffee bar. You?"

"No, I'm always here. Well, not *every* day, I mean not all the time. . . I mean, no."

He stopped, embarrassed by his sudden timidity.

She looked at him with warm, amber-colored eyes, a tiny smile in the corner of those gorgeous lips.

"What are you drinking?" she asked him.

He looked back at the table he came from, his Notebook still open, the half-empty coffee cup unattended.

"Uh, I was drinking a *café au lait*. You?

"A pumpkin spice latte, soy milk, no foam."

"Can I get you another?"

"Yes, that would be nice. This one is almost finished."

He raised a finger and motioned toward the man behind the counter. "Ruben, can we have refills here?" Lyle looked at her slender fingers caressing the cup. "Um, soy latte pumpkin spice, uh. . . ."

She giggled. "No foam."

"Right." He turned to face the counterman. "Reuben can—"

The barista nodded. "I know. I got it."

Andrea squinted across the tiny table. "You *do* come here often, don't you?" she asked.

He shrugged. "I guess so. Been coming in since they opened."

"You live around here?" she asked.

"Two blocks up, one over from Delancey."

"So what do you do, Lyle? I mean, that you can spend so much time here?"

"I'm a playwright."

"Really." She arched an eyebrow, seeming impressed if not truly interested. "What have you written. . .that I might have seen?"

"Not much, actually, at least not that you're probably aware of. Mostly regional theater, national competitions, some summer stock."

"What kind of stuff? Dramas, mysteries, musicals. . . ?"

"None of the above. Experimental, mostly. Had a piece in *The Fringe* last year. Another one up at the Cape last summer. Got good reviews, but no producer interest beyond that."

"You working on anything now?" she asked, a bit too earnestly, he thought.

Lyle shifted the focus away from his limited professional success. "So what do *you* do, Andrea? What brings you here?"

She produced a brief pout. "Okay, then, so don't tell me." He was sure his heart skipped a beat. A vamp, an honest-to-God vamp, he thought. This one is a heart breaker. Beware. His mind was racing. He wanted to make hot, passionate love to her right there on the table, coffee cups and newspapers flying, patrons aghast, the two of them oblivious to their surroundings, hungrily gasping, grasping, groping, howling in ecstasy.

Holding the image in his mind for the briefest moment, he refocused on her question. "Okay, okay, yes, uh, I'm finishing up a two-act, politically motivated, sci-fi love story."

She stared at him, not sure if he was serious, thought better than to pursue it at the risk of offending, and said, "What do *I* do? Not much of anything right now. I've been a model, a pole dancer, neuro-surgeon, a diamond cutter, concert violinist, and a—" she started to laugh, reached across and ever so lightly, touched his hand, and looked into his brown eyes framed by black horn-rim glasses. "Just kidding," she said. "Seriously? I'm only visiting. My sister and her husband live on Avenue B. I've only been here four days."

He was crestfallen. "How long are you staying?"

"Not sure. Just considering my options—stay or go to Hollywood. I have offers, you know?"

Hollywood? Was she still just kidding, or was she for real? His eyes fixed on hers before he gradually, so as not to be too conspicuous, shifted his gaze downward where he could delve into the cleavage peeking out of the top of her spaghetti-strap tank top. When he saw she was watching him, he blushed a hot crimson and quickly averted his eyes. She looked directly at him, a knowing smile on her lips and gently tugged upward on the thin straps.

"Here y'go," said Reuben as he set the two mugs on the table. Andrea tilted her head upward. "Thank you, Reuben."

"Uh, yeah, thanks," Lyle said without looking up, trying to avoid eye contact with her.

There was an awkward, momentary silence while they pulled their cups closer and lifted them to their mouths, but she never looked away from him.

His thoughts were running amok. He wanted her in every way imaginable. In just the few minutes he had been with her, he was already prepared to do whatever he had to. He wished he was rich and famous and could just carry her off into some romance- novel setting. For a few moments, he wondered how and where. *Hollywood. Was that for real? Maybe she'll stay, now that she's met me. She did say she wasn't sure what she would do.* "Um, Andrea. . . ."

She had shifted her focus to something behind him, and her face suddenly registered fear.

Before he could turn, she recoiled, and a figure appeared beside him. Reaching across the table, a tall, heavy-set man grabbed Andrea's wrist and pulled her to her feet, upending the coffee mug and nearly toppling the table. Lyle started to intervene, but the bulky figure shoved him back with his other beefy hand and growled, "You sit down!"

He yanked the cowering girl toward him, not letting go of her hand. "You're coming with me. What'd I tell you about wandering around in this city by yourself?"

Lyle protested. "Hey, who—"

"Shut the fuck up! You know how *old* she is?"

Before Lyle could say anything more, the man began pushing Andrea toward the exit and looked over his shoulder, scowling. "Fourteen. She's fourteen!"

IT WAS A FULL MINUTE BEFORE Lyle could register what had happened—the revelation, the craziness. He rose almost in shock, weak in the knees, stomach queasy, and shuffled back to his table, closed the laptop, stuffed it in his canvas briefcase, heaved the strap onto his shoulder, shook his head in disbelief, and walked out.

THE CAROUSEL

THE MORNING BROKE BLEAK and drizzling, with flat light, the sky over Paris white as an unpainted canvas; a morning mist hung above the Seine as barges slid lazily along the river.

Maurice stood at the window, scratching at his crotch, a cup of coffee in his free hand, an unfiltered Gitanes dangling from his lips. Antoinette stirred on the sofa where she had fallen asleep after their perfunctory lovemaking.

He searched the horizon for a break in the clouds, knowing that, if it remained gray and dismal, he would not paint. Across the courtyard, rainwater was cascading down the green rooftops, and laundry hung drenched and heavy on clotheslines.

Maurice's tiny garret consisted of a paint-splattered floor, its original color no longer discernible, two straight-back wooden chairs, the sofa on which his raven-haired model "Toinette" lay, and a cot wide enough only for one, unless, of course, you slept one on top the other, which was often the case with Maurice.

From his studio you could see across the Boulevard St. Germain to the Notre Dame. In winter the room was frigid, a hothouse in summer, which is why he preferred spring and fall, except when it rained and the sun was hidden and he couldn't work.

The smell of freshly baked croissants and brioche wafted up from the *boulangerie* five stories below, and it made Maurice's stomach growl. Perhaps he could convince Gaston, the proprietor, to give him a few on credit. But then, he already owed the rotund man at least three hundred francs, and the wine merchant Dubois an equal amount. Sadly, Dadou, the café owner, had refused to carry him any longer, and Maurice's finances were beginning to look bleaker than the sky.

He sighed loudly in despair, and Antoinette opened her eyes. She purred like a kitten and looked as soft and buttery as one of the flaky breakfast treats he was craving.

Stepping away from the window, he shuffled to the sofa. "*Bonjour*, Toinette," he said tenderly. "Did you sleep well?"

She sat up, rubbed her eyes, and glanced around the studio and up at Maurice. Rising from the divan, she ran a hand through the tangled mass of curly hair hiding half of her face.

"*Café?*" she mumbled.

"*Oui*, but not much I am afraid."

It was not starting out well. The painting he had begun the day before looked rushed, as in fact it had been. Moving as if in a trance, he went to pour her a half-cup of coffee, all that was left in the press.

"I'm afraid this is all there is—and it's not even hot."

She made a face and reached out to take the coffee from his hand. "*C'est bon,*" she whispered in conciliation. "I have had worse."

He sat next to her without saying a word, shoulders

drooped, head bent in dejection. "I am afraid I am finished, Toinette. I have no money, I have no new ideas. . . I am done for. I have not sold a painting in over a year."

"What will you do, my sweet?" she replied. "You are an *artiste*—you must paint. It is your. . .your very being."

"Perhaps so, but if I cannot eat, I cannot paint, and if I cannot paint I cannot eat. Do you see?" He was speaking to her as though she was a child, and at nineteen she wasn't far from it.

She sighed and peered into the cup, brought the cold coffee to her lips, and drank it down. Cathedral bells began to chime and Toinette leapt from the sofa. "*Mon dieu,* I must go. I am modeling at *l'ecole* this morning. So sorry. Forgive me."

She dressed quickly, kissed him on the cheek, and slipped out the door. He could hear her stomping down the stairwell and watched from the window as she scurried up the alleyway. For Maurice, it seemed as if everything was leaving him behind.

He walked to the easel, squinted at the unfinished painting of Antoinette, stepped back a few feet, reached for a brush, and pushed it listlessly into a dab of titanium white—but he found it had hardened overnight and was in need of linseed oil to restore its malleability. He shook his head and dropped the brush in a tin among the others. He stood motionless, transfixed by indecision whether to paint, go for a walk, beg for food, or throw himself into the Seine.

After a few more contemplative moments he dressed, threw a scarf around his neck, and trudged down the wrought-iron spiral stairwell to the street.

The Boulevard was alive with activity—shopkeepers sweeping the sidewalk, the *Rive Gauche* book sellers tidying their bins and setting out prints and postcards, children being shuttled off to school. Dadou, who was standing outside the Café Balzac, tying an apron around his waist, nodded curtly in Maurice's direction and stepped back into the bistro. Brushing past a recently occupied table, the artist caught a whiff of strong Moroccan coffee and the hint of a half-eaten *croque monsieur,* which he was tempted to pilfer as he swept by. Too embarrassed to do so, he turned in the direction of the Pont Notre-Dame, hoping his mood would change by the time he crossed the river to Ile de la Cité. He liked walking around the cathedral, in the shadows of the buttresses and gargoyles, taking pleasure in the towering serenity of Notre Dame. He rarely went inside, preferring to commune with God on his own terms without priestly guidance.

He sat forlornly on a bench overlooking the waterway, his stomach hollow and wanting, his hunger to eat now more prevalent than the hunger to paint.

Seeing a copy of *L'Espresse* in a wastebasket, he rose from the bench and deftly lifted it out, returned to his seat, and absently turned pages, glancing at headlines and photos until he came to the employment opportunities, pages of them. He hated the idea of getting a "real job," but was beginning to believe he had failed as a painter and had no other choice. Most of the offerings were for skilled office personnel or people experienced in fields he had no clue about. He exhaled, hoisted himself off the bench, and headed across the bridge in the direction of Montmartre and Le Sacré Coeur.

By the time he had ambled the three miles to the base of the church steps, the carousel had opened for business, and children were lined up. More than the childish chatter, he was struck by a hand-written sign attached to the ticket booth:

Recherché Operature. Somebody wanted to hire an operator. Being in the shadow of the famous basilica, a short distance from the Moulin Rouge and the street artists and peddlers soliciting tourists, he thought working at the carousel would be a an ironic job opportunity. To him the idea was preposterous, but he quickly reasoned that he'd only have to do it until he could pay his back rent, settle up with Dadou and Gaston, feed himself, buy supplies, and give Antoinette, who never asked him for the money, her back wages for modeling. How she survived as an artist's model was a mystery to him, but he loved having her around; she was good company and a willing lover.

He began circling, taking pleasure in the ornate decoration of the carousel building, the intricately carved horses and the elaborate cabriolet-style seats for two. Before inquiring about the job, he considered the boredom of literally going around in circles all day long. In the end, the idea of regular employment was anathema to him and he trudged instead into 18th Arrondisement, where he came across an artist he recognized from Dadou's. The man was sitting on a fold-up stool, completing a portrait of a tourist. Maurice watched from a few yards away until the session was over and the artist was paid.

"Ah, Claude," he cried out. "How goes it, my friend?"

The man, in his mid-fifties, looked up and squinted at Maurice for a few seconds before the moment of recognition. "Oh, my dear Maurice, what brings you to Monmartre? Are you peddling portraits, too?"

"No, no, I'm taking a break."

"Painting not going well?"

"No, no, I'm just. . .taking a break."

A knowing smile came to Claude's face, but he said, "That's good, I suppose."

"Yes, it is, Claude. But tell me, do you. . .do you make much money doing this portrait painting? I saw that he gave you three hundred francs!"

"Most of them don't understand the money system. And I don't tell them. Last week I made two *thousand* francs! Can you believe it? I never made that from my paintings."

Maurice was astonished.

"I see that you are surprised," said Claude, "but truly, it is like taking candy from a baby. I sit in the sun, wait for someone to approach me, and spend a few minutes scribbling...and *voila!* I have rent money, dinner *and* a bottle of beaujolais!"

Maurice gestured at the other artists. "Do you *all* make that kind of money?"

Claude shrugged.

Maurice weighed the prospects of operating a carousel versus making money as an artist, even if it wasn't the type of art he preferred. Claude, like the others, was making a living, and a nice one at that, so why couldn't he?

"My dear friend, how does one get in on this?"

"Just get here early in the morning and pick a spot. Some of us are here at five A.M.! The tourists start coming at nine, and we can work as long as we want, except when it rains. Those are my days off."

Claude stopped talking and busied himself counting his money while Maurice puzzled over the ease at which his contemporaries made ends meet.

"Tell me," he asked, "do you need a license or something to do this?"

Claude stopped counting, folded the money, and stuffed it into his pocket. "Yes, yes, but it is simple to get. Just pay the fee, and the city will issue one. You don't need anything more than your identification, not even a portfolio."

"...What's the fee?"

"Only five hundred *francs*. Can you imagine that? You can make that on your first day, *n'est-ce pas?*"

For Maurice it might as well have been a million. He pursed his lips, shook his head, and started to back away.

Claude looked up, shading his eyes from the recently returned sun. "You don't have the money, do you?"

Maurice didn't answer, just shrugged and gave a sheepish grin.

Claude nodded and started fussing over his materials.

After an awkward silence, Maurice gave him a half-hearted wave, said, "*Au revoir, mon ami. Merci*," and walked away.

Claude called after him, "*Bon chance, Maurice!*"

Maurice stuffed his hands in his pockets and headed back toward Sacre Coeur.

The following day he began his job at the carousel.

LIFE FORMS

D R. CARLTON NAGAS tossed a pencil on his desk and sat back in the chair. He clasped his hands behind his head and thought about the reporter's question, knowing it wasn't easy to respond in terms the public would comprehend.

While he considered his words, the journalist, Nick Alset, looked around the room at the stacked books, the piles of papers and folders, the blackboard with cryptic symbols scrawled across its surface. The room was the quintessential college professor's office.

Nagas was a professor emeritus at Peabody Institute, a former department chair at the University of Intergalactic Studies, and winner of two Nexus prizes in Astrophysics. His theories on extra-terrestrial intelligence had opened the door to major government funding and led to many discoveries in the search for other life forms.

His work had been instrumental in identifying the more than two thousand planets and moons capable of sustaining life as we know it. The frustrating part was that no contact had ever been made, which had ultimately prompted Alset's question.

The reporter returned his attention to the professor and started to pose the query again, "Let me rephrase the question."

"Oh, there's no need. I understood," replied Nagas. "It's just that my answer is complex, and I was trying to simplify it."

"I appreciate that, Dr. Nagas, but our audience is rather sophisticated, so there's no need to—"

The scientist raised his hand in protest. "Believe me, I know your audience. I've spoken at your conferences on many occasions. Your question asked why, if there is intelligent life out there, we haven't been contacted by *them*."

Having been invited to the interview by Nagas with the promise of a monumental announcement, Alset nodded in anticipation, hoping for a journalistic coup.

"Well, for one thing," offered Nagas, "how do you know for sure that we *haven't* been?" Alset rubbed his hands together in excitement and sucked air in through his teeth, making a hissing sound. Although they were the only two in the room, Nagas whispered, "This is off the record."

Alset leaned in to turn off his recorder, "Sure. Okay. What can you tell me?"

Carlton scratched his head, rested his elbows on the desk, and clasped his hands.

"We have been sending radio signals into the universe for almost two hundred years. We've been sending space probes into the cosmos for half that long. In all that time, micro-organisms have been discovered on asteroids, planets, and moons. We've even found ice or liquid water on some. We've recorded volcanic activity, livable atmospheres, and possible vegetation, but never other life forms as we know them." He took a breath and added, "At least that's the public's perception."

Alset raised his eyebrows. "Wait—are you saying there *is* life out there? That we know of for sure?"

"That is precisely what I am saying."

"Uh—do you care to elaborate?"

"I am not at liberty to say more."

"That's not fair. You tell me *this*, and you won't let me *write* about it?"

Nagas had a concerned look on his face. "It's more than I'm allowed to say."

"Allowed? By whom?"

"By GovCom."

Alset shook his head. "You're telling me we've known about life on other planets, and that we've been aware of it for—how long. . .years?"

"I don't recall saying that exactly, but yes. Unfortunately, Government Communications has forbidden public disclosure."

"So why are you even telling me this?"

"A good question," responded Nagas, a slight smile forming in the corner of his mouth. "Let's just say I don't agree with the government. We've spent an awful lot of money and time to get this far. A lot of good people devoted their lives to the pursuit and never got credit or were given their due. They died in obscurity, unheralded for all their work and discoveries."

Alset leaned forward in his chair and reached for his recorder, but Nagas placed his hand on top of the device and shook his head. "No, this goes unrecorded. The story cannot be attributed to me. I will disavow any knowledge of our meeting."

Alset sat back in exasperation. "Whew! Why me? Why now?"

"Listen to me carefully, and don't write anything down," cautioned the professor. He swiveled his chair around to face the window and remained silent for a long while before turning back to look at the reporter.

"What I am about to tell you has been documented, and a copy has been sent to this address." He reached across the desk and handed a slip of paper to the reporter. "You can retrieve it fourteen days from now. Do you understand?"

Alset glanced at the paper. The address was unfamiliar. "How do I get it? The file?"

Nagas handed him an envelope. "Inside you will find an identification code. Memorize it and burn it. You will be asked for the code at the address I have given you. The file will be released to you at that time. You can then determine if, how, and when, to publicize it."

Alset stifled a laugh. "All very mysterious, don't you think?"

"With good reason, young man. My life isn't worth much after word gets out about this. And it *will* be traced back to me."

"And me? What about *my* life?" asked Alset. "Won't they come after me, too?"

"Probably."

". . .Are you kidding me?"

Professor Nagas was suddenly dour. "It is no joking matter. The decision to publish will be yours. After today, you will no longer have access to me or my files."

Alset, caught off guard by the change in tone, finally realized that Nagas was using him to get his message out.

The professor peered over the top of his glasses and added, "Don't think you're the only reporter I've spoken to. In fact, there are four others, and each has a different address to go to. So you'll have to race to get the story in print."

"So what exactly is the story, Professor? You haven't told me anything newsworthy."

"I have gone into great detail in the recorded file. But you are right, I should share some of it with you." He paused, took a deep breath, and then very deliberately said, "Government has been very diligent about keeping our encounters top secret. They fear large-scale panic if the information were to get out, so it had to be handled accordingly."

Alset sniggered, "Why would it cause panic? Are we going to be invaded by aliens?"

Nagas remained grim and narrowed his eyes. "Look, I don't have a lot of time here, so let me just brief you and end the interview."

Alset sat back in his chair without another word.

The professor continued, "Initial space exploration within our star system yielded no proof there is or ever was life, intelligent or otherwise, other than our own. Probes were sent out years ago, and in most cases have billions of miles to go before completing their fly-by missions. There have been radio signals and gamma ray bursts, even laser detection from distant galaxies, that show promise, but nothing conclusive. Until, that is, the Intergalactic Optical Search Institute detected an object outside our galaxy. That was almost twenty-five years ago. Two years ago we were able to snare the object and bring it back for study. It turned out to be a rudimentary craft that contained a message from an alien world."

He stopped to peer at the reporter to make sure his re-marks were being followed. Alset's mouth was ajar.

Nagas reached for a folder on his desk, opened it, and went on, "The object included numerous oddities and a message that took us almost the entire two-year period to decrypt. Here is what it said:

> *This is a present from a small distant world, a token of our sounds, our science, our images, our music, our thoughts, and our feelings. We are attempt-ing to survive our time, so we may live into yours. We hope, someday, having solved the problems we face, to join a community of galactic civilizations. This record represents our hope and our determination and our goodwill in a vast and awesome universe.*

Alset sat in awe, wide-eyed, until he finally asked, "Is this for real? Where did it come from?"

"Yes, it is real and I can only answer where it came from by telling you we are still exploring the origin of the craft they call *Voyager*. It originated in a place they designated as Earth, third planet from their sun, in a galaxy called Milky Way."

MATEO, ENRIQUE, AND CARLOS

OFTEN ENOUGH, A FRUSTRATED and angry Soledad Ortiz grabbed her son Mateo's ear and led him to confessional in St. Ignatius Catholic Church. One day, before sequestering him in the tiny booth, they came face-to-face with Father Alvaro on the entrance steps. She released her grip on the slight boy. *"Padre!"* she beseeched the young priest, "please *do* something! God forgive me, I cannot control him. He lies all the time."

The cleric, still in his robes from morning mass, nodded almost imperceptibly, placed his hand on the boy's shoulder and smiled gently. "So, Mateo, how can I help?"

Nine-year-old Mateo was rubbing his ear and not looking at his mother or the priest.

"What do you say to Father Alvaro?" asked his mother. It was more a demand than a question. The boy shrugged, and Soledad sighed and glanced at the priest, her eyes moist.

He bent just enough to look into the boy's eyes. "Come with me, son. We'll talk inside. Will that be all right?"

In response, Mateo gave an exasperated sigh and took a step forward, twisting his shoulder from under the priest's hand.

"Mrs. Ortiz, you can wait in the parish house if you'd like. We shouldn't be too long." Father Alvaro motioned to the boy to follow him, and they disappeared into the low, unassuming stucco building adjacent to the church.

Once inside, Father Alvaro sat in a straight back chair, clasped his hands as if in prayer, and faced the youngster. "Sit down, Mateo. You are safe here. I will listen and help you if I can. So tell me, what's happened *this* time?"

It took a while for the boy to relax, his hand instinctively rubbing his ear, which was red but otherwise unharmed. He finally exhaled in relief and mumbled, "Something got stolen."

". . .What was it?"

Mateo didn't look at the priest but stared instead at a picture of St. Ignatius hanging on the wall above the priest's desk. "Cigarettes," he muttered under his breath.

"Cigarettes?" repeated the priest. "I see. Did you take them? You don't smoke, do you?"

The boy shrugged in response but didn't reply. Alvaro studied the young face for a sign of remorse but saw only anxiety.

"You can tell me, Mateo. I won't judge you—that is for the Lord to do."

Mateo looked up at the priest and seemed about to speak, but held back, then shifted his feet and shook his head. Father Alvaro sat there calmly, waiting for him to offer an explanation, but none came.

The church bell, salvaged from a 17th-century mission, broke the silence with a loud, deep clang, making conversation almost impossible. Startled by the noise and the vibration in the building, the boy tried to answer the question, but his voice was lost in the clamor.

Never taking his eyes off the boy, the priest waited for the ten peals to finish and then said, "The bells always catch me by surprise. I hope they didn't scare you."

Mateo fidgeted in his seat, shook his head, but then said, "A little."

Alvaro gave a knowing smile. "Yes, they do that to me sometimes, too." He straightened in the chair and made a motion to get up.

Mateo, thinking the priest was going to leave, blurted out, "Carlos took them."

"Carlos? Who is Carlos?"

"A boy."

". . .I see. Then why are *you* in trouble?"

Mateo grimaced and looked away. The priest considered this reluctance and intuitively asked him, "Mateo, is he the same boy who broke the window at school last month?"

"Yes."

"And when money was taken from the cafeteria, was that Carlos, too?"

"No. That was Enrique."

"I see. Tell me, Mateo, why do they do these things? And why does your mother blame you?"

With eyes still downcast, Mateo's lower lip began to tremble, and a tear rolled down his cheek.

Father Alvaro pulled his chair closer.   "Are these boys pushing you around?"

The boy shook his head.

"Do they hurt you, Mateo?"

He replied in a tiny voice, as if he hadn't heard the question, "I'm a *gusanillo*."

"...A little worm?"

"Yes."

"Why do you think that?"

The boy suddenly pulled back, afraid to say more.

"Talk to me, son. Is that what they call you?"

Mateo avoided answering the question and instead muttered, in a low, guttural voice, "Soledad is a—"

"Soledad? Your mother?"

"She's a whore."

"...That's a terrible thing to say. Where do you get that from?"

Mateo had a faraway, unfocused look, as if he was in a trance. He didn't respond to the priest, who was puzzled by the sudden transformation. He watched, alarmed, waiting for the youngster to speak. Minutes went by before Mateo glanced up and asked, "Why am I here?"

"You are here because your mother asked me to help you. Don't you remember?"

"No."

Father Alvaro rose from the chair and reached out to place a hand on the boy's shoulder, but Mateo pulled back and stood up. "I want to go now."

The priest nodded, not wanting the boy to feel imprisoned. "Of course, my son, but you can come to talk any time. Will you do that?"

Mateo began rubbing his ear and turned to leave, saying nothing in response.

"Okay, let's go get your mother. She's waiting for you."

At the parish house Father Alvaro asked Mateo to wait while he spoke to Soledad and motioned to her to follow him into the vestibule.

"Mrs. Ortiz, your son seems troubled in ways in which I may not be able to help. Can you come talk to me in the next day or two? Would that be possible?"

Still distraught, she could only manage to whisper, "Yes."

Soledad Ortiz worked in the Dollar Store as a checkout clerk, a job she had taken two years earlier when Mateo's father, her live-in boyfriend, left in a drunken rage and never returned. In all that time she had never been able to truthfully explain to Mateo why his father left or why she always seemed to be nursing bruises from "falling at work," as she put it.

A few days after the priest asked her to meet she went to St. Ignatius and sat with him in the tiny courtyard adjacent to the church.

"Thank you for coming, Mrs. Ortiz. I know how difficult this must be for you."

"Father, I am afraid for my son. He tells lies, and he's getting into so much trouble. He won't talk to me about anything, and he doesn't seem to have any friends."

"Mrs. Ortiz, I—"

Soledad held up her hand.

"Forgive me, Father. I have not been truthful with you. I was never married to Mateo's father, so calling me *Mrs.* Ortiz is not proper."

The priest considered her comment for a moment. "That is a matter for another time. For now, it is between you and God. We are here to talk about your son."

She crossed herself, held back tears, and thanked him for his kindness.

"As for Mateo," the priest continued, "he seems quite distressed, but I'm not sure I understand. You say he doesn't have any friends. Who are Enrique and Carlos?"

On hearing the question, the blood seemed to drain from her face, her hand rising to her mouth in shock.

". . .He told you about them?"

"Yes, he did. Who are they? How does he know them?"

"*Ai, dios mio*," she exclaimed. "I have no idea who they are. He blames all his bad things on them. And none of his teachers know who those boys are."

Surprised by her answer, the priest studied her for a few seconds. "How long has he been saying things like that?"

"Since he was six years old. He spent a lot of time by himself, even hiding, mostly from his father. He started getting into fights at school."

"And the lying?" asked the priest. "When did he start doing that?"

"Things would happen at school or around the house that I know were caused by him. He wouldn't take responsibility for any of it, telling me he didn't do them."

"And when did he start blaming Enrique and Carlos?"

"A few months ago, and then the other day, when I found the cigarettes in his drawer, he told me he didn't know how they got there. I got so mad, I didn't know what to do. . .and, God forgive me, I smacked him."

The priest sighed heavily but didn't admonish her. "Please go on."

"When he took the money from the cafeteria, he said he didn't do it. Then he said he didn't remember. Father, I think he believes what he is telling me, and that frightens me even more."

The young priest pondered for a moment and then stood up. "Mrs.—*Miss* Ortiz. . .will you let me talk to a friend of mine about Mateo? He is a child psychiatrist at the university hospital. I think he can help."

"Do you think my son is crazy?"

"No, no, not at all. I don't think he's crazy, but I think he may need help neither you nor I can give him."

"Then, yes. Please, I want so much to help my son."

"Good, good. I will talk to Dr. Scanlon. In the mean time, say a prayer for your son."

"I pray for him every day, Father. Every day, for the past three years."

"Then trust in the Lord that all will be well."

ALMOST TWO WEEKS PASSED before Soledad and a reluctant Mateo had their first appointment with Dr. Scanlon. He had offered to see them as a favor to Father Alvaro. The three of them talked in a tiny outer office until Scanlon asked Soledad to wait while he and Mateo went into another room.

For the next thirty minutes, Scanlon managed to get him talking. What he learned unnerved him, particularly because Mateo was so young.

On the third visit, Scanlon recognized symptoms that suggested Mateo was an unusual subject. The youngster came to the session angry and appeared somewhat detached. Ten minutes into their exchange, he stopped responding to questions and didn't look at the doctor. "Mateo? Mateo, do you hear me?"

There was no response. Scanlon stood in front of the boy and in a low voice, so as not to startle him, repeated, "Mateo?"

The youngster suddenly jumped up and shoved the doctor so hard that the man fell backwards, and then growled at him in a raspy voice, "What do you think you're doing?"

Scanlon quietly asked, "Where's Mateo?"

"I don't know any Mateo,"

The psychologist instinctively understood. "Who are you?"

"I'm Enrique! Who the fuck're you?"

"Dr. Scanlon, a friend."

"How did I get here?"

"You came with your mother," he offered.

He stared at the psychologist with no hint he knew what the man was talking about.

Scanlon watched him carefully, looking for a sign, some indication that Mateo was present. What he saw was unsettling. The boy's posture and facial expressions had changed. He stood with fists clenched, jaw jutting out, eyes narrowed, as if ready to do battle.

"Enrique, would you like to tell me why you are angry?"

"Get away from me!"

Scanlon waited for the anger to subside until it was safe to end the session. When they rejoined Soledad, the boy Mateo had re-emerged. Scanlon whispered to his mother that he needed to talk to her in private and that she should call him as soon as possible.

A distraught Soledad slept fitfully that night and waited nervously the following day until her break time at work to make the call.

Fortunately, Scanlon was able to take the call. "It's still too early to be certain, but I believe I understand your son's condition. I need to ask you some difficult questions, perhaps very personal, but it will help your son. Will that be all right?"

She hesitated briefly. "...Y-yes. Okay."

"Is it at all possible that your son has ever been subjected to some abuse. . .something traumatic, perhaps physically or emotionally?" She didn't answer. He could hear her weeping. "Mrs. Ortiz? . . . I'm sorry. I know this must be painful for you, but it will help me diagnose your son."

"Do you mean," she haltingly asked, "was he *molested* or—"

"Yes, that is what I mean. And if that's the case, do you know what happened and when?"

Her voice began to tremble, but between sobs she shared secrets she kept to herself for the past three years.

"His. . .his father was. . .dangerous—"

"What do you mean, 'dangerous'? Like violent?"

"Yes," she said, her voice stronger, more determined. "When he was drunk, I was afraid of him. After Mateo was born, Ray hit me all the time, and before my son could even walk, Ray started hitting him, too."

"I see. And was this ever reported to the police?"

She was silent for a long stretch before meekly replying, "No."

The psychologist understood this, so he didn't pursue it. He wasn't the police; he was trying to help a troubled child.

"Do you have any idea what—" he paused briefly— "what Ray did to him?"

"Yes."

Scanlon exhaled audibly and took a moment to gather his thoughts, almost afraid to ask his next question.

"I know this is not easy, but can you elaborate, please?"

"Sometimes I would find Mateo hiding under his bed or in the closet. I would see bruises and even blood on him."

"Where?" he inquired.

"Where what?" she asked.

"Where was the blood, the bruising? What part of his body?"

Soledad started sobbing uncontrollably, and Scanlon waited until he heard her take a very deep breath before asking, "Do you have contact with your ex? Do you know where he is?"

"I haven't heard from him since he took off. I have no idea where he is." She added, "I hope he's dead."

"Tell me more about Mateo's bruises."

"I'd find them everywhere. Sometimes he was bleeding from his mouth, sometimes his nose; even from his. . .his behind."

Scanlon inhaled deeply. "Do you mean his rectum?"

"Yes." Her voice quavered. "But by the time he was eight, he began wearing only long-sleeved shirts and wouldn't let me in when he was taking a bath. He always kept himself covered and would disappear for hours at a time. When his father came into the house, Mateo would stop talking. I was worried sick."

Scanlon glanced at his watch. "Mrs. Ortiz, I'm sorry, but I have another patient. But let me consider all of this and talk to a colleague. I will not mention your name or Mateo's. I will contact you in the next day or two. But do not hesitate to call me if there is a major change of any kind."

"Thank you, doctor," was all she could muster.

LATER, WHILE SHE WAS MAKING SOMETHING for the two of them to eat, she heard Mateo talking in his room, except it didn't quite sound like him. At first she thought it was the radio or someone outside the window. She pressed her ear to the door and became alarmed because the person speaking didn't at all sound like her son; he sounded much older.

"Listen to me, *gusanillo*," commanded the voice. "Your mother's a whore. She won't help you. And *don't* listen to Enrique."

Soledad, her heart racing, not sure what to do, pounded on the door. "Mateo, Mateo. . .open the door! Open it now!" she shouted.

Silence followed for a long while and she knocked again, this time more softly.

After another minute the door opened a few inches. She pushed it gently and saw her son sitting on the bed, his mood almost buoyant.

"Hi, Mom. Is it time to eat?"

MEMORIES

THE MOURNERS, A FEW DOZEN of them, could see snow starting to fall just beyond the chapel's large, high window, a backdrop that only added to the sadness of Lucille's passing.

Delores McCann dabbed at her eyes with one of the lace handkerchiefs given to her by Lu for her eighty-second birthday, only a few months before. She remembered her friend's words as she looked at the hand-made square, "I bought these just for you at a little shop in Galway when Sean and I went to Ireland in—" she had hesitated, searching for the year, then smiled weakly and handed over the box.

Delores and Lucille had remained friends from the moment in 1943 when they met at Fort Des Moines as newly enrolled WACs. Between them, over the decades, they'd had a total of three marriages, four children, and nine grandchildren. Their symbiotic connection was beyond measure; in the sixty years since World War II, not a cross word between them was ever spoken. They buried husbands, children, and pets, and though they lived miles apart, each journeyed to the other's side during the tragically difficult times as well as for the happy moments.

Now, Delores grieved alone, sitting in the pew facing that big window, finding it difficult to focus on the wooden box in front of the pulpit. She sat, tears staining her face, the hands in her lap wanting more than anything to grip Lucille's fingers, needing her comforting closeness, the knowing nod, the calm demeanor that dear, dear Lucy brought to such circumstances.

The idea that she would not, could not, sit next to her oldest and dearest friend ever again left her with an unfathomable despondency. Lucille's immediate family occupied the front pew and had asked Delores to join them. The kids all knew her as Aunt Delores, as was Lucille known in the McCann family. They'd all heard the story of the two women and at group gatherings reveled in their wartime adventures.

One Thanksgiving at the McCanns', Lucille started to chuckle. "This one time—I don't think you've heard this one yet. We were on board a troop ship. Thirty-three WACs and two thousand soldiers and sailors steaming across the Pacific."

"Lu!" screeched Delores. "You're not going to tell that story about me and the petty officer, are you?"

"Well, it *is* kinda funny."

"Yes, yes, tell it again," shouted one of the older children.

Delores sighed loudly, exasperated, but smiling nonetheless.

Lu started again. "Well, we'd been at sea for about three days. I was up on deck alone, looking out over a calm sea and a big yellow moon illuminating the night. I saw two figures making out under a lifeboat and watched for awhile to see who it was. I didn't know the guy, of course, but the girl turned out to be our very own sweet, innocent Delores."

The table full of people sat rapt waiting for more.

Lucille put a finger to her lips. "On second thought, maybe

I better not."

A dissatisfied *Aww* arose as if in one voice.

IT WAS A SMALL, DIGNIFIED BURIAL, but Delores, not emotionally or physically up to attending, asked her son Brendan to drive her home.

He took the less trafficked but slower route to the assisted living facility where his mother had been the past two years and walked her inside to her bedroom apartment.

"Mum, you going to be alright? Do you want me to stay?"

"Oh, no, dear, that's alright. You should go. Martha and the boys will be waiting."

"You sure? I mean, it's okay, I can stay a while. We could have dinner together. Would you like that?"

Ever the stoic, she touched his arm, smiled gently, and gingerly sat on the sofa. "Not today, sweetheart. I'm...very tired. You know, this is—this was—" She stifled a sob and took a breath. "I'll be fine, really. Thank you, dear."

Brendan stood motionless, looking down at the still- beautiful woman who brought him into the world, and wondered just how much longer she would actually be "fine."

He gave her hand a squeeze and kissed her forehead, held her gaze for a moment, and said, "Call me if you need me for anything. Promise?"

"I will."

Delores dozed off five minutes after he left and slept in a seated position on the sofa for almost half an hour. The slumber was a welcome escape from the day's ordeal, but memories began flooding back soon as she woke.

Although it was only 4:30 in the afternoon, she changed into her night clothes, put on a robe, and made a cup of tea.

While the water brewed, she retrieved a scrapbook from the closet and placed it lovingly on the kitchen table. Once tea was poured, she opened the album.

On the first page was a faded photo, the corners tucked neatly into four triangular black paper brackets glued to the page to hold the pictures in place. Two young women in WAC uniforms, their arms around each other, smiled back at her from the sepia-toned image. Under the snapshot, written in parochial school penmanship, was a caption that read *Lu and Del, Ft. Des Moines, April 1943.*

Delores smiled at the patriotic young girls, ran her fingers lightly over the image, and sighed. She took a sip of tea, went to the cupboard, took down a box of Lorna Doones, and returned to the table.

Page after page of photos of the twenty-two-year-old women followed, one with soldiers at a USO canteen in San Diego before they all shipped out. That ocean voyage, the one on which she made out with the petty officer, landed Delores and Lucille in New Caledonia at the beginning of 1944, making them among the first WACs to arrive in the Pacific. From there they went to Sydney, Australia, before the war finally ended and they were discharged.

For a while they shared an apartment in San Diego, found jobs, met future husbands, and moved away. They stayed in touch by mail, an occasional long-distance phone call at holiday time and birthdays, and visited each other when most appropriate or a special need arose.

The album photographs chronicled the sixty-year friendship and highlighted weddings, birthdays, christenings, and the myriad other milestones that mark a person's life.

As she turned each soft, yellowing page, Delores stopped

to touch the picture, laugh out loud, sob at a particular remembrance and sigh at another, while tears ran slowly down her cheeks.

She'd put the album together for her and Lucille as she did other scrapbooks for the family narrative, but this one was a special reflection of more than a close friendship—it was a visual record of two transcendently kindred spirits.

Just after her husband was killed in Korea, Lucille, pregnant with their first child, had come to visit Delores and her young family in Indiana. At that time, the album only contained pictures from their WAC service, and the two friends reminisced over them with fondness and shared laughter.

Delores closed her eyes and recalled those two weeks when Lucille was so crushed and afraid. She took a modicum of comfort knowing she was there for Lu and probably saved her from a total collapse.

Page after page, photo after photo, were added over the years, and, ironically, the last photo in the book, from eleven years ago, was of Lucille waving good-bye as she boarded a flight back home after a Christmas visit.

DELORES SAT QUIETLY WHILE THE TEA got cold and her eyes grew tired. She worked her way to the bedroom, pulled the cover down, and got in. She dreamt of Lu, as might be expected, and woke in the dark feeling as though an anvil were lying on her chest. The tingling in her fingers and numbness in her arm frightened her, but she was too weak to get to the telephone. She lay there trying to regulate her breathing and stay calm, hoping the sensation would go away or at least subside. In time she was able to sit up, regain her composure, and swallow two aspirins before falling back asleep.

The following morning the pain had disappeared, but Delores instinctively knew it had been a warning.

Fretting over calling him, she finally dialed Brendan at work. "Bren, I'm sorry to bother you, but I had another incident."

"When? What happened, Mom?" He said it lovingly, but he was anxious.

It took some convincing, but she agreed to see the doctor, who, after an EKG and examination, diagnosed it as a myocardial infarction and wanted her in the hospital right then and there.

After Brendan admitted her and had a consult with the doctor, he went to her apartment and brought some of her things back to the hospital, among them a framed photograph.

Frailer than he'd ever seen her, with a weakening pulse, she faded in and out of sleep for the next few days, spoke little, and ate even less.

Allowed only short visits, just one or two family members at a time stood by her bedside, telling her how much they loved her and asking her to get better. None left the room without tears in their eyes.

The first Saturday of her stay, Brendan got to the hospital early and sat at her bedside, reading to her from *The Greatest Generation*, with its tales of World War II veterans and their remembrances. She looked at him from time to time, nodding that she understood and remembered those days of long ago when she was young.

He put the book down, lightly stroked her hand, brushed the wisps of thin gray hair from her forehead, and leaned in to give her a kiss.

"Mom, I have to go," he said reluctantly, uncertain when

he would see her again. He saw that she was drifting off, not to sleep, but to a reverie of sorts.

"Memories," she finally muttered under her breath.

"What? What'd you say, Mom?"

"Memories," she repeated almost inaudibly.

That was all she said. He waited for more, but she closed her eyes and after a minute was asleep.

On the drive home Brendan thought about the one-word remark. Was that it, he wondered? Was life, in the end, only memories?

Delores McCann died in her sleep a week later. On the nightstand next to her bed was a framed photo of her family at her eighty-sixth birthday; she was sitting next to Lucille, holding her hand and a lace handkerchief.

MR. ABADDON

Ross Eriksson was teetering on the cusp of fame. He had been toiling for several years as a C-list actor and, according to his two former wives, would always be a "nobody," but that was about to change, or so he prayed. He had recently received high praise for a small yet key role in a much touted indie film. There was even Oscar buzz suggesting he was a front runner.

Soon after the nominations were announced, Ross began losing sleep, fantasizing at night about his acceptance speech, thumbing his nose at ex-wives and do-nothing agents.

The night before his inaugural walk on the red carpet, he lay awake practicing aloud, all the while believing he would not, could not, win. The air in his tiny apartment above the dry cleaner was stuffy; a helicopter chattered overhead, and car alarms punctuated the darkness. Around two in the morning, he finally fell into a deep, almost comatose state.

The voice began low and raspy, otherworldly, and it addressed him by name: "Ross? Ross, it's me, Abaddon. Wake up!"

"Who are you?" he groaned as he came awake. "W-what

do you want?"

A cloaked figure suddenly emerged from a thick, acrid cloud and came so close to Ross's face that the actor recoiled in terror. *"Whoa!"*

"Don't be alarmed," whispered the creature. "I'm not here to hurt you. I'm here to help."

"Help *me?*"

The figure curled into itself like water disappearing down a drain.

Ross bolted out of bed to search for the specter under the bed, behind the window curtain, in the closet, but found no trace.

He slumped on the edge of the bed and squeezed his eyes shut, trying to conjure the image of what he thought was more than a dream.

He knew it hadn't been caused by food or some other substance since he hadn't eaten too late or consumed any drugs and had had only one drink. Confused, he shrugged, drank a glass of water, and got back under the covers. He fell asleep almost instantly and, within minutes, plummeted into a stupor. An hour passed without so much as a twitch until what sounded like an atomic clap of thunder startled him awake.

Angry that his sleep had been interrupted yet again, he kicked the covers off, swung his feet over the side of the bed, and buried his head in his hands. "Damn it, I have to get some *sleep,*" he growled, and shambled off to the medicine cabinet to find a bottle of Valerian. Before taking one, he glanced at the mirror above the sink and screamed at what he saw standing behind him.

"I must *talk* to you," it hissed.

Ross gripped the counter tightly so as not to fall backward

or touch the thing. As he did, it grew larger until its head and shoulders were touching the ceiling, and then it slithered down the wall and onto the countertop, stopping just inches from Ross's finger tips. His heart pounded fiercely and he could barely breathe.

Trapped, engulfed, unable to move in either direction without touching the thing, he remained motionless.

"I am not here to harm you, Ross. I am not going to hurt you. I am here to help you," it repeated.

Ross raised his hands in surrender and began to tremble. His words popped out in a staccato rhythm. "W-what? Help me how? What are you? This is a-a dream, right?"

It began to glow, an eerie muddy green color at first that soon turned a putrid brown. The cloak it wore was slimy and appeared to ooze a thick gel that collected in a pool where its webbed feet and barbed tail hovered inches above the tile floor.

"Ross, do you know why I am here?"

"No! I have no *fucking idea*. What are you? Where did you come from? What's—"

In the blink of an eye, the thing grew voluminous, filling the entire room, and Ross, caught inside it, was rapidly swept to another place. He could feel the motion, swift, silent, forceful, and, sensing he was going to die if he wasn't already dead, he submitted.

Just as suddenly, all fell calm, and he found himself sitting in a large, brightly lit, contemporary office over-looking the Pacific Ocean. Opposite him, seated at a large oval desk, was Abaddon. Only now he had a human body and a handsome face, and he was dressed in an Armani suit, his hair jet-black and freshly cut, nails impeccably manicured.

"So, Ross," he started, "I'm here to help you. Do you want

that Oscar tonight?"

Ross, dazed, decided to play his part to find out what was going on or, better yet, just wake up.

"What can you do to help me?" he asked as calmly as he could.

Abaddon leaned forward in a conciliatory manner, clasped hands on the table, and said in just above a whisper, "Allow me first to inquire into your sincerity."

Ross nodded.

Abaddon smiled, and his eyes, almost aqua-colored, widened as he stared directly at Ross. "Mr. Eriksson, just how much do you *want* an Academy Award?"

"More than *anything!*"

"What exactly does that mean, Mr. Eriksson?"

"You mean the award, or what I'd do to get one?"

"Those are both very good questions."

Ross glanced out the window at the sun sparkling off the rolling surf and thought about how to respond without being melodramatic, but his excitement got the better of him. "I'd sell my soul for one."

Abaddon moved closer and searched his face for an indication of seriousness. A tiny smile curled the corner of his mouth before he continued tugging at his ear lobe, "I see. That's quite a statement you just made, but I'll take you at your word."

Abaddon rose and turned to the window; he seemed to become taller as the sunlight formed a glow around his shoulders.

"Suppose," he asked, "I could guarantee it would happen. Tonight! At the awards ceremony. What would you say?"

"How? How can you *guarantee* that?"

Abaddon sat down again. "Let's say I'm a very powerful figure in this town. I own a lot of people. And a lot of them owe me. . .big time!"

"So what're you, an agent? How come I never heard of you?"

"I'm known by a lot of names, but that's not important."

"I see," Ross said sarcastically. "So tell me, what *can* you do for me and how *do* you plan to do it?"

"I happen to know you did *not* win an Oscar tonight, but I can change that."

"Oh?"

"Leave it to me."

Ross covered his mouth in contemplation, and Abaddon, allowing him time to think, swiveled around in the chair to face the window and began to hum a metronomic beat.

Ross remained silent.

Abaddon addressed him without turning around, but loudly enough to be sure he was heard: "Tell me, Mr. Eriks-sion, what would you do were you to win an Oscar this evening? How would it change your life?"

Ross warmed to the subject a bit too enthusiastically. "First thing, I'd thank myself for all the hard work, I would diss my previous agents for doing nothing to move my career along, call out how unsupportive my two wives had been—"

"Oh, I'm quite sure you will make an outstanding *acceptance* speech, Mr. Eriksson, but I want to know what you would *do* with an Oscar. How would it change your life?"

Ross's response was a clear indication of just how much he had dreamed about it. "I'd be rich and famous, I'd make lots of movies, I'd be in demand. I wouldn't have to go on auditions, I wouldn't have to scrounge for tips at the dive restaurant I work in, I'd have dozens of women, fly my own Gulf-stream. . . ."

"And you shall, Mr. Ericksson, you shall indeed. Just tell me again what you are willing to do to *get* it."

"I'd sell my soul for it. I told you that. . .and I mean it."

"Are you willing to sign a contract with me, Ross?"

"You mean like you'd be my agent?"

"In a manner of speaking, Ross, yes."

"Tell you what. I get an Oscar tonight, and we'll talk."

Again a wry smile passed over Abaddon's lips, but this time it was accompanied by a low, raspy, laugh. Ross was too caught up in his musing to notice. "That is a risk you must be prepared to take, Mr. Ericksson. I will not provide an Academy Award without a contract, a binding agreement between you and me."

He opened the top drawer of the desk, produced a legal document, placed it in front of Ross, unscrewed the cap of a red fountain pen, and handed it to the actor.

"I give you my eternal word, Mr. Eriksson—no Oscar tonight, and you can tear up the contract. Do we have a deal?"

Ross sat upright and arched his back, glanced at the paperwork, did not read it, and signed where Abaddon pointed. The ink was as red as the case.

Abaddon rose even taller than he had appeared to be a few minutes before, tucked the agreement into his jacket pocket, and shook Ross's hand. We'll see each other in—um, later."

And Ross found himself back in his bed and, within seconds, sound asleep.

He woke in the afternoon feeling someone's presence.

"Good day, sir. I have been sent by Mr. Abaddon. He has provided a wardrobe for this evening, a limousine in which I will drive you to the ceremonies, and a young woman to accompany you."

Ross propped himself on one elbow and saw, draped over a mahogany clothes-horse, an Ermenegildo Zegna tuxedo and the accessories to accompany it.

By four in the afternoon, he had slid into the back of the Mercedes limo and been met by a blonde beauty dressed in a low-cut but tasteful Vera Wang white-on-white.

He fell into the role of an assured, sophisticated, toast-of-the-town movie star that he had always dreamed of being.

The line of cars leading to the Dolby Center stretched a mile back and crept along at a snail's pace as each car pulled up to the red carpet and dispatched its much-awaited cargo.

Far back in the cue, he looked at the row of buildings lining the street and at the signs, until the car momentarily stopped alongside a Greek Orthodox Church. He casually read the sign on the lawn:

TUESDAY LECTURE:

How Satan works to destroy societies and mankind: "They have as king over them, the angel of the abyss; His name is Abaddon." (Revelation 9:11)

RESTITUTION

B Y 12:40 A.M., THE ATN cable television newsroom had gone to sleep. The night shift had been perusing monitors for almost two hours, scrolling through the wire-service feeds, searching for newsworthy occurrences around the world. The room, tiny by major network standards, housed a bank of eight desks and computers, several digital clocks displaying international time zones, and six large television screens silently emitting images transmitted by other channels.

The low hum of hard drives, and an occasional cough, along with a few off-hand comments and low-key banter, were the only sounds in the room. On slow news nights, boredom often took over, and the younger staff would make crass jokes about what they were reading or throw an occasional wad of paper at someone.

Other than a coffee cup or other beverage container, desk tops were uncluttered because they were shared with the daytime crew. The lack of personal items created a sterile but professional ambiance.

Twenty-eight-year-old Connor Forsyth, an Ithaca College

Broadcast Journalism graduate, fidgeted with a pencil while he stared at the screen, scratching his nose with the eraser tip, grunting in response to the items scrolling before him.

"Hey, big art theft in London," he said to no one in particular.

Moments later, seated across from him, Molly Sharman, thirty and brilliant, admonished her co-worker, "No, Connor! It's in New York."

Annoyed, Conner shot back, "I can read, y' know. It says London!"

Within seconds, Peter Brodsky, thirty-two and a news anchor wannabe, shouted, "You're both wrong! It's in Buenos Aires."

Molly slid back in her chair, hands braced on the counter top. "What?" she cried. "Wait a minute. . .Connor, who's your source? What time was the London theft?"

"It's on Reuters. 0-four-thirty, GMT."

Molly turned excitedly to Peter. "What time does it say for Buenos Aires?

"O-one-thirty."

Molly peered at the time zone clocks above her head. "What the hell's going on? Those are the exact same times."

Peter abruptly stood up, almost upending his chair.

"Hold it! Here's another one, dateline Pretoria."

Molly shot a look at Connor and turned to face Peter, "Read it out loud!"

"*O-six-thirty: South African Police investigating a break-in at the Pretoria Gallery of Fine Art revealed that two Rembrandt etchings and a painting by Giotto had been—*" his head moved from side to side as he read from the monitor— "*removed from their frames sometime during the night and are presumed stolen. Agents—*"

Connor raised his hand to silence them. "Uh, I think we maybe. . .man, this is *weird!* Here's one from Vienna. It says four paintings were stolen from the Belvedere."

Molly hastily made hardcopies and yelled, "Bud, you better get out here!"

Robert "Bud" Kaminsky, nighttime newsroom editor, sauntered in from his office with a mug of coffee in his hand, blowing into the cup to cool the brew. "What is it? Korea? Iran? Afgh—"

Molly handed him print-outs. "Take a look at this. Five art heists in different countries at the same time!"

He stroked his chin. "Ideas, anyone?"

Peter jumped in. "It can't be a coincidence. I mean, five robberies in—"

Before anyone could say another word, Connor shouted, "Six! It's six! Another one, in Paris."

"Alright," said Bud, "this could be our morning lead. Stay on it. See if you can come up with some connection. Anything, I don't care how bizarre. There has to be a link."

Molly squinted at her iPhone, then back at the group.

Anybody know what happened today, November 9? I mean historically?"

Bud nodded. "Good thought. Do a search, see what you can come up with. The rest of you—"

Peter, barely able to contain himself, exclaimed, "Wait a minute! *Krystallnacht!* Today's the anniversary of *Krystallnacht*, the Night of Broken Glass."

"What the hell's that?" Connor asked.

Peter, gesturing with his hands, began to explain. "On November 9, 1938, the Nazis destroyed synagogues, Jewish-owned businesses, broke thousands of windows, burned stores, rounded up Jews. It was. . .the beginning of the Holocaust."

Bud calmly asked him, "Okay, let's assume you're right. What's that have to do with *this?*"

Peter, his confidence growing, slowed down just enough to say, "I know I'm right! I—"

Molly stared at him, trying to grasp his train of thought. "Peter, where's this coming from? What do you know about it?"

"I did my *dissertation* on it."

Connor asked, "What'd you major in, the Third Reich?"

Peter grew more serious. "Not really, Connor. I was a communications major and wrote about Joseph Goebbels, Hitler's minister of propaganda."

Bud focused his attention on the young researcher. "Peter, what are you thinking?"

"When the Nazis came to power," he started, "they began confiscating art belonging to Jewish collectors and sold it to finance the party's activities. Some of it was kept by high-ranking officials for their personal use—"

"So," Bud asked, "what are you saying? That these heists have something to do with the Nazis?"

"Well, in a way. . .yeah, but not really."

Molly made a face. "Meaning?"

An exasperated Peter began to raise his voice. "Meaning that, in some cases, Nazi sympathizers were allowed to buy the work at a pittance. Jewish-owned art galleries were—" he made air quotes with his fingers— "Aryanized and given to Nazi party members."

Molly and Connor stood transfixed.

"If they could," he continued, "some Jewish families sold

the art at a fraction of its value or bribed officials with it, just so they could finance their escape."

Bud, still not convinced there was a connection, asked, "And the art that was stolen tonight was taken by. . . ?"

Peter shrugged. "I don't know. But it might have some relevance."

Molly, struggling to make sense of it, sat down at her desk. "Who could orchestrate this? It'd take teams of highly trained accomplices to pull it off." She shook her head in disbelief. "And what would they do with the art once they had it?" Still skeptical, she added, "I mean, come on—it would be too hot to sell. Every intel agency on the planet is gonna be involved in this."

Bud, having heard, nodded in approval. "Okay, Molly, you and Connor see what you can pull up that might make sense of all this. Meet me at the conference desk in thirty minutes."

Connor asked, "What are we looking for, precisely?".

Bud glanced at the overhead television monitors to see if the networks were on the story yet. "See if you can find out what happened to the art taken by the Nazis," he suggested. "Where'd it wind up after the war? Is there a correlation with these six museums?"

He turned to Peter. "Brodsky, you keep following the story, and let me know if there are any more break-ins or new information."

They scurried to their workstations and, for the next half hour, clacked madly away on their keyboards. Not one of them raised a head until Bud interrupted. "Okay, people, let's go. Everyone, conference desk."

Chairs shot backward, and the three researchers pushed away from their computers, headed to a corner of the room, and took seats at the circular table.

"Okay," Bud wanted to know. "What've we got? Molly?"

She leaned forward in her chair, slid her glasses up the bridge of her nose, placed her elbows on the table, and began, "Sometime after World War II, lost or stolen art wound up in museums and in the hands of art dealers, all of it with no records showing how it was acquired, no provenance."

"Okay that's a start. Connor, what do you have?"

The young man cleared his throat. "In 1998, forty-four countries signed an agreement—" he paused, looking for the details— "Um, it's called, the Washington Principles on Nazi-Confiscated Art."

"And?" Bud murmured impatiently.

"Right, okay. Basically, museums around the world acknowledged that some work they had acquired between 1933 and 1945 had almost no provenance. The original ownership couldn't be traced or verified."

He put his notes down and looked at his co-workers with a pained expression. "Almost nothing's been done since to return the art to the rightful owners or their heirs, or even offer compensation."

EARLIER THAT EVENING, some six thousand miles east of the ATN newsroom, two men and a woman sat hunched over laptops in a dimly lit, windowless room. A shop-worn table and four chairs filled the space, with no other accoutrements but a large Mercator map and an Israeli flag.

With his face only inches from an Aspire S7 screen, its blue light casting an eerie pallor across his middle-eastern features, Davi Stein sat impatiently pumping his right leg and muttered, "Come on, come on. What's taking so long?" Then he abruptly leaned back and exclaimed, "Bingo! They're out. Paris is out. . .they have the art."

Middle-age and bearded Moishe Pederofsky, a pale blue *yarmulke* on his head, bolted upright and raised his arms in triumph.

"Okay, okay. Just got word from Vienna. We're good." He turned toward the woman, "Orit? Anything from South America? Africa?"

Israeli-born Orit Schiller, an olive-skinned, dark-haired beauty in her early forties, remained focused on her desktop, shaking her head in response.

"No. Nothing. I hope everything—wait, here it is. Pretoria is clear. They're out."

Moishe, not taking his eyes off the screen, grumbled to himself, "We should have heard from New York and London, Buenos Aires. . . ." He looked at his watch. "What's going on?"

Suddenly, he clapped his hands. "Hold it. I'm getting something," and then, with fists held triumphantly aloft, shouted, "Good, good. New York is out!"

Grim-faced, poised over the monitor, Orit murmured to no one in particular, "That leaves two."

An anxious Davi pleaded with the screen, "Come on. Come on."

Orit turned to look at him. "What's with you? I've never seen you so edgy. Calm down, it'll come. Take it easy."

"Yes," Davi said over his shoulder, "but this. . .all the planning, all the years. We must succeed. We have to."

Moishe glanced at him. "You always succeed, Davi. You did in Iraq, in Palestine. At least," he laughed, "no one is shooting at us now."

Davi waved the comment aside and haltingly replied, "Not the same thing. This is for *justice*. This is *our* retribution. This—"

Moishe put one finger up to stop him. "Hold on. Here's South America." Exhaling loudly, he made a fist and pounded the table once. "It's done. They have it."

Orit moved her face closer to the screen and, tears in her eyes, sobbed, "London is complete. That's all of them!"

Simultaneously, as if pre-arranged, they rose and high-fived each other.

Davi declared, "The museums were never going to relinquish that art. We're finished with their empty promises."

Orit, relieved, declared, "Finally! Now the art will be returned."

Davi slapped each of them on the shoulder. "All these years of stalling, their legal mumbo-jumbo about statutes of limitations. The museums just thumbed their noses at the families who lost everything. They'll never take responsibility for the art they acquired. They'd never provide restitution."

Orit dabbed at her eyes and quietly said, "If only. . .if only the victims had lived to see this."

Moishe nodded in agreement. "The hardest part is over. Now we have to get the art to the heirs. They've been waiting a long, long time."

They momentarily embraced and Davi looked toward the ceiling with moistened eyes and avowed, "Never again! Never again!"

RESURRECTION

I N April 2003, the Human Genome Project gave mankind the ability to read nature's complete genetic blueprint for building a human being.

Decades later, a secretly funded program in DNA reproduction would forever change the world. In simple terms, the experiments attempted to harvest DNA material from known, but long deceased, ancestors' garments and then match it with their living descendants.

As more sensitive and delicate extraction procedures were developed, fabric samples from ancient burial shrouds were selected for experimentation, resulting in startling finds.

The news first went public at a presentation to the International Genomic Sciences Symposium in Oslo. The two prominent NHGRI scientists who led the program and championed the results of the experiments lobbied for further exploration, only to be met by unbridled ridicule. Strong opposition from most of the world's religious groups voiced objections to "humans playing God," and eventually the experiments were halted. Or so it was thought.

The developers of the project, Doctor Abdul Chadhoury,

professor of genetics at the University of Karachi, and Isaiah Lazarus, professor emeritus of genetics and DNA studies at the University of Tehran, were cajoled into secretly continuing their work.

ON A TEPID SEPTEMBER EVENING, Chadhoury received a phone call at his home on the outskirts of Lahore.

"Yes?"

"How do you do, kind sir? I am contacting you in good faith and have a proposition for you that I believe will be to your complete satisfaction. May I continue?"

Thinking it was a hoax, Abdul was immediately skeptical, but his scientific curiosity took charge.

"Yes, yes. . .what is it?"

"Our venture will allow you to proceed with your DNA processing," continued the voice. "This is a legitimate offer and not a prank, as you might call it. . .and we offer it in complete confidence. You understand?"

Intrigued, Chadhoury murmured, "Go on."

"My colleagues are contacting your associate, Dr. Lazarus, in Tehran, and would like you both to meet with us."

Abdul raised his eyebrows. "I cannot promise that Dr. Lazarus would be interested. You must know, we were both let go from our positions after the program was halted."

"Yes, and I am sorry the organization and universities were so narrow-minded. But you have a great many admirers, and important people are willing to fund your projects and see that they succeed—at any cost."

The last comment caught his attention. "Why? What possible concern is it of yours?"

"Sir," the voice continued, "in due course we will explain

everything. However, allow me to say you would both be compensated beyond anything you could imagine. A laboratory will be constructed to your exact specifications—" the speaker paused for a few seconds, as if to emphasize his next remark—"And you and your families will have whatever is required to live a carefree life."

Abdul was silently considering the offer and wondering how much he could trust the unknown voice, or its origin, and the proposal. Too good to be true, he thought. "I will have to think about this."

"Yes, yes, of course," came the reply. "We would not wish you to act hastily. We understand the magnitude of such a proposal. We would expect no less from you."

"How much time do I have, and how can I reach you?"

"We will contact you in one week. Speak to no one of this. Good-bye."

Before Chadhoury could react, the phone line went dead.

He sat quietly in his study, contemplating the call and its mysterious content and what it was really about. After retrieving a bottle of Kingfisher beer from the kitchen, he sat down and perused his contact list, found the number he wanted, and keyed it in. It rang once before the serene voice he knew so well answered, "Good evening, Isaiah Lazarus speaking."

"Isa," said Chadhoury, "it's Abdul."

Lazarus exclaimed, "Ah, yes. I thought you might call."

"Then you have heard from him as well?"

"You mean the mystery man from nowhere?"

"Yes. What do you make of it? Do you think—"

"I think it is exciting, but I have no idea if it is *genuine*. Although now that I know you have been called too, well. . . ."

"What did he tell you?"

"Not very much, I'm afraid. That he represented a person of great wealth who was interested in our work and wanted to fund the program so we could continue. He said that they would build a laboratory, access the equipment and whatever else we needed to proceed, and that our families would be well provided for. Oh, and that we would be paid more than—"

"Beyond anything we could imagine!"

"Yes, yes, exactly. Indeed, what do you make of it, dear Chadhoury? Is it real? Can it be?"

"Perhaps we should pursue this. Do you agree?"

Lazarus was quiet, considering the idea, uncertain how to, or whether to, proceed.

Abdul continued, "Did he give you a name or number to call with your decision?"

"No, he did not. I checked the number with caller identification and then the phone company, but had no luck. And you?"

"No. He gave me nothing and said only that he would call *me*. Have you told anyone else? Jafra, or your mother?"

"No, not a word to anyone, but it only happened a few minutes before you called."

"Hm. Perhaps, Isa, we should remain silent until we know more. Do you agree?"

"Yes. Let's speak again after one of us gets the next call. Until then, *As-salamu alaykum.*"

Abdul replied softly, "*Wa-Alaikum-Salaam*, my dear friend."

WITHIN TWO MONTHS of the first mysterious call, Chadhoury and Lazarus were ensconced in a secret, state-of-the-art laboratory three stories below ground in the Abdali district of

Amman, Jordan. They, and a team of other genetic scientists, were given access to a variety of fragments excavated by Amman Governorate archeologists. The tiny samples were discovered at 'Ain Ghazal from sites inhabited as early as 7250 B.C.

Six months of exhaustive, inspiring experiments showed promising results. One day Abdul and Isaiah were summoned to a meeting.

It soon became clear that the people in the room were the money behind the project. Chadhoury and Lazarus were seated next to each other at a conference table with two men; a third man remained standing. Another, armed with an Uzi, guarded the door. At the opposite end of the room, on a table, sat a large, flat, rectangular box covered with a blanket; another gunman stood next to it.

For the first time since being recruited, Abdul and Isaiah felt frightened and cast furtive glances at each other. Nothing in the past few months had prepared them for such a scene or suggested any impropriety requiring the presence of weapons. They had always been treated with great respect; all the promises made to them had been kept, and they had not once feared for their safety.

One of the men started to speak, but then leaned in and whispered into the ear of the smaller man seated to his left. Dressed in a dark suit with a white shirt buttoned to the top, he nodded once.

"Good morning," said the first. "It is a great pleasure to meet you. "My name is Amir Hammad." He looked in their direction and turned slightly toward the diminutive man next to him. "This gentlemen is your benefactor and a great admirer, as we all are, of you and your work." He motioned to the guns, "Please do not be alarmed by the, uh, precautions."

Isaiah raised his hand. "Why are they necessary?"

Hammad smiled a bit sardonically, "As I said, they are precautionary."

"Yes, but for what purpose?"

"Dear Dr. Lazarus, do not be concerned, you will soon understand."

"Surely," Abdul interjected, "you can trust us. We are committed to the program. . .but in all honesty, we have been working in a vacuum. We have been given no clear goal or objective other than to scrape, if you will, some old cloth for DNA material and record our results. Your people remove the genetic material we collect and take it God knows where, and we never learn if it has been matched. We have not asked for anything or taken anything from the labs or asked to be released from our agreement. Perhaps it is time we know why we have been . . .why this project is so, so *secret*."

"Nothing has changed," Hammad insisted. "The objective has always been to recreate a human being from the DNA harvested from the cloth we give you, some of it dating back to a time before Christ. One reason we solicited you is that you have never thought of genetic transfer as 'playing God.' The other is that no one else on Earth has the knowledge or ability to achieve the result we seek."

"Which is what, exactly?" Lazarus asked him.

At that very moment, the smaller man held up his hand to halt the discussion. Everyone turned toward him. Hammad took a seat.

The man spoke in a low voice, deliberate and expressionless.

"I am Abd al-Yasu. Do you know what that name means?

It means 'slave of Jesus,' and that is what I have been all my life. You must remember that. It will help you to understand everything. You have asked two very important questions. I will answer them. As to the first, the guns are an unfortunate addition, but you will understand their presence as soon as I answer the second."

He motioned with his chin to the opposite side of the room, where the box lay. "You have been sequestered for quite some time without access to the outside world. You have been most accepting of these term, and we are grateful. It is vital that we avoid any divulgence of information related to our mission. We have come to the moment when everything you have achieved will be put to the ultimate test. We believe you are now ready to proceed with the final phase of the program."

Chadhoury and Lazarus looked at one another and then leaned in to hear what the man was about to say. Al-Yasu motioned for the blanket to be removed. The two geneticists remained seated, attempting to catch a glimpse of the contents, but restrained themselves from getting up.

Abd al-Yasu nodded in Hammad's direction, at which point the man opened a briefcase and spread out a front page of the *Gazetta del Sud* from the previous week's edition.

"Allow me to translate for you," said Hammad. His finger ran over the letters as he spoke, "Tragic Theft in Turin. World Outraged by Greatest Heist in History."

Under the very large headline was a photo of the revered Shroud of Turin; on it, the presumed, distinct, but hazy image of Jesus Christ laying prone, with hands covering his genitalia.

Again Lazarus and Chadhoury looked at each other, this time longer and with fear in their eyes. They rose as one and approached the box, gasping in unison at the sight of the first-century burial cloth. As they turned to face the room they were joined by Hammad and al-Yasu, who also peered into the box and then went back to the table.

"Please join us," Hammad insisted, motioning to the table.

They returned to their seats, and al-Yasu gestured to the guard to cover the box and then open the door, allowing an attendant to enter with a tray of figs, dates, tea, and biscuits.

The clatter of cups and saucers, and hum of the air vent, were the only sounds in the room, except for Abdul and Isaiah's anxious breathing. Hammad never took his eyes off them, and when the beverages had been placed in front of each and the tray of sweets passed around, he cleared his throat and addressed the scientists. "So, now, my dear professors, you finally know what all this has been about, and your questions have been answered, yes?"

Chadhoury was dumbstruck and sat as if in a trance. Lazarus' voice quavered when he spoke. "W-wait. Are you saying this is the real shroud of Turin? How did you. . .how did you get this? What do you plan to do with it? . . . What do you want *us* to do with it?"

They both knew the answers, but hearing it from the man himself was critical to believe what was occurring.

Abd al-Yasu continued to speak in a low, controlled voice with a tinge of smugness. "The plan was and always has been the same—to gain access to the shroud. Once thought to be a thirteenth-century fake, carbon testing was conducted, but it was mishandled in the most irresponsible way. However, I believe the cloth is authentic. So when I learned of your DNA processing techniques and your success in regenerating life from the chromosomal material, I knew I was the one to see to it that Jesus was reincarnated. Brought back, as he himself had promised. . .and had predicted. Together, we can do it! Extracting DNA material from the shroud and reprocessing it, developing the DNA matrix, harvesting the chromosomal material, producing a living, breathing Jesus—just think of it! He will have risen! The world is more in need of Him now than ever before, and it is *we*—I—who will have made it happen."

He sat back, satisfied that he was in like company, that his dream would become reality. It didn't seem to matter how he had come by the shroud, or that he was meddling with the past and the future at the same time.

The scientists both stood up in protest, but when the click-click of the two weapons filled the room they froze.

"Sit down!" ordered Al-Yasu. "This no longer your project. You will follow directions, do as you are told, and reproduce the living, breathing, holy son of God. . .and He shall once again be King of Kings, the almighty savior, the one and true heavenly Father. Is that clear?"

Abdul and Isaiah were stunned by the rapid turn of events. Protesting was out of the question, and they knew it.

"Gentlemen," offered Hammad, "surely, as men of science, as human beings, you see the significance of such a mission. All your efforts and work, your discoveries and gifts to the world, have led to this point. This is a crowning moment for the marriage of religion, science, and technology, the opportunity to save mankind from self-destruction."

A tomblike quiet followed these remarks. The two researchers sat grim-faced, unable to speak, deep in thought, contemplating what they were being asked to do.

After several minutes, Hammad rose to his feet. "Come, now, let us not be so glum. We must set the final stages in motion. You can view the journey as a giant leap in human evolution. We will leave you, so you can discuss it between yourselves. When we return, you will please have your answer."

Chadhoury, his forehead damp with perspiration, finally spoke. "What if we don't agree to do this? Who will you be able to turn to for your devious plan? What will happen to us?"

Al-Yasou consolingly replied, "I am sorry you consider this devious. As to what happens without you—nothing. You are the only two who can achieve the resurrection. You would be free to go."

Abdul stared at him, incredulous, unsure if the man was serious. He turned to Isaiah, scanning his face for an indication of what his colleague was thinking.

"But before you decide," said Hammad, "I want to share with you some very important information about our relic here." He gestured toward the shroud. "Al-Yasou alluded to the carbon dating that took place with inconclusive results. DNA testing done several decades ago, in 2002, physically damaged the cloth. A tiny piece was removed during a so-called restoration process. It is highly probable, too, that the cloak itself was contaminated, as were the microscopic blood particles they removed. My associates and I decided to ensure that no further destruction has taken place, and that you will have complete and total access to all the material you need."

The geneticists listened attentively, and Lazarus said softly, "Please, give us a few minutes."

Hammad, still standing, looked toward Al-Yasou for approval. It came in the form of a single nod.

"Yes, by all means," he answered. "We will return in fifteen minutes—but Mustafa will remain to guard the shroud."

They then cleared the room.

GOOD DAYS, BAD DAYS

Abdul and Isaiah turned to the far corner, where they could confer in private away from the prying ears of Mustafa.

Isaiah asked, "So, my dear Chadoury, what do you think? Is this crazy? Can we really leave without being harmed, or worse?"

"Ah, dear friend," said Abdul, "I fear we are in a very dangerous situation either way."

"Yes, yes, but if we proceed, and more importantly, succeed, then what? We are talking about The Christ. What would happen? How would it affect mankind? The implications are immense. What if. . .what if it turns out that He is not the son of God, and only a myth? No one would believe where he came from, and all our work would be for naught."

"Yes," responded Abdul, "but what if He truly is? Then what?"

Chadhoury began warming to the idea. "Let's say we go forward and find the DNA material we need, confirm its authenticity, and then reproduce. . .*Him* in all His glory? Suppose, just suppose, He is real, and we have been chosen by God to create the resurrection, the second coming. Perhaps," he mused, "we are part of a grand design."

Lazarus smiled. "Suppose, indeed. We *must* proceed Dear Chadhoury. This is our destiny. It is the world's destiny. I think Al-Yasou is right. There is no one else who can achieve this. Think of it, Abdul, my friend, science and religion collaborating—isn't that what we always wanted? We have waited for this all our lives. We must do it. Will you, *can* you, agree?"

Abdul tugged at his lip as he always did when deep in thought. In short order, he began nodding. "Yes. Yes, we must've been chosen for a reason. I have always been a man of science, but without my faith in something larger than life,

I would not have reached this point. Yes, let us do this."

They shook hands and uncharacteristically hugged each other.

Moments later, the door opened, and al-Yasou came in with Hammad close behind him. They were followed by the man cradling the Uzi.

"And so," began al-Yasou, "what have you decided?"

Lazarus gestured for Chadhoury to reply. "Yes, we will do it, but we must have a plan of action and be in complete charge of the shroud and how it is to be used."

"Agreed, but it must never leave the laboratory, and you will be in the presence of an armed guard at all times. We expect daily reports on your progress. Is that clear?"

Understanding that they would be accomplices to both the greatest crime and also the most important scientific experiment in history, Lazarus and Chadhoury resolutely agreed.

Hammad declared, "Everything in your laboratory will be transferred to a new location one level down. It is a climate-controlled facility designed specifically to preserve the holy cloth. All your instruments and work to date will be transferred there. Every precaution to avoid damage or disruption will be taken, but what matters most is the integrity of the Resurrection Project, as it will now be known. Nothing you have done to date is as significant. We begin today."

THE GENETICISTS WERE IMPRESSED with their new laboratory space and immediately started researching the shroud.

Soon, following their preliminary investigations and the beginning of the extraction process, Chadhoury explained his and Lazarus's findings and concerns to Hammad and al-Yasou. "We discovered minute samples of blood and were able to retrieve ancient gene signals, which we amplified through polymerase chain reaction—"

Abd al-Yasou held up his hand. "I do not need the specifics. Just tell me what we can expect and when."

"...I am afraid," replied Chadhoury, "we must work without any certainty that it will be Jesus."

"I understand," said al-Yasou. "But when will you be ready to move to the final phase—the resurrection?"

Chadhoury ran a hand across his mouth. "A few months, if everything goes well."

Abd al-Yasou sat back and clasped his hands, a smile slowly forming on his lips, his eyes filled with excitement. "And then?"

"And then," said Isaiah, pausing for a very long time, "if we are right, if Jesus is resurrected and He is the Lord... there will be the foretold battle between good and evil. We will have Armageddon."

SIBLINGS

THEY WERE BORN AN OCEAN APART to same mother and father, only at different times in their parent's lives. Marcus was older by four years and had come to live in Paris those first years when his father was a foreign correspondent for the *Herald Tribune*. Patrick, the youngest, had come into the world after his parents moved back to the States—Washington, DC, to be exact.

The boys' differences could be attributed to more than geography; living at the center of American government, Marcus's dual citizenship gave him credentials among his peers and in later life would work in his favor when he entered diplomatic circles.

The gap in age compounded the disparity from the beginning, and as adults they were on opposite sides of the political fence. In fact, everything about them took on a competitive significance. They fought over toys, chores, pets, and television programs, and eventually politics.

Patrick inherited his mother's sweet temperament and compassion; Marcus conveyed an air of authority and a touch of arrogance to go with it. He was bright but rigid, whereas

Patrick was artistic and open to new ideas.

The father, Eric, was a workaholic by nature, a Pulitzer Prize-winning journalist who liked being in the thick of things, but it often kept him from his family for weeks at a time and even longer when he was on international assignments.

Like so many people during the Viet Nam war, the two brothers had taken opposing sides. There was no middle ground, no shared vision. You were either a "dove" or a "hawk," and for them it was a foregone conclusion who would be what, and so the rift between them became a chasm.

Against his mother's wishes and father's admonishment, Patrick took off for San Francisco and dissolved into the commune lifestyle and, between peace marches and clashes with the police, shared joints, food, and beds with a succession of nubile girls. Marcus graduated law school, married a senator's daughter, and moved into a carriage house in Georgetown, a wedding gift from his father-in-law.

The brothers' lives remained separated by more than miles. Marcus, being geographically close, became the family anchor when Eric's cancer spread rapidly though his body.

Making only an occasional pay-phone or collect call to his parents' home, and having no mailing address of his own, months passed before Patrick learned of his father's impending doom. When he finally did call, his mom put Marcus on the phone because she became too emotional to speak.

"You should be here, you fuckin' hippy dipshit," was the way his brother phrased it—the first words between them in three years.

"And how have *you* been, big brother?" Patrick replied.

Marcus snorted into the receiver and shook his head in disgust. "The only reason I'm talking to you is because Mom put the phone in my hand. So listen good and listen carefully, dirt bag. Your father is dying, and you better get your ass out here if you ever want to see him again."

If he sounded militarily gruff, it was no accident; though Patrick didn't know it, Marcus had already done a tour in Nam and lost a hand in the process.

For his part, Patrick was dumbstruck by the news of his father's illness and offered no retort, which his brother misinterpreted as disinterest. "Goddamn it, Patty boy, I don't give two craps if I never talk to you again, but you better do this for Mom and Dad, or so help me. . . ."

A few more seconds passed before Patrick spoke. Holding back tears that his brother could not see, words catching in his throat, he steadied himself against the phone booth wall. "I-I'll be there soon as I can," he managed to say before hanging up.

With no car or money to fly home, Patrick loaded up a knapsack, stashed some weed in the bottom next to a bag of trail mix, and scrounged a few dollars from his commune buddies, which he slid into the toe of his shoe. He hit the road the day after the call.

Looking much like the vagabond he was, not many cars or trucks stopped for him along the highway, and all told he walked close to a hundred and fifty miles during the nine days it took him to reach Washington.

He appeared on his parents' doorstep in Arlington during a steady rain, late enough at night so the house lights were off. Not wanting to frighten them, not knowing for sure if they were home or if his father was alive, he crawled under the back porch and slept in his bed roll.

By morning, smelling every bit like a wet skunk, with scruffy beard and stringy hair, sniveling from the damp and his drained emotions, he rang the bell.

Several minutes passed before the door curtain was swept aside and his mother Joyce, in a bathrobe, peered at the derelict standing hunched over and shivering, her prodigal son returned.

"Oh, God," she screeched on recognizing him, and fumbled at the door latch for an anguished few seconds before getting it open. She threw her arms around him, almost knocking his exhausted body to the ground, "Patrick, Patrick, my boy. My sweet boy."

She held him tightly, afraid he would vanish if she let go. She stepped back and looked him up and down. "My God! What's happened to you? You look dreadful. When did you eat last? Your clothes, your hair. Dear God, Patrick!"

She pulled him inside and quickly closed the door.

He glanced around the foyer and instinctively looked up the stairs leading to the second floor of the brick Colonial.

"Is he. . .am I—"

She shook her head slowly and took hold of his hand. "Your father is very sick, Patrick, but you are in time."

"Can I—"

"Please, wait a bit. He sleeps a lot, and he's been sedated for the past two weeks." She smiled meekly but demanded, "You better get cleaned up first. Give me those clothes, and I'll wash them while you take a shower. Use the guest room. I'll make you something to eat."

Patrick, suddenly feeling as if he'd never left, almost wept a curious mixture of sorrow, fatigue, nostalgia, and happiness that he hadn't arrived too late to see his dad.

While he was in the shower, she stepped into the steam-filled bathroom and left shaving implements and a scissor, hoping he'd cut his hair and remove the two weeks of facial growth. She left his father's robe and a cup of coffee on the countertop and quietly returned to the kitchen.

The trepidation that had lurked within Patrick's mind was being replaced by a sense of relief. Fearing he would be shunned as their black sheep, draft-dodging son, he had instead been welcomed unconditionally by his mother.

How his father would react, if he recognized him at all, was another matter.

Shuffling into the kitchen, Patrick inadvertently startled Joyce. Recoiling from the stovetop, she let out a yelp and almost upended the pot she had been stirring. "Oh, dear, you scared me."

"I'm sorry, Mom."

She smiled warmly at his voice and motioned for him to take a seat by the table. "I made some oatmeal. Coffee is on the counter."

"Thanks, Mom. When can I see Dad?"

"He has a little bell on the night stand and rings it when he wakes up. We can go up together."

They sat in silence while he spooned the cereal into his mouth, her hand resting on top of his. Cradling the mug of coffee just under his chin, Patrick savored the warmth of it in his hand, the aroma, the all-encompassing sense of feeling at home. He realized, for the first time since leaving, that it was not the family he had run from but the need to be his own man, to find his own identity, to be Patrick Dougherty, not just Marcus Dougherty's little brother or Pulitzer Prize-winner Eric Dougherty's youngest boy.

The jingle of a tiny brass bell woke him from his reverie. Rising from the breakfast nook, Joyce murmured, "That's your father. He's awake."

She lightly touched her son's shoulder. "Come with me. But let me go in first."

She motioned for him to wait outside the bedroom door as she approached the bed and kissed her husband of thirty years on his forehead.

"You have a visitor," she whispered, and stepped aside so Patrick was visible from the doorway. Eric raised his head just enough to see over the footboard. He squinted and momentarily seemed confused before his lips parted and a muffled groan rose from deep inside him, followed by a series of phlegm-ridden, gurgling coughs. "Mother of God if it isn't my little Patrick. You came." He raised his arm and motioned to him. "Come here, son. Let me look at you."

The young man came to the bedside and knelt so his face was inches away. Tears slowly made their way down his face as he leaned in to rest his head on his father's chest. The two remained quiet for a few minutes, Eric's hand smoothing his son's hair, which had been dutifully cut a few inches shorter only minutes before.

Joyce left the room without either of them noticing and returned to the kitchen, where she lifted the phone and dialed a number. Still early in the morning, she knew Marcus would be at home.

"Good morning, honey," she said cheerfully when he picked up. It was rare for her to contact him so early in the day, and he immediately thought the worst.

"What's the matter?"

"Your brother's here."

Marcus exhaled loudly, and although he was exasperated by the news, he felt oddly relieved that Patrick had somehow gotten there in time.

"How's he look? Has he seen Dad yet?"

He hadn't uttered Patrick's name in almost three years, pre-ferring instead to refer to him as 'the hippy.'"

"Y-yes, they're upstairs now," she stammered. "He—he looks good. Undernourished perhaps, a bit sallow, but other-wise the same."

Marcus sighed but said nothing.

"Will you come see him? Please?"

A long silence followed her plea until she finally begged, "Marcus. Do it for your father. We may never have the chance to be together again. Please, please let him have that much."

She fidgeted with the phone cord, waiting for him to say something and then finally heard him clear his throat. "I'll do it for you Mom. . .and for Dad, but not for him."

Resigned, she said, "Thank you, Marcus," adding as an af-terthought, "Come soon—by yourself, not with Naomi or the kids. Just you. It will be less commotion for Dad."

"Give me an hour." He hung up.

WHEN SHE RETURNED TO THE UPSTAIRS BEDROOM, Eric had fallen asleep, and Patrick was sitting in a chair next to the bed. The nightstand was laden with orange pill containers, some crumpled tissues that had missed the wastebasket, and a water bottle. Eric's breathing was labored, and he coughed from time to time. Patrick rose when he saw his mother and motioned for her to wait outside, then went to her.

"How bad is he, Mom?"

Her eyes moistened on hearing the question. "Patrick—I'm sorry. We had no way to reach you. He, uh—" her knees buckled slightly before she caught herself by grabbing the banister. "Maybe a week, maybe two."

It was not the answer Patrick had expected and the words slammed into him. He hesitated, trying to comprehend the time frame, finally realizing his father could have died before he got there.

"Mom, I'm sorry. I'm sorry. I should have called sooner. I should've been—"

She reached for his hand. "You're here now. That's what counts."

They stood together in the bedroom doorway, whispering while watching Eric sleep. The gurgling sound in his throat was like a death rattle, and every few minutes he would cough and stir, but they remained outside in the foyer.

A little while later the downstairs door opened and Marcus called out, "Mom, I'm here."

Patrick turned to look down the flight of steps, caught sight of his brother, and immediately felt a tightness in his chest. He had no idea what they'd say to each other, or if they'd talk at all, or if Marcus would turn around and leave as soon as he spotted him.

He grimaced. "Mom? Did you tell Marcus I was here?"

"I had to, Patrick. You need to put your differences aside, to be here for your father—and for me. All of us together." She called down, "We're upstairs, son, come up."

Marcus climbed the stairs, pacing off each step as though he were counting them, until he was face-to-face with his brother. They stood staring at each other until Patrick raised his hand in a half-salute and then held it outward for Marcus to shake. It was only then that he saw the hook attached to his sibling's right forearm.   He let out a gasp and dropped his hand to his side just as Marcus reached out with his left arm and said, "What's a matter, dontcha want to shake your brother's hand?"

Patrick's mouth was agape as he tentatively, awkwardly, reached for his brother's left hand. He cringed and squawked, "Jesus, Marco, what the fuck—sorry, Mom—what happened to you?"

"Nam."

Patrick winced. "When? I didn't even know you were there."

"That's probably because you were too busy burning your draft card."

A touch of embarrassment flushed the younger brother's face, but before they could get into an argument, Joyce said, "Boys, boys—this is about your father. Forget your differences, at least for now. At least while he's. . . ."

The two men—sons, brothers, adversaries—stared silently into one another's eyes as the anger gradually faded from their faces. Then in unison they turned to look at their father, who was attempting to rise up on one elbow.

He spoke in a weak and raspy voice. "Boys! My boys, together. . .in the same room. Joyce, honey, look at that. We're all together again. And it ain't even at my funeral," he chortled.

They laughed nervously at Eric's attempt at good humor and moved closer, Joyce on one side, holding his hand, the two brothers at the foot of the bed. Eric smiled; tears filled his eyes as he lay back onto the pillow and closed his eyes. The smile remained.

He died in his sleep that night.

AT THE FUNERAL, JOYCE HELD her sons' hands and wouldn't let go until the first spadeful of dirt was cast onto the coffin. She turned to them then and embraced them before taking hold of their hands again and whispering, "Boys, please stay friends. Make peace with each other in your father's memory, and keep this family together."

Patrick smiled crookedly at Marcus, who then poked him in the chest with the hook and said, "Better get used to this thing, 'cause it ain't goin' away," and then added, "And neither are you."

PATRICK NEVER RETURNED to San Francisco.

SUBVERSIVE

THE THREE FLIGHTS OF STAIRS leading to Gil's Greenwich Village apartment were an obstacle course of bodies— not corpses but people sitting, talking, and smoking weed. The August night was stagnant with the stench of garbage wafting up from the alleyway.

Gil was the first in our Mountainvale Academy of Art class to find a job in the big city. He was also the first of our bunch to move out of the commune-like living quarters we all shared on Second Street and Avenue B.

He called me late one afternoon and said, "Hey, Steve, come over and see my new pad. B.Y.O.B. and anyone you want." That last suggestion was what caused the turnout and congested stairway.

Graduating a semester ahead of me, Gil had had a head start finding work, although I never thought he was that talented, but then neither was I. To me art wasn't a career choice, it just seemed like a cool thing to do, and if you got paid for it, why not? Gil had a job designing book jackets for a second-rate publishing house. It paid a hundred and fifty bucks a week, which in 1966 was pretty okay for entry level. His walk-up studio apartment cost eighty a month, so he was ahead of the game.

Stepping over people I didn't recognize, I followed the Rolling Stones blaring from the open door and made it to the third-floor landing, turned sideways to squeeze passed a sweaty, bespectacled, bearded guy in the entrance, and joined the throng.

The room was dank, smoky, and dimly lit. People were strewn across the sofa, sitting on the floor, leaning against walls, some with beer cans in their hands, others fanning themselves against the humidity.

I acknowledged the people I knew by waving in their direction and then spotted Gil by an open window leading to the fire escape. He was standing inches away from a very attractive girl I didn't know but instantly wanted to.

"Hey, Gil, what's happenin', man?"

He shouted above the racket, "Hey, Steve, glad you could make it," and then he moved closer to the girl.

She was wearing a gray Barnard College T-shirt and a pair of cut-off jeans, her brown hair pulled back in a pony-tail, eyes the color of amber. She didn't seem as engaged in the conversation as Gil was and possessed a rather vapid look hovering somewhere between boredom and allure.

"Hi," I shouted, trying to get her attention. Not my best opener, but it was enough to elicit a look in my direction and a tiny smile of acknowledgment, just enough to make my heart race.

Gil, noting my interest, reached across her and pressed his arm against the window frame, effectively shielding her from my potential advance. Glancing at me sideways, he muttered, "See ya later."

I spent the next ten minutes exchanging perfunctory con-versation with a guy I barely knew, bummed a Chesterfield, (not my favorite) from the bearded guy still standing in the doorway, and sought refuge in the kitchen, where, as luck would have it, I found Miss Barnard standing by the open freezer door, her face practically inside.

"Looking for something to eat?" I asked.

She answered in a languorous drawl, "It's too hot to *live*," which, in addition to totally captivating me, felt as if we were characters in a Tennessee Williams' play.

"Yeah, it is hot, isn't it? . . . Uh, what's your name?"

She pulled her face away from the freezer. "Marita Craw-ford. You?"

"I'm Steve Klein. You a friend of Gil's?"

"Jus' met him. Paul, my roommate, is a friend of his." She nodded in the direction of the bearded guy at the door.

"Oh! You live with beard?"

"Yup, him and five others from Columbia."

". . .You're South American?"

"No, Columbia, as in University."

"Oh, so where *are* you from?"

"Crawfordville, Florida."

I strained to hear her above the music—Otis Redding, I think. "Crawfordville? You own the town or somethin'?"

"My family did. Way back when."

"Wow, really?   Where's it?"

"Near Tallahassee."

"What's it like?"

"Hot 'n' sticky, lots of bugs, and not much to do."

"Sounds lovely. How'd you get *here?*"

"Daddy's the county judge? Wants me to be a lawyer.

So—" she pointed to her T-shirt— "Barnard."

I leaned closer. "You wanna get outta here?"

She shrugged.

I motioned to the door, from which Beard had mercifully vanished. "C'mon. Let's go where it's quiet and not so hot."

She moved with the slow grace of a feral cat. As she brushed by me, I became intoxicated by the smell of her sweat-dampened hair—like the pungent, musky odor following heavy sex.

We emerged onto Bleeker, moved down Hudson to the river, and sat on a bench. The lights from New Jersey reflected off the placid water, a tugboat chugged toward the piers up-town, and a few gulls bobbed near the dock pilings. I wondered what a small-town Southern girl thought of it.

"What do you think of New York?"

"S'all right," she managed to say and then did the unimaginable. She tilted her head so it rest on my shoulder, causing in me a confused mix of lust and paternal feeling. I was afraid to move, concerned that it would break whatever mood it was that we were sharing.

I found myself sitting as still as I could while my arm yearned to shift from under the added weight of her body, however slight.

I had no idea what time it was, nor did I care—it was a dream I did not want to end. I kept saying her name to myself, "Marita. Marita," liking it more than any girl's name I'd ever heard. In fact, I must've said it out loud, because she raised her head and asked, "What?"

Embarrassed, I stammered, "I-I didn't say anything."

"You said my name."

"Uh, it's a pretty name."

"Thank you."

The conversation began to flow more easily the longer we sat there. After an hour we walked to the Empire Diner, ordered coffee, and shared a dish of butter pecan ice cream. At one point she told me about some of her on-campus activities and mentioned people I'd only vaguely heard of—Tom Hayden, Mark Rudd, Abbie Hoffman, and Stokely Carmichael. She asked if I had burned my draft card and what I thought of Johnson escalating the war. Her demeanor slowly changed from soft-spoken belle to intense rebel. She praised the Civil Rights Act but said it was flawed. She said things like "up the establishment" and referred to the "new left," all of which caught me by surprise and none of which I'd expected to hear from the likes of her.

As for me, I wasn't that involved in college politics, or the war for that matter; my main concerns were finding a better job and getting laid. She had deep issues with LBJ's policies, equal opportunity employment, and the war on poverty. "How is it going to be paid for," she demanded, "if he spends all our money on a war in Viet Nam?"

We speculated on who had been behind Kennedy's assassination and how divided the country had become. As dawn approached, we took the uptown subway to her group-shared apartment on 110th and Broadway. The place was a messy, unhealthy-looking five-room apartment awash with scattered clothes, books, and piles of dishes stacked in the sink. The other occupants, including the Beard, were asleep, some in the same bed; others sprawled across the sofa or in a chair.

She led me down the hall to a tiny room and whispered, "We can sleep here." There was no door, just rows of beads acting as a curtain. There was a single bed and a dresser with a lamp and a card table strewn with her text books. She sat on the edge of the bed, pulled off her T-shirt, exposing her perky, braless breasts, removed her shorts and bounced backward holding out her arms for me to join her.

I crawled in and we spent the next two hours wrapped in each other's arms until I woke to arguing voices coming from the other side of the apartment.

"Man, you don't know what the fuck you're talking about!" screeched one, followed by another person's more controlled retort,

"There'll be plenty of us there to put up a fight, but don't go if that's the way you feel."

The first voice angrily replied, "Off the pigs, man! I ain't spending another night in a detention cell because of your stupid protests."

Marita, startled by the sound of the yelling, sat up straight, realized she wasn't alone, and fell back.

"Oh, hi. You're still here?"

"Yeah, I'm still here. What's all the hollering?"

She turned to look at the small alarm clock on the table and sat up again. Pushing aside the hair that had fallen across her face, she reached for her shirt, slipped it on, and climbed over me to get out of bed. "St-Steve, right? Listen, I gotta get ready. We're planning a sit-in today." She squinted at me and lightly touched my arm. "You wanna come with us?"

I immediately felt a conflict. There was no question I wanted to spend more time with her, but not at a protest sit-in. It was also a work day for me, and while I didn't like my job, I needed it.

"No can do," I told her, "I have to go to work?"

She actually pouted and then dismissively said, "Okay.

Well, nice to meet you. . .Steve."

"Hey," I said, taking hold of her wrist, "can I see you again?"

She pulled my fingers from her arm and nodded. "Sure," she said, but made no attempt to offer her phone number. I sat on the bed, awkwardly watching her gather her clothing, hoping she would say more.

She gave an exasperated sigh. "Look, I need to get in the bathroom before the others or I'll never get out of here. I like you, okay?"

Taking that as an approval and my exit cue, I rose from the bed, kissed her, hugged her, and gave it one more try. "I like you, too, Marita. I really want to see you again."

She stood silently for an anxious few seconds, finally nodded, and walked to the table. She scribbled the apartment's communal phone number on a corner of a yellow legal pad, tore it off, and handed it to me.

"Best time is at night," she said and leaned in to kiss me full on the lips. My heart pounded.

THE SIT-IN AT THE PROVOST'S OFFICE lasted for three days, ending in a tear-gas assault, tussles with the police, and numerous arrests, among them Marita Crawford's.

She told me all this on the phone when I called the day after her release, the sweet Southern voice all but gone, replaced by antipathy for the "establishment," as she, once again, put it.

"I'm done with non-violent protest. Nobody gives a shit. They're goin' down!" she hissed.

"Who exactly are you referring to?"

"All of 'em. . .the pigs, the faculty, the politicos—all of

them!"

The tone of her voice actually frightened me. It was hostile and, worse, she sounded serious.

It was clear I knew nothing about this girl, yet couldn't deny I felt something more than pure lust. "M-Marita," I stammered, "calm down. You need to rethink what you're saying." She didn't respond, but I heard her agitated breathing and waited a few seconds before adding, "Maybe we can meet up somewhere and talk."

"I'm done talking. You don't know what they put me through in that place. What they called me. Nothing they did is legal, and we're not standing still for it. Look, I gotta go. I'm sorry." She hung up.

I tried calling her over the next few days and finally went up to 110th Street, hoping to see her. Her roomies said she had moved in with a guy that was active in the anti-War movement. Paul, the Beard, reluctantly told me he had no idea where she was living or who the guy was, only that she had met him at a Eugene McCarthy campaign rally.

THE NEXT TIME I HEARD about her was a couple years later. I was working as an associate art director at McCann-Erickson Advertising. A *New York Times* article about an explosion in a house raided by the FBI listed her name as one of the casualties. There was no further information.

THE ORGANIST

MARRIED A YEAR AND A HALF, with a child on the way, rookie police officer Oswald Nesbitt just came off his daytime shift. He stopped for a moment to take in the cool Utah air and, with it, the hint of damp autumn leaves. He loved that time of year, and it brought a smile to his face as he slid behind the wheel of the Honda Civic. Before he turned the ignition key, his cell phone vibrated; it was 6:08 and his wife Trish was calling. "Hi, hon, I'm just leaving. What's up?"

"Hi, Ossie. Would you pick up some ice cream on the way? We don't have anything for dessert."

"Sure, baby. What kind?"

"I don't care. I just have a craving."

"You got it. Be home soon. Love you."

"And me you," she said, and hung up.

He thought of stopping at the supermarket to pick up some flowers for her along with the ice cream but decided it would be better to go to the convenience store, so the ice cream wouldn't melt before he got home.

It was dark by the time he pulled into the parking lot at

Mike's Mini-Mart; the street lamps were already bathing it in harsh halogen light. The only other car in the lot was far from the entrance, with the motor idling, a silhouetted figure in the driver's seat barely visible except for the glow of a cigarette. Always aware of his surroundings, Ossie reasoned it was someone waiting for an employee or customer.

As he reached for the door to enter the mart, two men rushed past him. The car at the far side of the lot suddenly roared toward them, wheels screeching.

"Go, go," shouted one of the running men.

Officer Nesbitt, in street clothes, quickly looked into the store and saw the counter man slumped across the register. He wheeled around, drew his service revolver, and shouted, "Police! *Freeze!*"

The two men jumped into the car as it careened toward him with one door still open. Nesbitt had a fraction of a second to jump out of the way as he fired into the windshield. It hit the driver in the forehead, causing the car to swerve radically and jump the curb, crashing into the store window. The other two leapt out of the car and ran across the lot. Oswald took after them and fired a warning shot. One of the guys stopped, turned, and shot back at him several times. The first bullet hit Ossie in the stomach, a second his chest; he fell to his knees and then sprawled on the pavement. Before passing out he managed to call it in: "Two-eleven! Officer d-down! Mini-Mart Clinton and Dorset—"

A near-by patrol car responded immediately and spotted the men running from the scene. The patrolmen gave pursuit and were able to cut them off, exchange gunfire, and kill one. The second, the one who had shot Nesbitt, was wounded and taken into custody.

Three squad cars, sirens wailing and lights flashing, raced into the Mini-Mart lot. Two cops, guns drawn, went into the store while the others attended the fallen officer who lay unconscious, blood leaking profusely from his wounds; it was 6:18 PM. The EMTs pulled up and began to work on Nesbitt before loading him onto a gurney and then racing to the ER, where doctors rushed him into an operating room.

Twenty-three minutes later, Trish Nesbitt appeared with a police escort and stood vigil, shaken and almost catatonic.

The procedure to remove the bullets, one lodged in her husband's kidney and the other in his right lung, took several hours. Fragments from the projectile had shattered his rib cage and torn into his liver. The loss of blood was profound, and he remained in a coma for twelve days, clinging to his life.

Trish lost the baby.

During the course of his convalescence the young officer's remaining kidney began to fail, and he was placed on dialysis. OPTN—the Organ Procurement and Transplantation Network—was notified about his condition, and he was placed on a waiting list for a kidney and lung transplant. But he had type B-negative blood, and it would not be an easy match; only about two percent of the population was type B-negative, and an even smaller number was listed as organ donors.

Although Nesbitt was lauded as a hero and given recognition by the force and the community, he could not be given priority for organ donation. Complicated by his rare blood type, even if a kidney and lung donor were to be found, the organs had to be delivered and transplanted without delay.

Dr. Peter Cameron, the chief surgeon at the hospital and a representative of OPTN, met with Trish to explain the situation.

He was perfunctory but compassionate. "Mrs. Nesbitt, your husband is in need of a dual transplant, but we are dealing with some very difficult conditions."

The OPTN rep interjected, "Once removed, a lung has only a four-to-six-hour life-span, and a kidney about a day to a day and a half, in which to be used. So if—" he cleared his throat and started again. "*When* we locate them, everything has to be efficiently performed." Trish sat motionless, listening, nodding, sobbing gently, her hand rubbing the spot where her child should have been.

TWELVE WEEKS INTO THE HOSPITAL STAY, the Police Benevolent Association raised enough funds to purchase a dialysis machine and provide nursing care for young Nesbitt so he could be moved home.

The months dragged on without a donor, and during that time Ray Flores, the man who had shot him, robbed the store, and killed the clerk, was convicted of murder in the second degree along with a host of other felonies and sentenced to life in prison without parole. At twenty-two years of age, Flores had previously served time for aggravated assault, drug possession, and grand theft.

Trish heard about the sentencing from the police captain, and said she wanted to tell Ossie about it by herself.

Later that day, she sat at his bedside and quietly said, "Ossie, sweetheart, I just heard from Captain Swayze about the guy who shot you."

He stared blankly at her, not making a sound, waiting for the information. Trish took his hand before looking into his eyes. "The guy was a . . . was a—" she had a hard time forming the words or knowing just what, or how much, to tell him.

"It's okay, hon, it doesn't really matter, you know?"

She studied her husband's handsome face, which has grown taut and pale, and said simply, "He was sentenced to life without parole."

Oswald blinked once and nodded in comprehension, but said nothing and then turned away. They didn't speak of it again for a long while.

A RECURRING LIVER INFECTION from minute, previously undetected bullet fragments plagued his recovery, and when the organ began to malfunction, a liver was added to the organ transplant list.

A lung donor was eventually identified, and Ossie was rushed to the hospital, prepped, and put under anesthesia while the lung was airlifted from Nevada, but the flight was forced to return to Laughlin due to a storm in the Wasatch Mountains. By the time the flight could get off the ground, eight hours had elapsed; the organ tissue began to deteriorate, and it was deemed questionable, at best, for the Nesbitt transplant. OPTN acted quickly when a recipient in Barstow, California, was identified, and the lung was delivered there instead, in less than an hour.

Ossie's health faded along with the winter, but he refused to talk about it and put on a brave face for Trish; she took to crying in the garage, so he couldn't hear her.

THE PRAYED-FOR CALL WAS ANSWERED the week before Easter. A match was made with a donor in Utah, just an hour away. A lung, liver, and kidney were being rushed to the hospital. A nine- person surgical team was assembled and worked on him for seven hours. They gave Oswald Nesbitt's life back to him.

Trish and Ossie were told that the donor had signed an agreement to provide his name, if it was requested.

The OPTN representative assured them, "Correspondence, if there is to be any, will go through our network so we can avoid any unforeseen issues or problems and also to maintain confidentiality, if desired. There is no time limit for you to do this."

They both wanted to know who the donor was so they could express their gratitude to the family for giving Ossie his life back.

It turned out the donor was not unknown to the Nesbitts. In one shocking moment they were told that Ray Flores, the man who shot Ossie, had died from stab wounds while serving a life sentence in the Utah State Penitentiary. In an apparent epiphany only a month before his death, a remorseful Flores, hoping for redemption, had signed a document donating his organs.

THE PLAN

THE CAR'S BALD TIRES SKIDDED to a stop just under the carport. Harlan pulled himself out of the Cutlass, its blotched paint pelted by the hot Floridian sun, rust eating its way around the door panel. One step at a time, he climbed the three lopsided wooden stairs leading to the mobile home.

Angela, already in her waitress uniform, was sitting on the sofa, a hair brush in one hand, her feet propped on the thrift-store coffee table. Without looking away from the TV, she nodded in his direction.

Harlan shuffled to the small fridge, extracted a beer, and tugged at the ring tab. He tossed it into the sink and sank onto the sofa next to her. "You goin' to work?"

"Yeah, I'm goin' . . . why?"

"S'late, ain't it?"

"I'm doing a double shift. A few minutes won't mean anything."

"Uh, huh," he said without looking at her. "So you won't be back until tomorrow morning?"

"Right."

He leaned forward, made a motion to get up, and slumped back.

"You know," he mused, "We can't keep doin' this. We're working our asses off and got nuthin' to show for it. We don't even own this miserable trailer, fer Chrissake."

"Well, let me know when you have a better plan, big shot, because no one's gonna pay the bills for us," she grumbled in reply, and then stood up, tossed the brush on the table, and said, "I gotta go."

He smirked and reached for her, but she squirmed out of his way and left. Harlan spent the next several hours clicking from one TV program to another, between trips to the fridge to grab another beer. By the time the last of the six PBRs were drained he had fallen asleep.

Angela shuffled in at six forty-five and found him still in his clothes, mouth agape, dried spittle on his chin, his shoes and socks strewn across the floor.

She didn't try to wake him; moving about the cluttered, cramped space was disturbance enough.

Harlan sat up and rubbed his face vigorously, then belched. "You back already?"

"Harlan, it's almost seven o'clock."

"Oh, shit, really?"

"Really."

"Crap. I better get ready for work. Mike said if I came in late again, I was toast."

"Then you better get your ass moving."

"Yeah, and good morning to you, too."

HIS JOB AT MIKE'S DISCOUNT TIRE had been given to him as a favor by his long-time friend, Michael Maltese. It was the third job Harlan had had in the past two years, and he knew he was close to losing it as well, and with it his best friend. Harlan wasn't a big drinker, except for a six-pack every now and then, and he didn't do drugs (maybe a joint if someone offered it to him), and he wasn't a malcontent; he just wasn't all that bright.

At the end of the workday, after he had installed fifteen sets of tires, a good day for the place, Harlan went for a beer with his boss and tried to smooth things over.

By the second brew, Harlan screwed up the courage to mention it. "Mike, I'm. . .I'm sorry about bein' late so much. I can't seem to get my act together."

Mike nodded, but it was more in agreement than understanding. "Harl, you never *had* your act together!

"Aw, c'mon, I was doin' pretty good when I married Martha, right? I mean she was pretty good for me."

"Yeah, and you screwed it up."

"Well, it wasn't *all* my fault. I mean, she wanted kids and stuff."

"That's what married people do, Harl, they have kids and stuff."

They sat in silence for a minute before Mike slid off the stool. "I gotta go home. I'll see ya tomorrow. Good job today, Harl."

"Wait!" urged Harlan. "I wanna ask ya somethin'."

Mike sighed and sat back down. "Yeah, what is it?"

"You ever hear anything about Martha? Like how she's doin' and all? I mean, I know she got married a while back and moved to Boynton Beach. Husband's a millionaire or somethin', right?"

Mike swiveled on the barstool and stared into his friend's

eyes before taking a deep breath and audibly exhaling.

"I don't know what good it's gonna do ya to know."

"Know what?"

Mike continued to stare into Harlan's eyes, trying to determine what to say or whether he should say anything at all.

Harlan laid his hand on Mike's forearm. "Please, Mike. Tell me what you know."

Mike shook his head in exasperation. "You're still in love with her, aren't ya?

Harlan smiled. "Nah, I was for a while, but I love Angela now. It's just that. . .it's hard. We just can't seem to get out of debt. There ain't never enough money. We're pissed at each other all the time."

Slowly grasping that he was talking to his employer, Harlan tried to explain. "I'm not sayin' I want a raise. You've been good to me, Mike. You always was. I'm glad to have the job." As an afterthought he added, "And I promise ya, I won't be late again."

Mike nodded and made another attempt to leave, but Harlan said, "Hold it, Mike. Don't go yet. Answer me this. What's with Martha? I'm just curious."

"Awright, but then I gotta go."

"Sure, sure, I'm just askin'."

"I dunno the whole story. I heard her husband was killed in a boating accident or something, about a year ago. Left her a fortune. She lives in a big house on the water."

"She got any kids?"

"Not that I know of."

Harlan sat in silence, his head filling with wild ideas.

Mike moved toward the door. "So now you know, okay? I'm outta here."

"Thanks, Mike. I'll see ya tomorrow."

Harlan nursed another beer and considered his crushing debt, his wife Angela, his dismal life and limited prospects; the revelation about Martha, her being a widow, a rich widow, stayed with him.

By the time he drove into Shady Glen Trailer Park, Angela had left for her shift at the diner. He wasn't sorry; he wanted the time alone. After an hour and three more beers, he was satisfied that he had mapped it all out and was eager to tell Angela but decided to wait until Sunday, when they were both off work.

Sunday morning, he told her to get dressed, that he was taking her out to breakfast.

Still groggy, she grumbled, "I just want to sleep. Okay?"

"No, babe, this is special. You can sleep later, but you probably won't want to. I have something real exciting to tell ya."

She shook her head in dismay; she hated surprises, especially his, which were usually not worth the bother. "Why don't ya just tell me now and let me go back to sleep?"

He was persistent as a little kid and tugged at her until she relented.

He drove to the café they went to when there was some extra cash, a rarity.

"Order whatever you want," he said with an air of bravado that she recalled from when they were first dating.

With a broad, self-satisfied grin on his face, bursting with excitement, he couldn't contain himself any longer and blurted it out before the coffee arrived. "Angie. I got this idea. It's bitchin'! Just hear me out, okay? I mean, don't say anything until I'm finished."

She sighed, already annoyed. "Oh, jeez, I'm all ears."

He began to lay it out. "Okay, so you remember my ex-wife Martha, right?"

". . .Oh, God, what have you done?"

"No, no, nothing, yet. Listen, this is good. We're gonna be okay. We'll have lots of money, and it's all legit."

Angela stared astonished at his enthusiasm and wondered aloud, "Is this gonna be another hair-brained scheme of yours?"

"No, no, this is good, it's gonna work. I promise."

He searched for a flicker of acknowledgement, of her willingness to accept. She continued to stare, waiting. Harlan told her what Mike had said and repeated the point about Martha's wealth. "She's got millions, Angie, millions. And she's all alone in that big house on the beach. I mean. really, isn't that just perfect?"

"What're you thinking, Harlan? Why would she even give you the time of day, let alone money?"

He scraped his chair closer to the table, leaned in, and looked around to make sure no one but his unimpressed wife was listening.

"Look, here's my idea," he jumped right in with no preamble. "I go see her, right? Not like to ask for money, but to pay her a con-do-lence call."

Angela shook her head, "Yeah, and?"

"And I get into her good graces, rekindle our relationship, and then woo her." He loved that he'd used the words *condolence* and *woo*; it made him feel smart.

Angela was astonished by his naiveté, his limited intelligence. Her mind wandered to their courtship, how she had been at a low point in her life, falling into depression and grasping for survival after her husband was killed in Iraq.

He interrupted her thoughts. "Babe? Babe, you listening to this?"

"Yeah, I'm listenin'. So what's your idea?"

He began to salivate and ran a hand across his mouth. "I get her to marry me!"

Incredulous, she could hardly speak, "What? How? Harlan, you idiot, you're *already* married."

"I know. I thought about that, but it's simple. We just get divorced."

Angela raised her hand. "Wait, what the fuck are you saying? *We get divorced?* Are you nuts?"

"No, no. It would just be temporary. Look, if I'm her husband, I'm entitled to half her money, or all of it. . .if something should happen to her."

He sat back smugly, certain he had it all figured out.

Angela was aghast. "Harlan, you are certifiable, you know that? You're crazier than I thought."

"Why? It's a great plan. And here's the best part—I divorce her and get an alimony settlement, and you and I get remarried." He sat back and folded his arm. "Pure genius, right?"

She stared at him, amazed that he thought it could work, that it made sense, that Martha would have anything to do with him, let alone entertain marriage. "Harlan, your stupidity is mind-blowing."

He sat looking at her, crushed. He pouted and fidgeted with the sugar and condiment packets, his eyes downcast, looking up only when the coffee arrived.

She finally broke the silence. "Harlan, I'm sorry. I know you mean well, and you're trying to figure a way out for us, but this really is—it's just plain scary. What are you planning to do? *Kill* her?"

She could see he was hurt, teary-eyed, but there was no way she would let him go down that path. "Well," he started, "I wasn't gonna do *that*."

"How how did you think you would get the money from her? And why, why in god's name, do you think she would even see you, let alone remarry you?"

He peered into the coffee cup as if the answer might be in it somewhere, floating to the top like a toast crumb. "You never let me finish," he said dejectedly.

"You mean there's more?"

"I hoped we could figure it out together. You know, plan it, so it would be foolproof."

The waitress returned, took their order, and shuffled off after refilling the cups. By then, Angela was amused and decided to play along to see where he would take it.

"All right, continue. Let me hear your idea."

He felt instantly better and moved in closer. "I was thinking I'd go there and just casually run into her. I mean, I'd scope it out and all, so I knew her routine and where she hangs out . . . . I could make it look like a chance meeting and strike up a conversation. You know, act like I didn't know anything. I ask her out for a drink and get her to see how much I'd changed, and I can be very charming when I want to be, you remember that, right?"

"Yeah, sure, charming. So let's say she falls for your bullshit, what are you doing about *us*?"

"I asked around, and Florida is a no-reason state."

"You mean no-fault?"

"Right, a no-fault divorce."

"And who's gonna pay for that? Assuming I agree."

"It's only like a couple hundred bucks."

Harlan was beaming with pride that he had the answers and had already investigated it on his own.

"Uh-huh," she grunted. "And where are you gonna get that?"

"Maybe I can borrow the money from Mike. Tell him I need a operation or somethin'."

She grimaced. "You really are special. You don't have a clue, do you?"

"What is that supposed to mean?"

"Nothing, it's just that you—oh, never mind." She shook her head, dug into the omelet in front of her, and refused to discuss the plan any further.

For his part, Harlan was convinced the idea was stunning, that it would not only work but was the answer to all their problems. For the next few weeks he immersed himself in his scheme. When he told her they could get divorced on-line for $159.00, Angela flat-out dismissed the whole idea. "Harlan, you're an asshole, and I am done talking about this. Just drop it. It's a stupid idea, and it's not gonna happen."

He knew she was serious but was convinced she was wrong, that his idea was brilliant, and that she'd come around in the end; he just wasn't sure how to get her to agree to the temporary divorce, or how long it would take to wrestle the money away from Martha.

As far as Angela was concerned, the subject was off the table and her hapless husband had moved on. He hadn't. When time permitted and he was left alone in Mike's office, he'd scour the internet for information that would help him locate Martha. Eventually, he discovered her married name, her address, her Facebook friends, and, from her timeline, places she often visited in Boynton Beach. The best part was he was only 163 miles from her house and figured he could drive there to scout it out when Angela was at work and still be back before she knew he was gone.

The hard part was getting gas money for the round trip, so he devised a plan to cut back on beer and cigarettes and was astonished at how fast he could scrape together fifty bucks. The plan was working great, so he thought, and he was very proud of how clever he was being, but sorry he couldn't tell anyone, most of all Angela.

HIS FIRST STAKE-OUT OF MARTHA'S HOUSE didn't yield anything and he couldn't find her at any of the places he thought she might be. Undaunted, he planned on making a return visit as soon as he could get away again from the trailer park in Hardee County.

A few days after that first trip to Boynton Beach, Angela called him at work, an unusual occurrence. Mike, not happy about it, came into the garage to tell him.

"Harlan, Angela's on the phone for you. You know, I don't allow calls during work hours, but she sounds upset."

Harlan placed the air wrench on the worktable, wiped his hands on his overalls, followed Mike into the office, and picked up the receiver.

"Hey, babe, what's up?"

"My sister has to have a biopsy done, and she's scared shitless. I need to be with her for a few days."

"In Kissimmee?"

"Yeah."

"Jesus, Angie, how're ya gonna get the time off?"

Stew Mosberg

"It'll be okay. I already told 'em."

His immediate thought was that he could use the time to pursue Martha.

"Harlan, you listening to me?"

"Yeah, sure. Uh, she okay?"

"She has lumps on both breasts. How okay can she be?"

"Hey, those things don't always turn out so bad. When're you leaving?"

He could hear her exhale, agitated at his seeming lack of compassion. "You could at least be concerned a little," she growled.

"I *am* concerned. Just busy, that's all. Sorry. So when are you leaving?"

". . .In a hurry to get rid of me, Harlan?"

"Nah, just want to know when, that's all."

"I'll drive up there tomorrow morning."

"Okay, then, I'll see ya at home later, right? Ya wanna get pizza?"

She hung up without answering him.

Harlan went back to the garage bay and the Subaru he had been working on. As soon as he tightened the last lug nut and let the car down, he walked back into Mike's office.

Mike, seated behind his beat up wooden desk, peered over the top of his glasses and grunted. "What?"

"Uh, Mike, I'm sorry, but I gotta take a couple days off."

"What's the matter?"

"My sister-in-law got cancer, and Angie's pretty upset. I gotta go with her to take care of business."

"Oh. Sorry to hear that. Yeah, sure. How long will you be out?"

"Dunno for sure. Probably a few days."

"All right. I think we can handle it. I can still pull my weight out there."

"Thanks, Mike. I'll make it up to ya. I promise."

"Okay, no worries. Hope she's okay. Look, there's only two more customers. A.J. and me will finish up. Go on home. Call me when you know what's what."

"Will do. Thanks again, Mike."

Mike waved, and Harlan left the office and headed to the back lot to get his car. It was where they stacked the used tires for haul away. Harlan got behind the wheel but slid back out before starting the engine. He knelt by the driver side wheel and looked at the worn tread, then did the same to the other three.

He stood up, made his way to the rows of used tires stacked like coils of giant Slinkies, and ran his hands over a few stacks until he found some that he could use on the Cutlass.

Why buy new when I can get these for free? he thought. They got better rubber than I have on mine. Anyway, he'd been driving on his bald Firestones for months, so another few days wouldn't matter. He made a mental note to come back after hours and load them into his trunk so Mike wouldn't know, but it could wait until he came back from Boynton. He stopped on the way home and bought a pizza, pepper and onion, the kind Angela liked.

Later that evening he told her. "Hey, Babe, in case you call and I ain't here, I'm probably bass fishin' with Rusty. So I'll call *you*. You know, just to see how things are with Madeline and stuff."

Preoccupied with her sister's health and the trip ahead, she only acknowledged him with a nod. Later in the evening, while she was asleep, he put some clothes in a bag and left it in the back of his car, then crept into bed next to her and lay awake, plotting the next few days.

Angela left in the morning before he woke up. She tacked a Post-It note to the fridge with her sister's phone number and a little smiley face followed by an "x" and an "o"; it was about all the affection she could muster. For Harlan, it was enough to feel everything was fine and he could go ahead with his mission. He would deal with their divorce once he made contact with Martha.

He left the trailer before eight, filled the gas tank at a Circle K, bought a container of coffee and a cinnamon roll for breakfast, and headed out. By noon he had completed his first drive-by of her house on Ocean Boulevard. Like other homes on the street, it was gated, but he could see the entrance and noted that there was a car and a van of some kind in the driveway.

In mid-afternoon Martha came out of the house and got into a silver Lexus. Her hair was lighter than he remembered, and she had put on a few pounds.

The gate slid open, and Harlan scrunched down so as not to be seen. He waited until her car was far enough ahead before pulling out to follow her.

Hoping she would go somewhere that he could accidentally run into her, he kept a close distance and felt like a detective on surveillance; it gave him a thrill.

After she stopped to run into a dry cleaner and then a florist in a strip mall, he followed her to the Boynton Beach Mall on Gateway Boulevard, watched where she parked, and pulled into a space a couple rows away. He trailed her inside the mall for twenty minutes, until he saw an opportunity to run into her.

He waited until she left a shop, passed her, and then turned around to face her. There was no hint of recognition on her face when their eyes met and she brushed past, then quickly swung around to look at him.

"*Harlan?* What. . .what are you doing here?"

He feigned wide-eyed surprise. "Martha? Wow! Hi!"

There was an awkward silence while she tried to process his presence, and he moved closer to put his arms around her, but she took a step back and turned her cheek to avoid his attempted kiss.

"So what *are* you doing here?" she asked again.

"I'm thinking of opening a discount tire store in Delray Beach, or maybe here in Boynton."

She blinked in disbelief and nodded a few times. "Well, that's. . .that's great, Harl. Good for you. I guess you've changed some, huh? Things going well for you?"

"Yeah, how about you? I heard—uh, I was sorry to hear about your husband."

"Really? You know about that?"

"Yes, I do. Must be terrible for you, being a widow and all."

Her face suddenly contorted. "What are you saying? He's not *dead.*"

It was Harlan's turn to be dumbstruck. He stood there, mouth open, a sinking feeling in the pit of his stomach, sweat beginning to drip under his arms. "What?"

". . .Harlan, what did you hear, and from who?"

"Uh, Jeez, somebody told me he was killed on a boat or somethin'."

"Well, he *did* have an accident on the boat. He was sailing solo to the Bahamas and was thrown against the mast in a violent storm and cracked his spine. He's in a wheelchair, but very much alive, thank god."

The surprise, it now seemed, was for Harlan. After a long, awkward silence he stammered, "Uh, that's g-great. Glad to hear it."

"Thank you. Well, tell me about you, what's been going on?"

When he started to pull away, she put out her hand. "Wait. Where're you going?"

"I gotta. Nice to see you. You look great, by the way. Bye."

He bolted down the corridor, ran outside to his car, and drove out of the lot as fast as he could, narrowly missing an entering Toyota.

It was beginning to rain, and by the time he turned off Gateway Boulevard and onto Old Conners Road, it was a downpour. Only one of his wipers worked, and his visibility was further diminished by the torrent of rainwater cascading off his roof. By the time he had gone thirty miles, the water was pooling on the two-lane heading west. The canal on his right was churning with waves, and drivers put on their head-lights. It wasn't letting up, and he found himself straining to see the road in front of him, the glare of approaching lights making it even more difficult.

Harlan was so upset by the turn of events that his anger boiled over, and he stepped on the gas to get as far away from Boynton Beach, Martha, and his dashed plans, as fast as he could.

Rather than heading away from the storm, he seemed to be heading directly into it. Lightning flashed in tighter inter-vals, but he didn't slow down or pull over.

His mind racing, tears filling his eyes, Harlan screamed at the top of his lungs in frustration. Nothing in his life ever worked out. Nothing!

Blind with rage he didn't see the flashing yellow light or the intersection up ahead until the semi pulled onto the black top and into his lane. By the time he saw the truck and slammed on the brakes, there was only about a hundred feet between them. His nearly treadless tires skidded across the pools of water like a hockey puck, the Cutlass spinning sideways and then flipping over twice, landing on the roof and sliding across the shoulder into the canal, sinking instantly with only its underbelly and wheels visible.

By the time highway patrol divers could get to the car, Harlan was long dead.

TOGETHER AGAIN

T
HE LIGHT WAS SO SEARING he had to squint just to look down the tunnel-like corridor. It was then he realized the voices he'd been hearing had diminished to almost nothing. He noticed too that he felt odd, as though his head and torso were no longer attached. He instinctively glanced at his body, but the harshness of the light made it impossible to see a thing.

What a dream, he thought. Way too real, but I should get up. As he customarily did when he first awoke, he opened one eye to look at the clock, hoping he still had time to doze for a few minutes.

Thing was, he couldn't see the clock, and then he realized that he wasn't tired—in fact, he'd never felt lighter. At the same time, there seemed no need to rush or to force himself awake. A feeling of warmth gradually permeated his entire being: not hot, just comfortable; sensual in a way.

Well, he sighed, might as well get out of bed. Everything he sensed, thought, and did miraculously occurred at the same time. It was as if it took only the slightest notion to complete anything he briefly considered. He gave a tiny shrug and was on his feet in an instant.

Heading to the bathroom, he became aware that he had already washed and dressed and must have eaten breakfast, because he didn't feel hungry.

He turned to kiss the photo of his wife Sophia, the one taken the year before she died, lifted it to his lips, touched them lightly to the image, smiled, and replaced it on the nightstand. There was no need to look in the mirror; he knew he was appropriately turned out for any occasion.

What happened next shook Raymond to the core, but only for the briefest of moments. In a flash the bright light dissipated, and he found himself, as if hovering, facing a field of clover, green and lush and sweet-smelling beyond any he had ever encountered. He entered it, and although he was wearing shoes, he could feel the tiny leaves between his toes, tickling his soles. A happy grin formed on his lips before the sound of waves caught his attention and the clover became warm, turquoise water lapping at his feet now nestled in soft white sand.

Rather than being frightened or curious, he completely accepted the moment and the manifestation of his every thought. Whatever triggered a vision became real; whatever transpired in his mind became tangible, incorporating all his senses.

Looking where the horizon and the sea melded into a shimmering haze, his eyes drifted upward to the swath of bright blue sky framing voluminous white clouds. He impulsively, implausibly, reached to touch them, and to his utter amazement he felt his fingertips brush their billowy edges. He raised his arm, extended his index finger, and poked at the azure expanse above him, feeling the sky as though it was dense, yet the softest of fabrics.

Ray, what's happening? he asked himself. I mean, it's like a dream, but real. I feel these things, I can touch them, smell them! Imperceptibly, his mind shifted, and he was standing before an enormous tree-lined boulevard, wider than any he imagined could ever be built. It seemed to stretch to infinity. There were no cars, no people, just a broad, pink cobblestone expanse leading to. . .he had no idea where. He wondered about the absence of people—and suddenly there were multitudes strolling quietly, smiling, all going in one direction. In their midst he saw that a tall, stately, serene woman had stopped and turned to face him. She had a parasol in one white-gloved hand and was motioning to him with the other, saying, "Follow me, she's waiting."

Without hesitation, he entered the concourse and approached her, but then she, along with all the others, vanished. Standing where she had been, he felt a current drawing him forward, urging him onward with the promise of absolute fulfillment.

He had no sense of time or how long he had been dreaming it, if it was a dream. What he did know was that he had no fear; he was aware of everything, no matter how fantastic. And he fully accepted it, all of it. There was no need to question what was taking place, no need to have answers or resolution; he just knew it was absolutely right.

He had the urge to sit and, oddly, felt the edge of a bench just behind him where none had been a moment before. Then he was seated and closed his eyes to contemplate what had occurred in the past few minutes—or had it been hours? He had no idea. It felt. . .timeless.

His surroundings seemed diaphanous as he looked around. He could feel everything without touching it. He sensed a current once again guiding him forward, but without any sense of urgency.

About to rise and follow it, he suddenly felt a jolt of energy and had a vision of some catastrophic life-altering experience from which he was both removed and part of, central to the action but aloof. He could hear a distant voice: "We're losing him! Come on, people. . .we're losing him." Then nothing. No noise, no people, no place. Ray was there and then he wasn't.

He rose from the bench and proceeded toward the horizon. The thoroughfare vanished, and he found himself standing under a large elm tree by a beautiful pond. The air was fragrant with springtime; a few magenta butterflies fluttered above him; across the pond, he saw a woman, but not the one he had seen with the parasol. This one seemed familiar, but she was too far away to be sure.

She waved to him, and her face lit up with a glorious smile, and even from his vantage point he knew in an instant who it was. Then they were facing each other, and he could feel her presence and held her hands before caressing her cheek, and they embraced. "Oh, Sophia, how I have missed you," he whispered in her ear.

"I know," she said softly, "it seems like a long time to you, but time has no meaning, it is infinite and finite all in one. For me it has been an instant, as it has now become for you. There is no past, no future only this—" she spread her arms and took in the vastness of all the light surrounding them— "timeless bliss."

"Are we dead?" he asked her.

"No, not dead, we are alive, more alive than before. We are soul mates and always have been. This is what we become, eternal souls. All creation is guided by love," she explained. "Two souls who have loved each other without restriction or objectives, without needs or transgression, two souls who shared in life what is offered in the beyond, will have it for eternity when they are joined together again."

TORMENT

TORI WAS STANDING in her living room, listening to the weather report, absentmindedly running her fingers through her hair, when Catherine called.

"Hey, big sister, whatcha doin'?"

"Good morning, Cat. What's up?"

Catherine sounded exasperated. "Would you believe Josh called and wants me to come in today? I mean really, on a Saturday?"

Tori knew instantly the reason for the call. "And you want to know if I can watch Bryan, right?"

"Could you? *Please?*"

"I'm going to the mall this morning," she replied. "Is it okay if I take him with me?"

"Sure, that'd be fine. I probably won't be done until three, though. That still all right?"

"No problem," Tori assured her. "...Have you heard from Jordan this week?"

"No. I'm a little worried. He missed our Skype yesterday, and his last letter was three days ago."

"Well, it's not like it hasn't happened before. I'm sure he's okay."

"Yeah, you're probably right. Just wish his tour was over, and he was home already."

"I know—it's been a long ten months. You dropping Bry off at my place on the way?"

"Yeah, I should be there in half an hour."

"Okay, I'll be ready."

"Love you, Tori. Thank you."

"Love you, too."

BRYAN, ALWAYS EXCITED to see his aunt, broke away from his mother and ran to Tori. "Whoa! You're getting so big!" she cried.

Tall, like his marine lieutenant father, the boy was dressed in tan pants and an oversized T-shirt that had the marine insignia scrawled across it, a baseball cap with a "B" embroidered on the front, and sneakers—all boy.

Catherine was eager to get going but genuinely sorry to drop the boy off on such short notice. Tori recognized her kid sister's conflict. "Not to worry, Cat—it's okay. We'll be fine. Go to work. I'll see you later."

Tori kissed her nephew on the top of his head and announced, "You and I are going to. . .the *mall!*"

"Can we go for Chinese food?"

"You bet we can."

Catherine smiled at the interplay, relieved that her son was in good hands. "I'll check in with you later, Tee. Bye." She waved and took two steps before turning and coming back to give Bryan a kiss. "Be good, Bry, and listen to Aunt Tori. Mommy loves you." She left without looking back.

AFTER AN HOUR AT THE MALL, up and down escalators, in and out of a few stores, Bryan stopped in the middle of the corridor and gripped his crotch. "I gotta pee," he said, so loud that a few passing shoppers laughed.

"Okay. Let's find a bathroom," his aunt suggested.

She took him by the hand and scurried toward the restrooms. Standing outside the facilities, she considered which to use— take him into the ladies' room, or let him go into the men's by himself? "Bryan, can you go in by yourself?"

"Yes! I'm eight."

"Yes, you are. I'll wait right here. Go on in."

Tori waited for what seemed an eternity until he came out.

"Did you wash your hands?" she asked.

"I did," he said proudly.

"Good boy. You *are* growing up, aren't you?"

"I am. I'm almost nine!"

She made sure he didn't get too far ahead of her as they cruised the mall; she stopped to buy cosmetics and a few other items and then went to Great Wall, as she promised. The place had a large open dining area and was chaotic at lunchtime— two birthday parties with children of all sizes, and a few kids running back and forth getting in the way of the waiters.

Bryan was delighted and chattered all the way through lunch. Before leaving, Tori asked him if he had to go to the bathroom again.

"Nope, I'm good," he said, chomping on fortune cookies.

"Well, *I* have to use the restroom, so wait here for me, Bry, and I'll be right back."

She pointed to the purchases on the seat next to her. "Keep your eye on these packages, okay?"

"Okay. I'll start reading this." He held up *Bridge to Ter-*

abithia, the book she had bought him earlier that day.

She stopped before entering the ladies' room and turned to wave at him, but he was staring at the book cover and didn't notice.

Tori had to wait a few minutes for an empty stall, washed her hands, and went back to get Bryan. Heading in the direction where they'd been sitting, she didn't see him and looked around to make sure she had the right spot. She saw her packages, but no Bryan—his new book lying face down on the table.

While scanning the room she called out, "Bryan!" but her voice was lost in the din of laughter and clatter of dishes. Not yet panicked, she scoured the restaurant looking for him. She went back to the restrooms, pushed open the men's room door and called out, "Bryan, are you in there?"

No answer. A teenage boy was about to enter, and Tori stopped him. "Excuse me. Could you please see if my nephew is in the bathroom? His name is Bryan."

"Sure, okay."

The boy went inside and Tori could hear him calling Bryan's name. A minute later he came out and told her Bryan wasn't there.

Tori began frantically shouting, "Bryan? *Bryan!*"

People looked up and noting her angst, the restaurant manager immediately came over. "Is problem, lady?"

"I can't find my nephew. He was sitting—" she pointed to the booth— "over there. I went to the bathroom and—"

"Oh, yes, yes," the man acknowledged. "Boy in marine shirt, yes? I was by door and saw him walk out with a man."

"Who? What man?" she asked, staring in the direction of the exit.

"Uh, man in suit. They look okay together, so I didn't think anything. You want me to call security?"

Tori shouted, "Yes!" and ran into the corridor, looked in both directions and toward the escalators, but didn't see them.

Her composure was beginning to unravel. *"Bryan!"* she screamed again.

People turned to look at her; two security men appeared from a side door off the main walkway and approached her. "You the woman looking for a lost child?" one of them calmly inquired.

Tori stammered, "Y-yes. He was here a few minutes ago, and now—"

The second guard stepped forward and gestured toward a bench in the corridor. "Please, ma'am, sit down here. Let me ask you some questions."

Tori took a deep breath and tried to compose herself, but couldn't stay seated.

"You said 'he'? How old?"

"He's nine—n-no, he's eight."

The guards glanced at each other. "Is he your son?"

"No. My nephew."

The guy nodded. "Were you here with anyone else besides him?"

"No."

"What is he wearing?"

"Uh—" Tori tried to think, momentarily confused— "a blue T-shirt, tan pants." She brought her hand to her mouth. "The shirt has a U.S. Marine logo on it."

The first guard pulled at his walkie-talkie and spoke into it. "Miki, we have a lost child. Eight-year-old boy in a blue shirt. Name is Bryan," he looked at Tori. "Did you say he's wearing tan pants?"

She nodded repeatedly. "And a baseball cap. Blue."

"Did you get that, Miki? Blue T-shirt, tan pants, baseball cap."

Within seconds an announcement came over the speaker system asking anyone with information to dial the operator on a red mall emergency phone or to contact any security guard.

One guard remained with Tori; the other was joined by a third in a golf cart and cruised off in search of Bryan. The parking lot patrol was notified and set out to scour the area as well.

Almost twenty minutes passed before the reports came back negative. Local police were brought, in and Tori nervously answered their questions, the first one being, "What is your relationship to the missing child?" followed by, "Can we contact the parents?" to which Tori responded, "I'll call his mother, she works about twenty minutes from here. His father is serving in Afghanistan."

TORI, THE POLICE, AND THE GUARD all went to the security office to look at mall surveillance videos spanning the time from when Tori and Bryan entered the restaurant until ten minutes after security arrived.

Afraid, but knowing she had to call her sister, she prayed that somehow Bryan would show up in the next few minutes. Based on the restaurant manager's remarks, they searched the video for a man in a suit and saw three of them in the restaurant at the time Tori and Bryan were there.

Two sat together on the opposite side of the dining room. The third sat alone, diagonally opposite Tori and Bryan. He glanced in their direction for a few minutes at a time, smiling, at one point moving his hand under the table, out of sight.

Tori could be seen leaving the table and heading to the restroom. When she disappeared from view, the man in the suit rose and came over to Bryan. He stood by the table with his back to the camera and, after a few seconds, sat down opposite him. They exchanged some words, and the man reached across the table, tousled Bryan's hair, took hold of his hand, and led him out of the restaurant. There was no sign of struggle or resistance on Bryan's part, but he looked over his shoulder toward the restroom before he was squired out of sight.

Tori made the dreaded call to Catherine. "Please listen carefully. I-I—" her voice broke and she began to sob— "Cath, you have to get to the mall right away. Bryan is, is. . .he's missing."

"*What!*" she screamed. "What do you mean, *missing? Where?* Oh, God! Oh, my God!"

"Maybe we should send a patrol car for her," offered one of the policemen.

Tori pleaded into the phone, "Catherine, wait until the police come for you. Please. You shouldn't—"

"I'm not waiting. Where are you?"

"Please, Cath. Just hold on for—"

"*No, Goddamn it!* I'm coming right now. Where the fuck are you?"

"We're in the mall security office. It's on the second floor, south entrance."

Catherine hung up.

WITHIN TWENTY MINUTES OF THE CALL Catherine burst into the office, out of breath and terrified.

Tori, seeing her, started to tremble. "Cathy, Cathy, I am so sorry, I was only gone for a couple—"

Cathy's eyes widened in disbelief, "You *left* him? *Alone?* What the. . .Tori, are you *crazy?*"

It took a long time before she was calm enough to be questioned by the police. Meanwhile, security searched every bathroom, every store, storage area, and food outlet, top to bottom.

Further investigation of surveillance videos captured an image of the man and Bryan in the parking lot getting into a car, but the license plate was obscured from view. An APB alert went to law enforcement with a vehicle description along with digitally enhanced images of the man and of Bryan.

CATHERINE AND TORI KEPT VIGIL at the mall office for hours until it became unbearable and the two of them went back to Cathy's house to wait for a phone call.

By nightfall, Tori had called the family doctor, a personal friend, who stopped by the house and prescribed something to calm them both down.

A little after eight a car pulled into the driveway. Catherine ran to the door, expecting the police, hoping Bryan would be with them. Tori came up behind her just as she opened the door and saw two marines in full dress uniforms.

One of them quietly asked, "Excuse me, ma'am, are you Mrs. Jordan Crenshaw?"

It took only a few seconds before she realized why they were there. "No! No! *No!*" she screamed and collapsed into Tori's arms before slipping to the ground.

Tori, momentarily dazed, stood there staring silently at the Marines before she asked for their assistance getting Catherine into the house, where they delivered the news that Jordan had been killed, made unimaginably worse by Bryan's disappearance.

Tori explained the circumstances, and that she was Catherine's sister. She rallied enough to take down the information about how Jordan died, when to expect his remains, and was given a contact number for the regional Gold Star family counseling group.

Catherine had fallen into a catatonic stupor, and a frightened Tori called the doctor again. By the time he arrived, several reporters and a television crew had gathered outside the home, seeking an interview about Bryan's disappearance and unaware of the newly added trauma.

The doorbell rang, followed by knocking. Thinking it was the doctor, Tori went to answer and found a reporter and a cameraman on the doorstep.

"Hello, we're from—"

"Get out of here! Get *away!*" she screamed, and slammed the door.

She called one of the detectives and begged him to keep the media at bay. After telling him about Jordan's death, he saw to it that a policeman was stationed outside the house to keep reporters from approaching.

Barely managing her own grief, Tori stayed to take care of her sister, to field phone calls and do whatever she could to comfort Catherine; an impossible task. Heavily sedated, Catherine remained bedridden, at times incoherent and minimally functional.

Two days later, the abductor was identified as a registered pedophile and sexual predator, but when police raided his home, they were told he had moved, address unknown, a direct violation of his parole.

A few more agonizing days passed and with it the hope Bryan would be found alive, but then on the afternoon of the sixth day the abductor was seen lurking outside a Chuck E. Cheese on the opposite side of town. A suspicious store manager called the police. "I'm not sure if this means anything," he told Dispatch, "but I've been watching this guy for a while and he's kinda creepy?"

The call was routed to the same detective Tori had spoken with, who, on hearing the description, recognized the guy as the suspect. He and his partner immediately headed to the location, arrived within minutes, and made the arrest. Their interrogation was a short affair, eliciting a full confession and leading them to a fenced-in, clapboard house on the edge of town, where Bryan was found locked in a windowless basement, shackled to a metal framed bed, terrified, but alive.

WHEN BRYAN RAN INTO THE HOUSE and threw his arms around her, Catherine screamed and exploded in a torrent of tears and mixed emotions. They hugged each other for a long time, and that night he stayed in the room with his mother.

They left telling him about his father for the following day. Coupled with his kidnapping ordeal, the shock of losing his dad was almost impossible for Bryan to process.

A few days later a military burial was conducted at the local cemetery, and mother and son were handed the ceremoniously folded triangular flag that had draped Jordan's coffin.

Neither fully healed from the loss or the abduction.

Tori's agonizing sense of guilt remained with her for the rest of her life.

TOUGH TIMES

HEADLIGHTS GLARED ALONG the two-lane black top adjacent to Cardiff's Bar & Grill; the afternoon light had dissolved into dusk. The regulars had been at the bar for hours nursing a beer along with their sorrows and complaints. Others straggled in soon after five o'clock with no place else to go.

As a tavern keeper, Cardiff McCracken wasn't much of a talker, but he nodded pretty well and every now and then poured courtesy drinks for what he referred to as "the local gentry."

Petey Maguire, like most of the others hunched over a draft or boilermaker, had been coming to Cardiff's long before the layoffs. Martha Figgs, a heavy-set, ruddy-faced woman of indeterminate age, sat at the far end, a cigarette poised mid-air clenched in chubby fingers. She had driven a mill truck before the closure.

Fact is, most of the men and women in the innocuously named Centerville had lost their jobs when the mill closed. Scraping by until their unemployment ran out, many ultimately became destitute. A few just up and left for the big city to find work and a hoped-for fresh start doing who knew what.

Centerville was an American cliché. At first, the mill lay-offs were minimal, mostly the older employees and then the newest hires, but soon larger chunks of the populace were cut, until only a handful of the original 318 workers were kept on, and then the whole place shut down.

The lucky ones, if you could call them that, got jobs at Boyd's Dairy Farm or the Home Depot two counties over; several others retired on meager pensions after thirty years of labor in the lumber yard. It was a familiar story for towns that didn't keep up with technology, where inhabitants held fast to a small-town mindset confined by narrow political and religious beliefs and no opportunity or desire to change.

McCracken had already given up trying to lighten the mood in the place; he'd even stopped buffing the mahogany bar or the brass fittings on its footrail.

Like the town, the bar's shabbiness was a sign of life gone wrong. Along the knurled edge of the counter, a series of burns marked forgotten cigarette butts; these were joined by nicks in the wood and initials carved with a pen knife when Cardiff had his back turned.

The plastic-cushioned stools, worn away in spots, were patched with mismatched colored tape. The linoleum tile flooring, put down by the first owner in '54, was broken and scarred from one end of the room to the other, some replaced with thin plywood squares.

The juke box records, all of them 45 rpm, hadn't been changed in decades, and playing one still only cost a quarter, if you could play them at all, which you couldn't because it had been inoperable since 1986.

THERE WAS A POOL TABLE in the back, coin operated, but that had been busted when a drunk biker, passing through, tried unsuccessfully to rip the money box out of the thing. It had taken Petey, Marcus, and eventually Daryl the Sheriff, to put the guy in the drunk tank for the night and send him on his way in the morning.

The tiny school had closed for lack of funding, and the state had decided to bus children twenty-six miles to Dunlap rather than to subsidize education for 640 inhabitants, only forty-six of them children.

And so it went, day after day, week after week, dismally trundling along, waiting for. . .what? Prayers to be answered, lottery tickets to pay off, some new factory to open?

Then it all changed. Petey had been grousing out loud one day about how other places became famous overnight, and big Hollywood movie companies came in with trailers and trucks and hundreds of people who filled hotels and restaurants for miles around, "Bringing lots of money with 'em," he said.

The gentry scoffed at first, brushing the notion aside like so many other ridiculous comments Petey made when he had a few, which was typically by five in the afternoon.

"Ah, Petey, whatta you know?" mumbled Marcus Tidswell, perched three stools away. "Why in hell would anyone want to make a movie here, or how'd they even know we was here? Who in hell ever heard of Centerville, except maybe folks who live here?" He squinted at Cardiff and added as an afterthought, "Hey, whadda you think, McCracken?"

Cardiff nodded several times, offered a crooked smile without a word in reply, and continued mopping up beer spills; Marcus shrugged.

Minutes passed without further comment before Petey

looked up from his half-empty glass, eyes suddenly alert.

"Just s'pose that was to happen. How much do ya think we're talkin'. . .money, I mean?"

"First place," Marcus replied, "We ain't talkin', and second place, it ain't gonna happen. So just forget it."

Petey, dejected but not quite over the idea said, "A man can dream, can't he?"

"You never was much more than a dreamer, Pete," Marcus shot back. "That's why you're still sittin' at the bar and not working behind it."

"Don't be so mean-spirited, Marcus." The scolding came from none other than. . .Cardiff McCracken, the first full sentence he uttered in longer than anyone could recall.

All eyes, wide with astonishment, were suddenly trained on the bartender.

"Let me tell you something," he started. "I listen to you folks day in day out, mumbling 'bout this and that, feelin' sorry for yourselves, not makin' any move to get straightened out. It ain't right."

He took a breath and looked at each of them one at a time, making sure they were paying attention.

"Listen, the mill shut down," he continued. "It's a fact of life. Happens all the time—businesses start up, businesses go out. They don't owe you nothing. They paid you for your work, and when they couldn't do it no more, they closed down." He shook his head. "S'all there is to it. They lost *their* jobs, too."

There was a long silence while the stool sitters shifted in their seats, not looking up.

After a few minutes, Cardiff started again. "I don't mean no harm. I know how hard it is. How little you all got left.

And I am truly sorry for that. You know I extend credit and don't ask for payment. You got bills to pay aside from your bar tabs. I know that, too."

He stopped talking as abruptly as he had begun. Nothing further was said on the subject, and shortly afterward, one by one, all the customers shuffled out into the night with a only a slight wave or nod in Cardiff's direction, a few dollars left by their drained glasses.

A COUPLE OF DAYS LATER, sometime during the wee hours of the morning, Cardiff's Bar & Grill burned to the ground. The cause of the fire was never determined and Cardiff Mc-Cracken was never heard from again.

TRANSPARENT

I T BEGAN WITH A PHONE CALL. "Swain! It is Ghareeb," cried the excited voice. "I have most special news." "Ahmad, my dear friend," replied Chester Swain, "how good to hear your voice. So tell me, what is this special news?"

Ghareeb animatedly replied, "It has been kept secret for several months now, but it is time that you know. A tomb has been discovered not far from the Hawara Pyramid, a few kilometers from Al-Fayyum. You *must come*...we need you most urgently."

"Slow down," Chester replied. "Nothing new has been discovered in that region for years. Where is it exactly?"

"It was just under our feet all this time. But you must *see* it. It is most fantastic. It fits into the same timeline of Amenmhat III, 12th dynasty!"

"...That is *quite* noteworthy, Doctor—but why the urgency for me to come now? It has been there for four thousand years."

Ghareeb could hardly contain his enthusiasm.

"We have just found glyphs suggesting it is the funeral chamber of the pharaoh's physician."

At this, Chester's interest was piqued. It was his area of expertise—ancient Egyptian medical practices.

"Ah, I see. Yes, yes, I am very interested. What have you learned?"

"Not much more than that. There are indecipherable symbols. Many we have never encountered. Perhaps you will be able to help. No, you *will* be able to help."

It didn't take long for Chester to make up his mind. "Give me a few days to tidy up some affairs, and I will fly to Cairo as soon as possible. I will call you when I am booked. My respects and good wishes to your beautiful Halima. *"Ma'as salaama!"*

"Es-salaam alaykum!" replied Ghareeb.

THREE DAYS LATER, AHMED MET CHESTER at Cairo International airport, and they immediately headed to the site. Several tents, and canopies for shade, marked the location abutting a low mound of mud-bricks barely distinguishable from the surrounding dunes.

A team of archeologists were hunkering over artifacts and photographs, as well as a series of images taken by robot. On one large table stood several pictures of the hieroglyphs Ghareeb had spoken of. Scanning them with a magnifying glass, Chester was awed. He looked up. "I concur," he said. "The symbols clearly suggest a physician is entombed here. When can I see the sarcophagus?"

A small, dark-skinned man in khaki shorts and a field shirt stepped closer to the table. "My dear American friend, I am Professor Ammon Elsayed. The burial chamber walls are very fragile, so we have waited until you arrived before attempting entry."

"That is a great honor, Professor. I am most grateful."

Elsaye smiled wryly. "It was not meant so much as an honor but a cautionary measure. You see, we have not been able to decipher all the markings at the entry, and. . .and fear there might be a curse."

Chester studied Elsayed's face to see if he was joking, but there was no hint of it. "I understand," he replied. "And you think I can interpret the meaning?"

"Yes, precisely what we are hoping, *Inshallah!*"

"Yes, if Allah wills it."

For several days, Ghareeb, Elsayed, and Chester gingerly entered and exited the chamber, taking photos, making notes, and discussing their findings well into the night. Images were sent to the universities of Alexandria and Cairo for opinions and comment. Various interpretations were suggested, but none were accepted until, like a clap of thunder, Chester himself shouted, "Ammon, you're right! It does suggest something will happen to the one who—" he hesitated, looked again at the icons, and muttered, "but I can't figure out what that something is."

Ammon stroked at his beard, peered at Ahmed, and nodded slowly. "Who's the superstitious one now?"

Chester grinned, glanced at the symbols in the photograph, and drew the magnifier across the pictograms until he came to a section damaged by time.

"I'm not sure it *is* a curse, but maybe it's a warning of sorts."

"Such as?" inquired Ghareeb. "Why a warning if there is no curse?"

"There's only one way to find out," Chester told him.

"I knew you were the man to do this," said his colleague.

"When do you want to go?"

"Tomorrow. We'll go tomorrow."

RESTLESS FROM ANTICIPATION rather than fear, Chester barely slept and was dressed at sun up. Downing a cup of pungent Turkish tea and *börek* filled with cheese and minced meat, he awoke the loudly snoring Elsayed and nodded at Ghareeb, who was sitting on a camel saddle in the sand.

The team was assembled; logistics for the entry were reviewed, roles and positions defined for each of the participants, and most important, contingency plans discussed should any extreme measures be required.

Within an hour, carrying halogen lanterns, they were inching their way along a labyrinth of tunnels toward the burial chamber, accompanied by two assistants, one bearing tools for opening the crypt, the other video equipment to record the event.

Standing outside the sealed entry wall, which they all thought must be where the tomb lay, Ghareeb gave the signal to make an opening through the partition.

"Wait!" cried Chester. "Let me do it. If there *is*. . . if there *is* something, let me be the one. I don't believe in spells or curses." In a more serious vein, he added, "But just in case."

The assistant handed him a large canvas bag containing excavating tools and then stepped away. Ghareeb and Ammon shook Chester's hand, joined the assistants, and moved a few meters down the tunnel. Ghareeb waved and said, "*Allah Merrech!*"

"Thank you," Chester called back. "I may need it."

His first thrust elicited a hollow thud, suggesting there was open space behind the wall. The second and third created a small opening the size of an orange through which seeped a miasmic blue green vapor that engulfed him. He dropped the tool and swiped at the gas, trying to avoid inhaling any, but it was too late. He coughed and spit, but nothing discharged.

"Chet, are you alright?" called Ghareeb.

Before Chester could reply, the wall in front of him collapsed and he was enveloped in the gaseous substance. Waving his arms to ward it off, he stumbled backward and fell to the floor. In the short time it took for the team to reach him, the mysterious fog had vanished.

"Mr. Swain!" Elsayed cried out. "Are you all right? What happened? What was that?"

Somewhat dazed but otherwise unharmed, Chester scrambled to his feet. "I'm fine, fine. Not sure what that was, but I feel fine."

They decided to take precautions, left the tunnel, and went back to the campsite, where Chester was attended to by the team doctor. All his vital signs checked out, and he felt no after- effects, but they decided to stay out of the tunnel for seventy-two hours.

Chester passed the time poring over the photos of the glyphs and reworking his interpretations of their meaning. He was puzzled by one issue in particular—the odor of the gas that had engulfed him, and what it might have been. The team decided to do a chemical analysis of the clothing he'd been wearing at the time and brought it back with them to Cairo.

The sarcophagus would be moved to Cairo and opened under the "strictest of conditions," insisted Elsayed before looking at Chester and telling him, "I am saddened you will not be in attendance for the opening."

Chester, clearly conflicted, said, "I, too, am sorry, my

friends, but I have run out of time and I am scheduled to return for the launch of my book."

Ghareeb assured him he would be in touch as soon as clothing analysis was completed. "I trust all will go well my friend. *Allah Merrech!*"

CHESTER'S BOOK ON ANCIENT medical practices and mummification was, appropriately, going to be unveiled in the Egyptian Hall of the Pharaohs at the Museum of Natural Sciences. Still jet-lagged from his journey, he took the elevator to the second floor rather than the ornate marble staircase.

A crush of people followed him into the compartment, seemingly unaware he was the main attraction for the evening. Feeling queasy and claustrophobic, Chester stood quietly at the rear, gazing straight ahead. The doors slid closed, and the box started its slow ascent.

As he stared into the back of a wide-bodied man only inches from his face, a startling vision occurred to him. Chester thought he was hallucinating, perhaps from exhaustion or the stifling air in the lift. From the time the elevator began to move until it came to a gentle stop, Chester could see the man's spine through his jacket—the vertebrae, every rib encasing his organs. He saw the man's heart beating, the lungs expanding and diaphragm moving up and down. He blinked twice and shook his head to rid it of the uncanny, all-too-real image. Last off the elevator, he headed directly to the restroom, where he bathed his face in cold water and took several very deep breaths.

The crowd of attendees, the introductions, and the cocktail chatter served to shake the peculiar experience from his mind— until he took the podium and began to speak.

As was his custom when addressing an audience, he looked at those seated in the first few rows and made momentary eye contact in an effort to identify friendly faces. A woman in the second row had her head down, reading the cover of his book. At first, he thought she was wearing a knitted hat—until he realized he was looking at her brain. He gasped, pulled back, and almost stumbled off the platform.

A few in the audience began to whisper behind cupped hands. Chester could see his editor rise from her chair and take a step forward, but he indicated he was quite well, and she stopped in the aisle. His eyes still fixed on her, he could see through the fabric of her fashionable suit and was stunned by the sight of her thumping heart, her lungs, her intestines and liver. . . and then he fainted.

While he was being attended to, a voice mail message appeared on Chester's home phone: "*Ma'as salaama!* Chester, my friend, it is Ghareeb. We have some good news. We have just identified two of the substances on your garment. Also, our cryptographers are very close to deciphering the symbols, and we should have a translation quite soon. Have a good evening."

By the time Chester was helped to his feet, he was a in a state of panic. Every person within his field of vision was transparent to him. He could see blood and body fluids coursing through their systems, food being digested, a pregnant woman's fetus, a man's lungs being eaten by cancerous cells.

He began to shake violently, perspiration poured out of him, and his face frighteningly contorted. Crazed with fear, he pulled away from any offer of help and raced out of the room, down the marble stairs, falling down the last three of them, scrambling to his feet, and out into the night.

Seeking refuge from people, from the horror he had just encountered, he rushed across the street and scurried into the park.

Afraid to sit under a street lamp for fear of being found, he hunkered down on the grass, gasping for air, under a towering oak. He sat with his head between his legs until his breathing calmed, and then he slowly sat up.

The moonless night gratefully shielded him from the outside world, and he used the solitude to ascertain what was happening. Was he actually seeing inside people, or was it some bizarre psychosomatic disorder?

He nodded off several times during the next few hours, each time waking with a start, still terrified by the experience, convinced it was real.

The light of dawn arrived, and with it Chester's ability to see his surroundings. He pulled his sleeve back to look at his watch and saw, instead, the cords of veins and sinew surrounding the bones in his wrist. The image thrust him once again into his terrifying, confusing situation. He squeezed his eyes shut and tried to blot the vision from his mind. An early-morning jogger ran past without seeing him, but Chester looked up in time to see what was becoming commonplace—the interior of the man's body.

Wild with fright, he jumped up and tore out of the park, screaming and running at full tilt, trying to escape the visions. A patrol car with two police officers caught up with and subdued him, and took him directly to the psychiatric hospital across town. Quickly sedated, Chester was placed under observation and later diagnosed as delusional and psychotic and was institutionalized indefinitely.

He never heard the messages left by Ghareeb. The last one

said: "*Ma'as salaama*! We are not understanding why you do not return our call. I have news. It appears the gas had two substances, sulfuric compound and silver bromide; both are used in the processing of X-rays. We are not sure why or how they could have come to be in the tunnel walls, so. . .if you have experienced any peculiarities, any health issues, you must let us know at once. Also, we have translated the inscription by the burial chamber entrance, but are not completely clear what it means. It says, *Whosoever shall enter will forever see inside.*

TRAVELING COMPANION

"D R. BARTOSKI WILL BE WITH YOU in a few minutes. Please have a seat." The nurse was obviously trying to be kind. "Can I get you a glass of water, a cup of coffee perhaps?"

Geoff Coleman barely managed to whisper, "No, thank you."

She left him then, her crisply starched, immaculately white uniform making a rough sound as it brushed against the desk on her way out.

It was the second time Geoff had been in the doctor's consultation room, where the pronouncements and explanations were proffered. There was little in it that qualified as decorative. It was, rather, officious: a desk, two green leather armchairs on one side, a high-back executive chair opposite them where the doctor sat, a group of certificates and diplomas on the wall indicating membership in a professional society, board certification, and degrees in specialized medical fields from institutions of higher learning.

The mahogany desk had the usual framed photo of a smiling wife and children, a brass table lamp with a green glass shade, and a large, leather-trimmed blotter. Did anyone still use a fountain pen? Geoff wondered. The walls were an insipid beige. There were no windows.

Being asked to return for a "chat" with the doctor didn't come as a surprise to Geoff; he had, after all, asked for a second opinion. Third, actually—the first diagnosis had been two months earlier, in Denver, where he had been living since his wife ran off with her ski instructor. Did women really do that? he wondered.

At that original consultation, Dr. Crimmins, who was listed as insurance plan-approved, had also sat behind a desk while Geoff awaited the results of the CAT scan and the MRI.

When he delivered his opinion to an anxious Geoff, Crimmins had lacked grace or anything remotely close to a bedside manner, and launched right into it. "Mr. Cole—" he had peered at the chart— "I'm afraid, Mr. Coleman, that you have a brain tumor."

The words had smacked into Geoff, rocking him to the core. The doctor had lifted the scan image and pointed to a dark spot in the corner of the oval that was Geoff's brain.

Stunned, speechless, Geoff had raised a hand over his mouth to keep from throwing up his lunch.

"Are you okay, Mr. Coleman?" the doctor had asked with unconscious irony.

An incredulous Geoff, his anger rising, almost hissed, "You just *told* me that I am not!"

The physician had looked away, not making eye contact, and pointed to the spot on the picture of Geoff's diseased cranium. "The lesion appears to be a tumor the size of a walnut. Unfortunately it has vascularized."

"It's *what?*"

Crimmins had sat back and recited the next sentence as if he was delivering a baseball score. "Geoff—may I call you Geoff?—the type of tumor this is, well, I'm afraid it's inoperable. It's become entangled with blood vessels, and as such it would just be too dangerous to remove."

The kiss of death, at least according to Rudolph P. Crimmins, M.D.

"Of course," he'd continued, "you probably want to get a second opinion. And I understand if you do."

Geoff had nodded slowly but had barely been listening by then, and as he rose from the chair, he had not reached across the desk to shake hands. "Uh, thank you. I will do that," was all he had managed to say before leaving the office.

The next several days had been a blur of confused thoughts, emotional upheaval, and fear. It had taken Geoff a while before he could muster the energy and focus to begin searching for a more experienced specialist to review his case, someone who might tell him how wrong Crimmins was—or so he hoped.

It had taken almost two weeks to find the highly recommended Dr. Bartoski, a specialist in brain cancer and a well-regarded surgeon. Another two weeks had passed before Geoff could get an appointment. The first visit was a consultation and review of the original MRI scans, after which new MRI and CT scans had been ordered, plus a biopsy, and that was how Geoff had wound up in the office for a second time.

With a full head of salt-and pepper hair, compassionate blue eyes, and a tall, thin frame, Bartoski appeared much younger than his fifty-four years, Geoff's age. The only telltale sign of it, though it may only have been a lack of sleep, were the dark circles under his eyes.

Bartoski ambled into the consultation room, chart in hand, crossed over to Geoff, and shook his hand. "Nice to see you, Mr. Coleman. I'm sorry it isn't under better circumstances." He sat in the chair next to him. "Given all that you've been dealing with the past few weeks, I hesitate to ask, but how are you feeling?" He said it without a touch of irony but with gentleness and sincerity.

"I feel all right, I guess, just exhausted."

"Understandable. Well, I suppose we must get to the business at hand. Shall we?" He didn't wait for a response. "Mr. Coleman, as I mentioned last time, our policy here at the Center is to have our team of specialists review each set of images individually before meeting for a group discussion. Our consensus is that, yes, you do have a malignant tumor. It appears to have grown infinitesimally since your first series was done, but that might only be an illusion. On the other hand—and this is the complicated part—it has indeed become entangled with blood vessels, and if surgery were attempted, it might do more harm than good. The location of the cancerous growth is such that removing it would most likely result in loss of speech. There is also the likelihood you would lose motor skills and some bodily functions." He paused and looked at Geoff. "Are you following me on this?"

Geoff heaved an enormous sigh, his shoulders drooped, and a minute groan emanated from somewhere deep within. "Yes," he all but sobbed.

Bartoski nodded and sat behind the desk before continuing. "I'm sure you have some questions. Take your time."

"How long?" he asked, wondering how many times a patient had uttered those words in this very office.

"Best case scenario, without any treatment, six months.

We might be able to extend that to a year, possibly longer."

"How?" Geoff was too stricken to speak more than one word.

"For one, there's radiation that can be done with pinpoint accuracy so as not to damage surrounding tissue. Then of course, chemotherapy or a combination of the two, but the side effects can be devastating. And as a last resort. . .surgery, but that would be invasive and we might find there is nothing we can do once we get in there."

Geoff upped his response to two words: "I see."

Minutes ticked by in silence before the doctor leaned forward on his elbows and clasped his hands. "I'm sorry, but I have surgery in a little while, and I have to leave you now. I know this is all too much to absorb at the moment, and you have a lot to think about. But please get back to me as soon as you decide how you'd like to proceed. And of course, you might want to consider another opinion. . .just to put your mind at rest. At least on what your approach needs to be."

"Thank you doctor, I. . .I'm not sure what I want to do right now."

They shook hands, and Bartoski left the room. Geoff followed a minute later, sat in his car, rested his head on the steering wheel, and cried.

TWO WEEKS LATER, he quit his job, sold his stocks, cashed in his bonds, and brought his will up to date. He had no children and only a few living relatives, most of them too old to understand what he was dealing with.

He mapped out itineraries for a trip around Europe, something he had always dreamed of but been too timid or busy to do.

At night, lying in bed, he sometimes thought he could feel the tumor growing in his head, yet for some strange reason, the original warning headaches had gone away.

During the day he felt perfectly fine, had no symptoms at all, and called Doctor Bartoski to ask if he might be in remission, but was told that, unless he had undergone the radiation therapy, it was highly unlikely.

As for the options given to him, Geoff decided he wanted none of them. He didn't want to live with the false hope that he'd be cured or risk being a vegetable if surgery failed. When the time came, and he knew it would, he would take whatever drugs were offered to ease the pain and simply let it take him.

What he discovered was a resolve to live life to the fullest while he was here, and he eventually came to realize that was all anyone could do, or should. He could be hit by a falling piano or safe; did anyone really drop safes from the top of a building like they did in cartoons? he wondered.

He read Eckhart Tolle, and the Zen masters; he practiced mediation and took his time shaving or lingered over a second cup of coffee.

He went out to dinner and to the movies, and, for the first time in his life, ran an ad in the personal columns under the headline *Seeking Traveling Companion*. Did anyone ever meet a love interest through those things? he wondered. Was it fair of him to even be doing it? The ad was honest—to a point:

Man seeking woman 45-50 years of age willing to travel. All expenses paid by interesting, attractive man. Objective: enjoyment, laughter, good conversation and, if the stars align, romance.

It was a perverse idea and would undoubtedly attract loonies, one of whom he now considered himself to be. But then, what did he have to lose? It might provide some interesting conversation and at least get his mind off the pending doom.

To keep a reasonable distance from inquires and avoid as much weirdness as possible, he gave only an email address, one different from his regular account.

As he expected, the initial handful of responses were odd, if not downright nuts. A few came from men, some men and women offered themselves as sex slaves, one woman was a dominatrix, and others were looking for an eccentric pen pal. He nixed all of them without so much as a reply.

Two weeks later, he received a short, but very promising note:

> *Hi, I saw your advertisement in the personal column and at first thought it was a joke, or worse, scary. I love to travel, just left my job after 23 years, and am intrigued. So please reply and tell me more. Michelle.*

Geoff was equally intrigued and for some reason believed every word of it, however brief. They began writing several times a day and, in the evening, longer, more detailed emails, and his heart skipped a beat when she suggested they meet; coffee at first, in a public place.

He knew that, whatever risk there might be, it diminished exponentially in comparison to the journey they would take together should she agree to do it.

The first week he and Michelle, which actually turned out to be her real name, spent several days together and then every day the following week. It was thrilling and quixotic, and if there was any problem at all, it was how and when he would tell her what he really wanted. By the end of the third week, they were as close to being in love as their short time together had allowed, and it only made his confession that much harder. He knew it must be said, that he owed it to her, and he expected to lose her right then and there, believing she would be angry, and had every right to be, about being strung along on a hopeless journey with a not-so-happy ending.

At dinner one evening, after discussing when they might go to Europe, she blurted out, "This is crazy. You know that, right?"

"Yeah, I know, but isn't it wonderful?"

They spent the next afternoon going over travel brochures, picking places to stay, things they wanted to see and do. He watched her face light up every time something caught her attention; the smiles and giggles emanating from her were lovable and charming, and he wondered for the hundredth time why she wasn't with someone else, how the timing of meeting her was both cruel and joyous.

They slept together that night, blissfully entwined, lovingly embracing each other until morning. The sunlight came streaming into the room, flecks of dust floating in it, warming the wooden floor and reflecting harshly into his eyes. And before he could kiss her good morning, an intense shooting pain bore into his head like a needle, followed by the sensation that his head was being crushed. He instinctively pressed his hands against the sides of his head and tried not to cry out.

Michelle sat up abruptly and stared at him in panic. "Geoffrey! What's the *matter*? Are you all right?"

He could barely respond, "Oh, God, what the—"

It lasted almost thirty seconds before subsiding enough for him to look at her.

"Geoff? Do you get migraines often?"

He turned to face her, slowly so as not to rattle his brain. His eyes welled up with tears, not from the pain, but because he knew it was well past the time to tell her. He took a deep breath. "Uh, no. . .yeah, I'll be fine. I'm okay."

He leaned in and kissed her. She was tentative, obviously concerned, but then returned the kiss, put her arms around his neck, and held him for a moment, kissed him again, and murmured, "That was a lovely night."

"Yes it was, and you are a phenomenal woman, and. . . ."

His voice trailed off; he disengaged from her grip and got out of bed. "I'll put up some coffee. You can get in the bathroom first."

He grabbed his briefs, pulled them on, and shuffled to the kitchen, listening for the bathroom door to close before he pressed the tips of his fingers hard against his temples. He took a deep breath and reached for the coffee canister only to have it slip through his numbing fingers, spilling the contents onto the floor.

He wondered whether she had heard the commotion; when the shower began to run, bent down to clean up the mess, scooped it back into the can, then doled out enough to make six cups.

Straightening up, he felt dizzy and almost lost his balance, regained his footing, and went gingerly to the bedroom to pull on a pair of jeans and a T-shirt. He returned to the kitchen, poured a mug of Arabica, and brought it to her.

An appreciative smile came to her face and she kissed him lightly. "Thank you my marvelous man," she purred.

"English muffin okay?" he asked.

"Yes, sounds good."

He brushed past her, quickly washed his face and hands, swished some mouthwash, and ran a comb through his hair. While he was in the bathroom, she dressed in her clothing from the night before.

Sitting in the kitchen, sipping coffee, he gazed at her and tried to read her expression to determine what he should tell her now and what could wait, or whether to say anything at all.

Before he could speak, she reached across and took his hand in hers. "So you want to tell me about that?"

He wasn't quite ready for the question, inhaled, let it out, touched her cheek, and almost started to cry but caught himself. He managed a conciliatory smile and started again. "Michelle, my Belle—" he'd taken to calling her that on their second date— "I am so, so sorry. I haven't been fair or completely honest with you."

The look on her face was one he hadn't seen before, a mix of fear and curiosity. "Please don't tell me there's somebody else." She said it in all seriousness, without a hint of humor or sarcasm.

For a moment Geoff wished he could say yes, and that that would be it. There'd be no talk of dying, no explanation other than to agree that he was a world-class asshole and deserved her wrath, so much easier to be guilty of infidelity than to tell her he was living on borrowed time.

"No, I'm not seeing someone else. I almost wish I were, because this is going to be harder than anything I have ever told anyone."

She sat back in the chair, waiting. Before he could utter a

word, she let out a cry. "Oh, God, Geoff, what is it? Are you—
?"

"I have cancer." He said it as if he was admitting to eating the last cookie in the jar—childlike, a little ashamed and frightened. It was the first time he had uttered the words aloud to anyone other than himself when he looked in the mirror, trying to get used to the phrase.

She sat there with her mouth open, in a state of shock. Grim-faced and hurting, he didn't know what to say next, so they sat in complete silence.

Tears of frustration began to fill her hazel eyes. "Geoffrey, what are you telling me? I mean. . .how bad is it? How could you plan? How could you even. . . ?"

Embarrassed and remorseful, he shrugged sheepishly and then began to shake. She reached across the table, took his hand, and stroked it. "Tell me, please," she implored.

He dabbed at his eyes with his free hand and swallowed. "I have a tumor. . .a brain tumor."

She gasped.

"They say—they say it's inoperable."

"Oh, my God." She clasped a hand to her mouth and pulled her other hand away from his.

Shaking her head in disbelief, she looked at him with a complexity of emotions running though her mind, sorrow and disdain, confusion and compassion, heartache and anger. She toyed with a napkin and didn't look at him for awhile. He fidgeted in his seat, feeling crushed, as if a huge weight were pressing him downward. He suddenly arched his back and began to speak. "I know, I know. I was wrong to—"

"How could you? How *could* you? When were you going to tell me? You are the most selfish human being I have ever met. This is so unfair."

The words spilled out of her, angry at first, and then that subsided. "Geoff, what is this all about? How bad is it? Are you getting treatments? Has it spread? How can you go on a *trip?*"

He heaved a sigh and told her the whole story: when he'd first started feeling sick, how he'd gone to Crimmins and then Bartoski, why he had decided not to have treatments, and what the doctors had told him about his chances and why surgery would probably not help and might even make it worse.

When the words stopped coming, he sat there meekly, wanting to say more but not knowing what.

Another few minutes passed before she rose from her chair. He thought she was going to leave without another word, and his heart sank. Instead, she came around to his side, put her arms around him, and cried into his chest. He began stroking her hair.

She straightened up and led him to the living room sofa, joined him on it, and turned so she could see his face. Not taking her eyes off of him, she cleared her throat and held up her hand. "Listen to me—and please don't say anything until I am finished."

With his lips pressed together and his hands clasped in front of him, he nodded. "As crazy as this has all been, and I mean crazy," she started, "I found myself falling for you after our first coffee date and was so excited about the possibilities that I just went with it, no matter where it was headed. For some reason I trusted you immediately."

He started to say something, but she held up her hand again. "You agreed to let me finish." He leaned back without a word. "Thank you. Geoff, if I understand this correctly, and if you feel anywhere near what I do about what there could be between us, what has already started, then I need you to let me be part of this. You don't have to go it alone, and I want to be there for you, and most importantly, I want us to go to Europe together, without any of this hanging over us."

He looked at her in amazement—at how beautiful she was, how calm and controlled, and how lucky he was to have found her.

"I hope you will agree to this," she continued. "If the doctors say chemo or radiation can help, or even prolong your life, then you must take that chance. If surgery is needed, than you must do that. Without them there is no chance at all, and you will. . . ." The word stuck in her throat.

He shook his head in acknowledgment, a half smile on his lips, hope growing in his heart, and a new resolve taking hold. He wanted to live—for her.

Tears trickling down her cheek, she took a breath and asked, "Can you do that? Can *we* do this together? No matter what?"

Geoff was so emotional he could barely speak. "I—I. . . yes, we can, we *will*. I'll call the doctor and make an appointment, and if you want to come—"

"Yes, I do, if it's okay. From now on we are in this together. Agreed?"

"Agreed."

They kissed then and held each other for what seemed an eternity: travelling companions wherever it might lead.

WHITE GHOST

HALF AN HOUR INTO THEIR TREK HOME, Patreak sensed the old Husky had stopped, and he turned to see if it was following him. A few yards back, Sorkay stood transfixed; ears back, tail down, a low whimper coming from somewhere deep within.

"What is it, boy? What do you see?"

Sorkay's nose twitched as he slowly backed up, keeping his snout to the wind. Patreak followed the dog's gaze. There, only yards away, stood a four-legged figure easily twice the size of Sorkay. It blended so well into the whiteness of the descending snow that he wasn't sure if it was a wolf or a polar bear. But Sorkay didn't want any part of it. The dog had already lowered himself to the ground and burrowed into a drift.

Patreak turned in the direction of the apparition and thought he saw it move, but then it vanished so quickly he wasn't sure if it had been there at all.

But Sorkay knew.

After staring into the void, squinting beyond the flakes the size of his gloved fist, Patreak wondered if the presence they felt could be what the Inuit call *Saupa Anernerk*, the White

Ghost. Apprehensive but determined to keep moving, he took a few steps toward the husky. "Okay, boy, come on, it's getting cold, and we have a long way to go before we reach Nungak."

The dog whimpered in dismay but stood up when his master approached. He ambled toward the young man, nudged his leg, and then tentatively walked ahead a few paces, turning briefly to make sure his companion was following.

Patreak yanked his backpack higher onto his shoulders, pulled his fur hat down to cover his ears, and shoved off. The rapidly accumulating snow, almost knee-high, was wet and heavy, and it made trudging onward as tough as he could remember it ever being. Trying to keep up with the powerful sled dog, he leaned into each step and focused on the paw prints in front of him so as not to lose sight of his companion or the course the Husky was taking.

From time to time, another set of tracks mysteriously appeared alongside Sorkay's and then vanished, only to reappear a few hundred yards later. They were as big as a polar bear's, but not the same shape. In fact, they were like nothing Patreak had ever seen before.

Uneasy at being in the vicinity of a predatory animal, Patreak knew they had to keep moving, because the village would be a safe haven from the cold, the snow, and whatever else might be sharing the night with them.

They moved across the frozen lake and over the encircling hills. They fell into a rhythm, with Sorkay pushing through the mounds in exhaustive leaps and Patreak high-stepping to keep his snowshoes from post-holing, making their way toward the town at the edge of the mountains a few miles ahead.

Patreak stopped when he saw the snow slowing and a patch of sky and stars appear overhead. He reached into his pocket for the compass. It was never easy to get an accurate reading that far north, but he looked at it anyway. The arrow trembled between W/NW, and he nodded, knowing they were at least heading in the general direction. If he could get to high ground, he might see the lights of Nungak, providing the snow let up long enough.

He returned the compass and glanced around for the dog, but there was no sign of him. He whistled and then shouted, "Come on, Sorkay, let's go."

When they were out walking, the husky often ran ahead and disappeared for an hour or more, but would always come trotting back. Patreak called out again, shrugged, and pushed on, expecting the dog to sidle up alongside at any moment.

After twenty minutes and a few more shouts into the darkness, the snow began to fall as heavily as he had ever seen it. He grew concerned over the dog's whereabouts, and that he himself might lose his direction or become disoriented.

He listened for a few seconds, then knelt and cupped his hands to his mouth. "Sorkay! Sorkay!" He tried to whistle, but it got lost in the wind. "Damn it. Where *are* you, pup?"

A low grumbling sound caused Patreak to swing around; startled and a little frightened, he called yet again, "Sorkay? Here, boy!"

He waited, listening for the dog, trying to determine where the noise had come from, thinking it might be the wind, but then he heard it again. This time it was longer and seemed closer, and it wasn't the sound of any animal he knew.

Heart racing, he grabbed the halogen headlamp strapped around his hat, held it away from his body and started a sweep of the surrounding area, but the snow was too heavy and the shaft of light only magnified the blizzard's intensity like high beams in a whiteout when the flakes head straight at your windshield.

When the two started out, the temperature had been ten above, but Patreak sensed it had already dropped to minus fifteen or twenty. With all the stopping to look for Sorkay, clammy from anxiety, he felt chilled and was uneasy about being so far from a fire.

He removed the neck gaiter from his backpack and pulled it over his head, adjusting it to cover his mouth and nose; snow on his lashes began to freeze, and his toes were starting to numb.

He heaved a heavy sigh, looked around one more time, and then kicked up one snowshoe, stepped forward, and started walking, unaware that the compass had fallen from his pocket.

While he walked, he thought of Sorkay and recalled how, ten years before, Ugalik, the owner of the trading post, had given him the runt of the litter from his sled team's Alpha.

The old Inupiat had said Sorkay was too tiny and timid to be a sled dog. Patreak had been happy, though, and scooped up the puppy and stuffed it into his coat so only its nose poked out. From that point on, the two had been inseparable. As Sorkay grew into adulthood he could hold his own against any creature. Once he had even stood his ground against a Kodiak bear they had come across in the forest; growling, snarling, and barking wildly, Sorkay had sent the beast hunkering off into the woods. Patreak smiled at the memory and felt comforted that the dog would be all right no matter what was out there.

The *thump, slap, thump, slap* of snowshoes moving through the drifts was the only noise Patreak could hear as he trudged onward until he saw a large, dark shape about ten yards ahead. He approached it cautiously, trying to determine if it was alive, a tree stump, or something else. As he got closer he saw a freshly killed caribou. He stopped, listened, and looked around, then approached the carcass. Blood stained the snow around the animal; its throat had been ripped open, its belly eviscerated. There was no sign of struggle and there were no tracks in the snow surrounding the carnage. No Eskimo would do this, he thought. They would never leave it there and would not have torn open its throat.

Patreak was cold, tired, and troubled by the way the caribou was killed. Frightened for himself and his companion, he screamed, "*Sorkay!*"

As suddenly as the snow had started, it ceased. A swath of night sky, with a few pinpoints of light flickering in its void, appeared on the horizon and silhouetted the ridge a short distance away. Patreak pulled the gaiter away from his face, sucked a long, deep breath into his aching chest, and headed for the knoll.

He reached the crest and panted deeply, the frigid air searing his lungs and pinching his nostrils shut. Reaching for the compass to take another reading, his stomach churned when he a realized it was gone.

In the distance, he thought he saw the lights of Nungak, but they were just blinking stars, and he dropped to the snow, pulled his knees up to his chest, and pressed his chin against his parka. Hugging himself for warmth, he wondered if he should dig a snow cave and crawl inside until daybreak. The aurora borealis reflected light on the snow around him, turning it a blue-green color—and it was then that he saw the paw prints. He followed them with his eyes, down the ridge he had just climbed, and then up over the top.

He jumped up and tracked them for a few yards, bent

down to look at them, and thought they might belong to the husky. The prints headed down the hill, then abruptly turned back, traversed the summit and stopped at a deep crater-like depression that looked as if something had fallen or dropped into it from above.

Perhaps an animal had been there, lain down, and left, but why weren't any tracks leading away from the site? Anything large enough to make that size hole could easily crush his snow cave, and Patreak knew it, and decided against building shelter. He glanced around, then forged ahead, hoping he'd find the husky and reach town within the next hour.

Then, almost magically, he saw dim shapes in the distance that could only be Nungak, and he moved as fast as he could to get to the safety of the village.

Most of the modest modular homes and trailers that made up the town were dark, but a pale yellow light was shining through the frosty windows of the building that housed the saloon, post office, and meeting hall. As he approached Edmund Peck Street, he could hear the wind whooshing through the alleyways, whipping the snow into rushing vortexes between the buildings.

Only two men were inside the hall—one, dressed in Carhartt overalls, was standing by a pellet stove, his backside almost touching the cast iron housing; the other, a scraggily, ruddy-faced man of indeterminate age, was tilted back on a chair with its front legs several inches off the floor, his own sprawled out in front of him, one hand grasping a bottle of Canadian whisky. When the door swung open, the chair legs hit the floor with a thud.

"Jeezus Christmas, Patreak, you scared the hell outta me!"

Words tumbled from the young man's mouth: "Bonard,

have you seen Sorkay?"

The other moved his head from side to side. "Hell, no! Ain't been outside since this morning. What'd he do, run off agin?"

The other fellow stepped away from the heater so Patreak could get to it and asked, "You look like you seen a ghost. What happened?"

Patreak removed his gloves and stumbled toward the stove. He pressed his curled fingers and bluish hands against the stove pipe and muttered, "I just maybe did. You know the White Ghost the Inuit are always talkin' about? I think it's out there. I mean—"

Koder, the other man, glanced at Bonard and then back at Patreak. "Yeah, well," he said, "I don't believe that crap. Them Eskee-moes are too superstitious. Ain't no such thing as a white ghost." He stretched the word out and wiggled his fingers. "Spooky."

Patreak shook his head. "Believe what you want, but I just saw a lot of things I never saw before. . .and so did Sorkay."

Bonard tilted the chair backward again. "Like what? What kinda things?"

"It doesn't matter," said Patreak. "I need your help finding my dog."

"All right, then," said Bonard, "let's go." He stood up, grabbed a rifle from behind the bar, and the two men put on parkas, scurried outside, and mounted Skidoos. Patreak sat behind Bonard and explained what had happened and which way to head. With engines blaring, headlights illuminating their way, they sped off.

They had covered a lot of ground in a few minutes when Patreak told Bonard to stop. Koder pulled up alongside and cut his engine. They scanned the vastness and listened for sounds of any kind. At first they could only hear their own breathing. Patreak got off the snow machine, took a few steps into the darkness, and waited.

Koder shouted excitedly, "Hey! Look at this!" He was pointing at dozens of deep indentations in the snow. "What do you think these are? I ain't never seen no paw prints like that."

Patreak knelt to look at them. "Those are like the ones I saw on the other side of the ridge."

He moved around, looking for more evidence. "See what I mean? They just stop. They disappear like something dropped from the sky and walked around a bit, then vanished."

Suddenly Bonard held up his hand. "Hold it. . .did you hear that?"

They fell silent. From a distance came a faint growl, then a snarl, and finally an angry barrage of loud barking.

"That's Sorkay," cried Patreak. "I know that sound. He sees somethin'. C'mon!"

They raced toward the noise until they spotted two large figures grappling in upright positions. Patreak pointed a searchlight in the direction of the commotion.

"Bears," shouted Koder, raising the rifle, but Bonard pushed the weapon downward. "Hold on, them ain't no bears. One of 'em's a wolf. I don't know what the hell that other thing is."

Patreak strained to see in the darkness. "Fire a warning shot," he said.

Koder pointed the rifle high above the brawling figures. There was a flash from the muzzle and a delayed cracking sound that echoed into the night. Then it was silent. A minute later Sorkay trotted toward them, no other creature in sight.

Patreak ran toward the dog and fell backward as they careened into each other. The husky licked his companion's face, and they rolled around like children in the snow.

Koder and Bonard tramped over to where the clash had been and searched for evidence of a second animal, but they found only one set of prints and nothing to suggest a struggle had taken place.

Koder rubbed at his chin, holding the rifle in the other hand. "I coulda swored there were two of 'em. I know I saw two of 'em."

Bonard said nothing; he just peered at the spot in disbelief, then looked up to the night sky and shook his head.

Patreak examined Sorkay for bruises, saw nothing, and patted him loudly on the flank. "C'mon, boy let's go home."

FOREVER

P EOPLE OF ALL COLORS and sizes were milling around the gate, speaking in so many different languages it reminded him of the Tower of Babel. It was pretty much just that. The number of people was hard to compute—easily thousands, probably more, stretching to the infinite horizon.

Silvio had no idea how long he had been among them. He just knew he was part of something much larger, more vast than he could ever have imagined back in his tiny Brazilian village, or even at the soccer stadium in the city of São Paulo.

He thought he'd been waiting a long time—by some calculations, even years—although that was too complex a theory for him to grasp; there was no nighttime or daytime to measure it by, for that matter. The entire area had a blue-gray atmosphere with no visible sky or ground, no trees, not even a shrub, no buildings, no entities of any sort other than the throngs of humanity.

On occasion, Silvio tried speaking to a few people around him, but the language barrier prevented anything more meaningful than a few hand gestures and facial expressions. A sense of resignation seemed to be the one common characteristic they all shared.

The amount of time it took him to move forward and finally approach the closed, solidly constructed gate was incalculable, but he eventually did and soon discovered language was no longer a problem.

Just outside the doorway he was told by a disembodied voice to stand under a shaft of light that was emanating from someplace he couldn't see: "Turn slowly and wait for the beep."

He followed the order, stood with his arms at his side and rotated 360 degrees until he heard the sound, which, he thought, was more of a chime than a beep.

"Step out of the beam," the voice said. "Walk through the gate and over to the table."

He did as instructed and moved down a long table with scores of people sitting behind it. Each had a tablet of sorts and was making notes as they questioned whoever was sitting in front of them. Silvio instinctively took the first empty chair and waited for an invitation to sit. It never came. Instead, another voice said, "Silvio Oliviera de Bargado, you have entered through the Gates of Forever. There will be no other welcome, only this brief orientation, after which you are on your own, as I have just said, forever."

Silvio was confused, curious, and a bit frightened. "Forever? I just waited forever to get this far." He grabbed the seat and sat down without being asked.

The person orienting him was of indeterminate gender, age, or ethnicity, was expressionless, and spoke in a perfunctory, detached tone. "Silvio to be clear, you are no longer among the Earthly bound. You can call it being dead if you wish, but there is no real designation for your new forever status."

Silvio was suddenly struck by where he was or at least seemed to be, but could not remember how he had gotten there. The notion occurred to him that perhaps he was in hell and not in heaven, where he had always prayed he would end up. "Can I ask any questions?" he inquired.

"Now's the time."

"How many can I ask?"

"I'm in no rush," the individual said, "but the sooner you get moving, the better off everyone will be."

There was so much he wanted to know—what he should expect, what was expected of him, what he needed to be aware of, what he could and couldn't do.

He stammered, "I-I. . .what is. . . . ?" He gave up without asking anything.

"Okay," the person said, writing something on the tablet. "You're ready. Just head down that passageway and turn left."

"That's it? That's the end."

"Yes, Silvio, it's forever."

Dumbstruck, he rose from the chair and headed down the corridor, turned at the end, and found himself in a wide open space not unlike what he had been in outside the gate—still blue-gray and unencumbered by objects of any sort.

He looked back in the direction he had just come from and wondered if he had misunderstood the instructions, or if this was all there would be. He decided to backtrack and, after a long walk, realized he had turned right instead of left and once more found himself outside the gate.

Frustrated and growing angrier, he joined the rabble and had to wait all over again for his turn at the entrance.

The procedure was the same until he got inside and was told to stand in the beam of light.

"Oh, wait. . .you were here already," the unseen voice declared. "Step forward and go to the desk."

Inside he saw the same long table, this time with different people doing the orientation. Having already had the experience, he felt more controlled and had a number of questions ready to ask. He took a seat immediately, but before he could protest, the individual said, "Silvio Oliviera de Bargado you have entered through—hold on, you were here already."

He was about to explain, but a hand rose to stop him. "You don't listen very well. You were supposed to turn left, not right. Go try it again. But turn left this time, or you will have to come back and start the process all over."

Silvio was thus dismissed without getting to ask his questions. Miffed by his discharge but eager to get on with it, he made his way down the corridor until he came to a left turn, took it, and then traversed another long hallway. This time he came out into a wide space with a hint of sunlight, or something like it, on the horizon.

He trudged along a narrow path on which many others were also moving and sped up to catch a woman ahead of him, touched her elbow, and immediately startled her. "What the fuck? Who are you?" she screeched.

Silvio pulled his hand back and contritely said, "I'm sorry, madam, I just need to talk to someone about—"

"I know nothing. No one knows anything. I don't even know where we are, or why, or how we got here. Leave me alone."

Utterly taken aback, he fell a few steps behind her and whispered, "I'm sorry."

The procession in front of him stretched to infinity, yet there was very little noise, no mumbling, grumbling, or discord, only an endless chain of people moving as if on a conveyor. In fact, he suddenly realized that was exactly the conveyance he was standing on, a moving walkway, like the ones in an airport, only much slower.

AT LAST HE REACHED THE END and stepped off the belt.

The multitudes he witnessed vaporized in front of his eyes, and when he surveyed the space around him he noticed that he too had vanished—at least his physical embodiment had.

For all intents and purposes Silvio was invisible to "living" people. Here, wherever here was, he soon learned, no one had the need for a material vessel. The thought process was collective, and when you pondered a question, someone responded. By the time Silvio finally figured that out, he'd forgotten everything on his mind and had to start all over again, a pattern, it seemed, that was normal around this place.

The first and foremost question that came to him was ubiquitous. "Where am I?" He followed it with a barrage of others, all of which were answered by myriad voices.

"You are in no place in particular," came a response.

"Wait," implored Silvio, "are you saying that you don't know, or that this place has no name?"

Authoritative answers came at him from different voices, and Silvio quickly learned to trust them.

"I was told I am not dead or alive either, for that matter. I just am. So am I in heaven or hell or. . .where?"

"There is no heaven or hell. You are here. Here is where you are."

". . .I'm confused."

"Look, there is no religion. Never was, never will be. It's fabricated. It always was. You leave the Earth or wherever you are from, and this is where you end up."

"I don't get it," he insisted. "Where are the others from, if not Earth?"

"From all the other places in the universe—billions of places, trillions of people. . .they've been coming for eons."

"Why here? What is here?"

"Listen, knucklehead, this is all there *is*. That other stuff is like dreaming, made up in your head. Doesn't matter who, what, where, when. Everyone ends here."

"What do we do now?"

"We just *be*. It's simple. There's nothing to do, nothing to worry about, no rules, no punishment, no sins, no heartache, no nothing, not even time."

"Sounds dreadfully boring," commented Silvio.

"Not really. You get used to it. In fact, you probably already have."

Silvio considered what he had just been told, all of it, including the getting used to it part, and, astonishingly, it felt right. He wasn't bored, and he didn't care. He had zero desire to do anything—eat, sleep, screw. . .well, to live.

He thought, I never would've guessed. Why did I bother to do any of it all that time? It didn't—it *doesn't*—matter. You live, and then you vanish into thin air and wind up here, where nobody cares, nobody exists as we know it, and nothing matters, and we're not bored. What a surprise.

After all the head-spinning revelations, he was as indoctrinated as anyone else and was able to answer questions asked by newcomers.

And that was it, forever.

ABOUT THE AUTHOR

Following a successful career in graphic design, Stew Mosberg migrated to the mountains of Colorado to write full time. In addition to the novel *In the Shadows of Canyon Road*, he is the author of two books on design and co-author of *Colorado High Country Anthology*. He is the former publisher of *The Cultural Times*, a monthly arts journal, and has written widely for national and international publications. He is currently a feature writer for the *Durango Telegraph*. His innate curiosity and zest for life have led him to adventures around the world—from a bull ring in Mexico to driving Formula II race cars, skiing on three continents, and scuba diving in the Caribbean, his travels have taken him to twenty-one countries. When not hiking the high trails of the Southwest, he can be found casting a line into a tranquil trout stream near his home in Bayfield, Colorado.